EXIT
STRATEGY

ALSO BY LINDA L. RICHARDS

Endings

The Madeline Carter Series

Mad Money

The Next Ex

Calculated Loss

The Kitty Pangborn Series

Death Was the Other Woman

Death Was in the Picture

Death Was in the Blood

The Nicole Charles Series

If It Bleeds

When Blood Lies

Anthologies

Vancouver Noir

Thrillers: 100 Must-Reads

Fast Women and Neon Lights:
1980's inspired mystery, crime, and noir short stories

EXIT STRATEGY

A NOVEL

LINDA L. RICHARDS

OCEANVIEW PUBLISHING
SARASOTA, FLORIDA

ISBN 978-1-60809-422-6

Published in the United States of America by Oceanview Publishing

Sarasota, Florida

www.oceanviewpub.com

10 9 8 7 6 5 4 3 2 1

PRINTED IN THE UNITED STATES OF AMERICA

"Sometimes even to live is an act of courage."

—LUCIUS ANNAEUS SENECA

EXIT
STRATEGY

CHAPTER ONE

Today

HE PROVES TO be a genial companion. I'd never doubted that he would. Across the table from him in a romantic restaurant, I can see his pale eyes are sparked with amber. Or is it gold? Maybe it depends on your perspective. A trick of the light.

So much of life, I've found, are those things: perspective and also light. Or maybe that's saying exactly the same thing.

He tells me he's in "finance," a term that is vague enough to accommodate a whole range of activities. I've done some research, though, and I know he is a hedge fund manager; that his apartment in this town is a playpen: weekends only. I know he is based in the City and that he flies down here for the occasional weekend, especially since his divorce, which was messy. He doesn't say that: "messy." But when he briefly skates over that episode of his life—the period of time in which "we" became "me"—he makes a face that is unpleasant, like he's got a bad taste in his mouth. I let it ride. Where we are going, it won't make a difference.

He tells me funny, self-deprecating stories. I reflect that he is someone I would date—in another lifetime. If I dated. If I still had a heart.

Faulty read

"This is a fun first date," he says in that moment, as though he has read my mind. His thick dark hair flops over his eye endearingly, and my heart gives a little flutter. I'd try to stop it, but I don't hate the feeling. That flutter. It feels good, in this moment, to simply feel alive.

"Yesterday, Brett. Wasn't that our first date?" I ask, more for interaction than anything real. Because, of course, the few moments on a rooftop we shared were not a date by any standard. Especially since I was trying to think how to kill him for part of that time. But he doesn't know that, so maybe it doesn't count?

"Nope," he says firmly. "That was a meeting. This—" he indicates our wine and the delicate nibbles between us—"this is a date."

"How does it end?" I ask pertly. Knowing the answer. Knowing he doesn't. Wanting to know what he thinks.

He looks at me searchingly for a moment, then smiles raffishly, a certain boyish charm bubbling through. It's a practiced look. He's used that smile before, to good effect, I can tell. He's probably done that his whole life. I don't dislike him for any of that. It distresses me slightly that I don't dislike him at all. It would be beneficial to me if I could find it in myself to dislike.

There is more conversation, just like that. An ancient dance.

After a while he excuses himself to go to the bathroom.

Once he's out of sight, I slip a vial out of my purse. It contains a powder I made myself. Oleander flowers, dried, crushed, and mixed with salt and a few strong spices, intended to cover the plant's bitter taste. I don't know how well those spices mask the taste. It's not as though I can test it, and none of my customers have ever complained.

I quickly sprinkle some of this concoction judiciously on the food that remains. I do it using natural motions. Anyone watching would think I was eating. A little OCD, maybe, but it wouldn't look anywhere close to what is true. I mix it quickly into the salsa, the guacamole. I salt the chips with it. Sprinkle it on what is left of the chicken wings. I don't dust the calamari. I'd noted he hadn't been eating that. It will give me a safe spot to nibble, not that I plan on needing much time to eat. All of this will happen quickly, my experience tells me that.

Before he returns, I have this moment of absolute indecision. I very nearly call out to a nearby server; have her clear the table. I'm not even super sure why I don't. All of this is going well. Textbook. And yet, I have qualms. Why? He's lovely of course, there's that. But beyond the way he looks or how he looks at me. Not long ago, things had happened that had made me resolve to do my life in a different way. Then I'd gotten an assignment and instinct had more or less kicked in. And it was easy to reason around it and to rationalize: if not me, then someone else, right? There would always be some other person ready to do the job. Viewed in that light, there was no earthly reason for me not to do what I do.

But still.

I don't call a server. And the moment passes.

He comes back looking refreshed, like he's maybe splashed water on his face or combed his hair, which is behaving for now. Not, for the moment, flopping into his eyes. I figure he probably did both—splashed and combed. He looks good.

He smiles when his eyes meet mine. A 24-karat smile that lights his whole face. My heart gives a little bump. "Fuck," I say. But it isn't out loud.

He takes his seat and starts talking again, picking up where we left off. He is easy. Comfortable. But I'm having trouble tracking the conversation; my mind is elsewhere. I'm thinking about what my next steps will be. After. And does it matter what he says right now? Really? If it does, it won't matter for long.

I try not to follow his actions. Try instead to listen to what he is saying. These words will be his last ones, I know that. And part of me thinks I should do him that courtesy. At least. The courtesy of attention. But it's difficult to follow his words now. I watch one corn chip as he picks it up, dips it into salsa. I watch him consume it, and it feels like all of it is happening in slow motion. All the while I am listening to his words—I am!—participating in the conversation, not wanting to miss any cues. And wanting to honor the small amount of time he has left. It's all I can do.

The chip is consumed. I detect no reaction to the bitterness, so that's a plus. He picks up a chicken wing, swirls it in the blue cheese dip, which makes me realize that, in my haste, I'd missed an opportunity by skipping doctoring the dip. He consumes the wing while we talk; a slight sucking, the meat peeling gently off the bone, all the while, the words flow, though it doesn't come off as rude. He seems adept at eating and talking so everything stays and sounds as it should.

I listen closely, interjecting as appropriate when I think it's necessary, all the while watching for . . . signs. I detect nothing until another wing and several chips later. His eyes are suddenly glassy. Sweat stands on his forehead. His hands shake.

"Brett, are you all right?" I ask, but it is pure form. I know he is far from all right. All right no longer exists for him.

"I don't know. I've never . . . never felt like this before."

I give it another minute. A little less than that. I know it's all we've got. I make the right sounds, the correct motions of my hand. Even when no one is watching, people are watching. Physically, I am unremarkable. A middle-aged woman, so some would say I am invisible, certainly there is nothing about my appearance that makes me stand out. But there will be a future, when questions are asked and people are perhaps looking for clues. I don't want them to be looking for me.

When he collapses, face directly into salsa, I scream, as one does. Not bone chilling, but an alarmed scream. Our server trots over, clearly distressed. The manager is on her heels. All as expected: it's pretty terrible for business when customers collapse into their food.

"My date . . . he's . . . taken ill . . . I don't know what to do," etcetera. All as one would expect. I don't deviate from the script.

An ambulance is called. Paramedics arrive quickly. The manager has already pulled Brett from the salsa, but it's clear he is not all right. They take him away, one of the paramedics offering to let me ride in the ambulance. I decline.

"I'll follow you," I say, heading for my rental. And I start out following, but a few blocks from the restaurant I make the turn I know will lead me to the freeway and then the airport. My bag is in the trunk and it's all mapped out: I am ready to go.

With this moment in mind, I'd left a ballcap on the passenger seat before I entered the restaurant. It is emblazoned with the logo of a local team. While I drive, I push my hair into the cap and wiggle out of the jacket I know I'll leave behind. These are simple changes—hat on, jacket off—but it will change my appearance enough. I don't anticipate anyone will be looking for me, but I like to think forward. Just in case.

I have no way of knowing for sure what will happen to him, but I can guess. From the amount of food I watched him consume, I figure he'll probably have a heart attack before he reaches the hospital and will likely arrive DOA. And at the age and heft of him, and with a high stress job, they will probably not test for poison. And the woman with him at the restaurant? I figure no one will be looking for a girl who doesn't follow up on the date that ended in hell.

From there it all goes like it's being managed by a metronome: tick tock, tick tock. Arrive at airport. Drop off rental car. Get through security. Get to plane while they're boarding. Claim aisle seat at the back of the plane. Keep my eyes peeled for both watchers or people who might recognize me from the airport. But everything goes exactly as it should. No watchers this time. No one looking at me in ways I don't understand. In fact, everything is perfect. Everything is exactly as it should be. Or maybe it is not.

CHAPTER TWO

Last week

I HAD NOT planned on killing again. That is, it wasn't in the plan. That's not to say it was an accident. You don't arrive for a date with a poison in your pocket unless you're preparing to do some bodily harm. But, as I said, that hadn't been the plan. Not before.

When the call came, I had been eyeballing my gun again. A darkness of spirit. A feeling I can't fight or name.

For a while I had spent a lot of time wondering why I kept bothering at all. In recent weeks, there had been darkness all around me. Times that, if it weren't for the dog, I wouldn't bother hanging around.

At times I wonder why I am still showing up every morning. For life, I mean. What's the big appeal? What is the motivating factor? Is there a mirror beyond the darkness? A pool; some reprieve. I don't know. Here's the thing, though: at this point, I'm less convinced that I need to hang around to find out. It's a battle I wage every day.

Most days.

Before the call comes, there are times it takes me a while to get out of bed. This is new. And when I do get out of bed, it takes a while longer still to orient. Motivating factor, that's the question.

Is there one? What is supposed to be motivating me? I don't know for sure. So I wait it out.

And the call doesn't come right away. First, and for a long while, everything is very silent. And not a churchlike silence. The sort one dreads when pieces fly together. First there was this and this and it all made sense. Then we added that other thing and we're done.

I don't know. I can't figure it out. I mostly don't bother anymore.

Why would one even bother anymore?

It wasn't always like this.

Let's put it that way.

There was a time when I didn't live alone.

There was a time when someone loved me.

Several people loved me.

I don't remember that time anymore. Not exactly. I'm like a ghost looking back at her memories from a previous lifetime. They are my memories, but they might as well belong to someone else.

Let me tell you this as I try to bring you up to speed.

I live at the forest's edge. My house is small and simple. It is all I need. My garden is incomplete, though it is occasionally vibrant. I am alone but for the company of a golden dog.

I am alone.

These are the things I think about. Vibrant gardens. Forest's edge. Seasons in motion. The padding about of golden feet. I don't dwell on the past. I try not to dwell on the past. For the most part, I have released everything that has happened. It no longer has a hold on me.

Mostly.

I have tried a lot of things to bring some sort of meaning to my life. Attempted. For instance, recently I have begun to keep a gratitude journal. It is a practice I read about somewhere. I try very hard to begin every day with that notebook, pen in hand. In gratitude. It changes the heart, I'm told. It changes the mind.

I have charged myself with finding five things every day for which I am grateful. It's like an affirmation.

It is an affirmation.

Some days it is easy. Five things to affirm. How hard can that be? I have air. Sufficient food. There is a roof over my head. The beautiful golden dog. Some days there is rain. On others, sun. Both of those are things to be grateful for. The air is clean. The ground is firm. All reasons to give thanks. Most of the time.

On other days it is more difficult. On those days I sit there, stare at the blank page. Maybe a tear falls. Or more than one. Sometimes I begin to write and then stop; picking up and putting down my pen. The past is closer on those days, I guess. The past is nipping at my heels; my heart. On days like that, I am filled with that unnameable darkness.

It is unnamed, but I recognize some of the contents. Guilt. Remorse. Regret. And variations on all of those things that incorporate measures of each. I don't believe in regret, and yet there it is. Regret does not bother checking in with me about my beliefs.

So my gratitude journal.

I am grateful for . . . and my heart turns over and I remember why I am alone at the forest's edge. I remember the things I promised myself to forget. On those days I can't look into my heart and find gratitude and I wonder how it is that I have tasked myself with this ridiculous burden: this burden of being grateful. I who have lost so much. Fallen so far. How can I expect myself to live in gratitude? How can I expect myself to continue to live at all?

You move forward. Simple? It is all I have left, some sort of forward momentum. It is all I can do. It is my privilege and my burden. My single track. I put my head down and go.

There are days when it is a close thing, this forward motion. Days when I wonder if it's worth it. Why I bother. Maybe there will come a time when I *won't* bother, that's what I think. But I don't know about that. Not yet.

It wasn't always this way; you'll have gleaned that. Once, I had a vocation. When that was taken away, I had a mission. Once that was completed, I was left with a profession. Not the one I was once trained for, but the one that now pays my bills. There are worse things, though probably not many.

The upside: it's not a profession that demands a lot of me most of the time. There are hours and days and sometimes even weeks where I am stuck with my own devices.

Stuck.

What do I do then? I cook sometimes, a creative art that amuses me and gives me some pleasure and satisfaction. Nourishes more than one part of me. And I have always been interested in nourishment of various sorts.

Other times I take rambling forest walks at a pace severe enough to raise my pulse and force a sweat.

Sometimes I sit at a rusted cast-iron patio set overlooking my fallow garden and think about what might be accumulating under the soil . . . what might be building there. I think about how things grow.

I don't watch television. Or Netflix. Or movies from any source. I don't watch things that might entertain me. It seems there is no longer anything that can come from the minds of humans that can give me joy. Not now. And turning on a television means possibly encountering some form of news, and I can't risk that. Risk is maybe the wrong word. I can't bear it, that's it. Sometimes there is news that I can't bear.

So I cook. Or I read. Or I walk. And occasionally I take up a short-term hobby when I knit or weld or sew or some other thing that makes me feel more full for a while and that passes the time.

I had said I would take no more assignments. Had turned off my phone, forgetting that I could be reached via email if usual channels didn't work. And so, after some time, an assignment arrives via email. I feel ready and rested. Why not, I think? I have forgotten the reasons I'd started turning work down; the truly heartfelt reasons. And life has gotten slow, in a way. Too slow, even for me.

It spells the end of another quiet moment in my life, time spent at the edge of my forest in reflection and small searches for meaning and even pleasure. And the timing is such that, maybe I am ready for that moment to end.

The email, when it comes, is from an unfamiliar sender, but I recognize the code. None of that is unusual.

"I've missed you. We should get together."

"Buzz off, creep," I reply.

I close my general mail app and open my Tor browser, then use it to log on to a special e-mail server on the DarkNet. As expected, I find a single note there from the person I think of as my handler, even though, for all I know, it is a whole team of people. Or maybe they are different people, or perhaps in different locations, tag teaming their operation.

The correspondences with me are all generated by a single user who in my mind is a man about my age, looking vaguely like an actor I once remember liking in some film I no longer recall. In my mind, I call this guy "Bob," though, in reality, there's a perfectly statistical chance it is not someone named Bob, or it is a woman, or, as I said, a whole group. I don't know. Truth be told, I *can't* really know. It would defeat the purpose.

The package I receive via email is, as always and like the text, completely cryptic. There is a name: my target. There is a photo of a handsome, strongly built man of middle years. In the photo his face is creased into a smile and thick dark hair drips engagingly onto his forehead.

Additionally, there is more information. There is a number that I know will be my fee, payable in cryptocurrency when the job is complete. Another set of numbers indicates the longitude and latitude where my target will most likely be found. I pay attention to the next set of letters, too: NPM. No preferred method, which means the whole thing will be at my discretion: no one cares how this one goes. For various reasons, that's always best for me. It's good to have options, that's what I think. It's good to have different paths through the same forest.

I feed the longitude and latitude they have supplied into a web page that deciphers those and am pleased when it indicates a city on the other side of the country that I've never been to but have always wanted an excuse to visit. I did not anticipate the reason I would finally manage to get there would be to kill someone, but if I've learned one thing, it's that life is full of surprises: You never know what might come up next. You can't be sure what is around the next bend.

The single hiccup comes from an unexpected source: it is a wrench to leave the dog. I haven't done so in a while. My constant companion. Logistically I can. Even if I'm gone for a few days, things are safe and complete for him here at the forest's edge, so it isn't the practical reasons that make me hesitate. He has become my constant companion, even though I've never before had one of those. He is my best friend, and on certain days he is my reason for living. All of that together makes it hard to leave him behind. In the end I do, reminding myself it won't be for long.

As I bump down my long driveway toward the county road that will take me out of town, I try not to think of the dog's dear, smart face on the other side of the front door, listening for this bit of activity and trying to puzzle out my next move. I tell myself he will be fine. No question. He has enough of everything he needs as well as access to outside. Barring some weird and unexpected medical emergency, there is nothing I need to supply that he can't get on his own. Still. I can't help but think of him. Then, after a while, I let it go. I have business to deal with.

CHAPTER THREE

As soon as I get to the airport, I feel like someone is watching me. I know the feeling is foolish, and it's not one I've had before. Also, I believe that someone watching me is not even a possibility because I am careful. To a fault. Always. And yet the feeling persists.

My instincts are well honed, from necessity and maybe even instinct. I think I was born that way. But I have that feeling, and so I respect it and hang back when it is my turn to board. I stay back and look around.

Everyone here is going somewhere. And so they are festive. Or bustling. Or joyous. Or morose. The moods are different, and you can feel them, but everyone is intense. That's the thing that connects them. They've got things to deal with, of one kind or another, but it's all at a high level of energy. And everyone looks different, of course, but that energy—that intensity—in some ways it makes them all the same.

At first, I spend some time chiding myself. I am being foolish. Needlessly so. Paranoid. There is nothing to see here. Nothing out of the ordinary. Keep your head down and go.

Still, I hang to the rear, watching, trying to bring a sort of stillness to the visual noise all around me. Trying to single out what it is. One thing. I know that's all it will take.

And then I give up. There is nothing. I'm being silly. I let it go.

I am about to get in line to board when I see him. And right away I understand why I nearly missed him. He does not appear worthy of recognition. He is paunchy and a baseball cap slouches backwards on his head. He is easy to miss: someone's brother/boyfriend/son. He appears to be without consequence. What makes me realize he's more than he seems is such a small thing, too easy to miss. And it's not how he looks at me, but maybe how he does *not* look that alerts me. It's as telling as if he had been holding a sign.

And now everyone on my flight has boarded but me. And the airline employees are eyeing me impatiently. I can feel the one closest to me gathering herself up to talk to me. And I see all of that. I see everything. But I see him most of all.

I have hung back from boarding and so I surprise him with a look. Right at him. And when he realizes he's been made, he turns on his heel and begins to sprint away. I don't have to reach very far for my reaction: I put my head back and I scream.

"That man! He stole my purse!" I wail it, while pointing at his retreating back, even while hoping that no one notices that I am still, in fact, holding a purse.

I can see his reaction in his response: he's heard me shout and sensed it is not good for his outcome, even if he is too far away to have made out the words. And he is going flat out: a paunchy sprinter diving against the clock or maybe a yearling steer in a pen: he can make the big move but, in the end, there is no way he's going to get away.

I see them grab him as the airline employee gets to me.

"Are you a passenger on this flight?" Her voice is curt, impatient, but I ignore that. She's just doing her job. And anyway, I've done everything I wanted to do. Everything I can.

"Yes, yes. I'm sorry. I'm coming right away." Last passenger to board.

I head toward the plane. They have made the last call for the flight and so I don't dare hang back anymore. I see them collar the watcher and then I have moved too far into the plane to see the drama. I'm about to turn the final corner when I stop and look back. As I do, he raises his head and looks at me. Our eyes meet and there is nothing there, but now I wish it had gone a different way. I'm no longer certain it's all danger. Had he been trying to kill me or convey some sort of message? As things have turned out, of course, I'm pretty sure I'll never get the chance to know.

CHAPTER FOUR

AT THE OTHER end of the flight, things are much more calm. At least that's how it seems. I keep a sharp lookout, but no one is waiting for me. No one I can see.

I move through the airport on full alert feeling ready for all eventualities, but I don't get even a hint of anything amiss. I make it through baggage claim without incident before taking the shuttle to the car rental area. There are no disturbances. There is no one watching me or too obviously not watching me, and I feel myself begin to relax, or at least the thing I do that is closest to that.

This is the first assignment I have taken in a long while. This will be the first time in recent memory that I kill. I feel mixed about that. Apprehensive, a bit. Not because I'm frightened of the outcome, but because I told myself I would not kill again. And yet, somehow, here I am. I'm almost not sure how it happened.

At the same time, I welcome the familiar thrill of excitement. Whatever anyone tells you, there is nothing quite like the hunt.

And this one will be different, too. I've been told that the client has not specified a means: how he dies will be my call. To that end I have come prepared. In my suitcase, in a compartment where one might stash their undies, is a small pouch that contains specially prepared oleander powder. I had dried the flowers myself a few weeks ago—hanging them upside down from the rafters of the garage until perfectly dry, mixing them with spices as I ground them. It strikes me as odd, now, that I had done that. I hadn't planned on killing again. Yet, on a certain level, apparently, I'd been making plans.

And here I am.

When I park the rental car at my hotel and begin to move my things inside, I feel a buzz in the air right away. It's a festival city, and the biggest fest of the year is in play. I curse myself for not researching that aspect and I feel a little foolish. Certainly, had I realized what week it was I would have put the whole thing off for a while. There had been no urgency around this job.

I walk toward the downtown core, joining the parade of people dancing in the streets. Here is singing, music everywhere. Color. Art is hoisted. Food is offered on street corners and consumed. Every inch of the city seems solidly covered in festival. There are times when I would love all of this, but I don't now. I have a bad feeling about all of it. It's not a feeling I've ever had before. Like a premonition, and I don't believe in those.

I think seriously about taking an audible: packing it in and heading home. But I remain frightened of turning down a job, an old-world work ethic instilled by my parents. Maybe this, also, is genetic. What if I say no and then nothing ever comes again? But I don't audible. I take a deep breath, soldier it out. Festival or no, this is meant to happen, and it will.

His home is above a main street—shops under, apartments above. Tonight, the street and the shop are furrowed with revelers. I see people in the apartment and the generous patio outside of it, watching, partying, enjoying what is below; making an event of it. I consider getting my hands on a gun and taking him out from across the street, but there's something a little too cliché about it—too grassy knoll and dead president and, anyway, it seems risky as fuck. A lone woman gunman—person—leaning off a balcony, keeping her firearm steady while she takes careful aim. No. While it *would* be surgical and over quickly—both pluses—the potential for disaster seems too great. I reconsider. In any case it is impossible, at this distance, to be certain which one is my target. And I certainly don't want to take them all out, gangland style. There might be times that would be the appropriate response, but this isn't one of those.

The partiers on the balcony are mostly male, I notice. Around my age. It gives me an idea. One that feels more workable than the one I have been—however lightly—considering.

I cross the street. Buzz the buzzer marked "Penthouse" and am surprised when I am buzzed right in. Once there, I can tell that no one is quite sure who I belong to, but I sense right away that my instincts did not lead me astray and there will be no problem. They are intent on their party and in a jovial mood: it's not the beginning of the evening. It's possible someone might have questioned my presence hours ago, but by now enough alcohol and perhaps other substances have been consumed and no one is interested in asking any questions.

Up close, it is not difficult to identify my target. He is one of the more sober of them; tall and lanky with dense dark hair that flops over an eye. A cheerful-looking sheepdog of a guy. He looks like the photo they sent me. I find myself liking him instantly. He has a ready smile and a cutting wit and I can't help but wonder who wants him dead.

"Penny," he says in a quiet moment.

"Hmmm?" I reply. I am standing on the balcony, listening to him joke with his friends and thinking about the rough lilt of his voice. Him addressing me directly has taken me by surprise.

"For your thoughts," he says easily. If he is curious about my identity or my presence, it doesn't show. "The penny, I mean."

"Is it still only a penny?" I reply pertly, noticing for the first time the gold flecks in his eyes. "Surely it's up to two bits by now."

He cocks his head at me in amusement.

"Two bits," he repeats. "I haven't heard that in a while. A good long while."

"That makes sense," I say. "I'm kind of an old-fashioned girl." I'm not, so I wonder what makes me say that.

He smiles in a warm way, then responds to a comment from one of his friends sitting nearby. While he does this, I admire his profile and the way the edges of his eyes crinkle when he laughs. There is a masculine beauty in him that I can't help but appreciate. And then that sweetly flopping hair.

"Figures," I mutter.

"Pardon?" he says, turning his body toward me and making me wonder if he has ears like those belonging to a cat.

"Oh, nothing," I say quietly. "The shadow of a memory from another life."

He examines me more fully then, like what I said was of interest or significance, though I don't feel as though it was.

"That's interesting," he says, confirming my thought.

"Is it?" I reply honestly. "It wasn't meant to be."

"Still," he says.

"Still," I reply.

And then we smile at each other foolishly without having a lot to say.

"I don't know you, do I?" he says after a while. "I feel I would have remembered you if we'd ever met."

"No," I say honestly. "I've crashed this shindig. I was on the street and you all looked like you were having so much fun that I came up and joined you."

"That's hilarious," he says honestly. The laughter hitting his eyes again.

"It kinda is, isn't it?" I agree.

"I'm Brett," he says, confirming what I already know. My heart sinks with it. It is the name of my target. I'd had a different hope.

"Nice to meetcha," I say. "It's your birthday?"

"You could say that, but not really," he says. "Say, want to get a meal some time? This doesn't seem like the perfect time and place to get to know each other. And I feel like I'd like to get to know you."

"Sure," I say, knowing that whatever we agree to will provide the opportunity I need; regretting that need, even while I keep an eye on the bottom line. "But I'm just in town for a couple days. Does tomorrow work for you?"

He brightens at this, like he'd been afraid I'd shoot him down and he can see now that I won't. It's a delicate one, this dance. And the risks someone takes at the ask are huge. Personal safety is one thing, but the heart, that's the thing. We risk a lot when we expose even the tiniest piece of our hearts. We live in perilous times. Even asking someone out can be dangerous.

"Yes, yes," he says. "I'd like that a lot." He names a restaurant and a time. I, of course, don't know the place, but I assure him I can find it.

The next time he turns away, I take the opportunity to slip out, back to the street. Knowing him better won't make what I've come to do any easier. At all.

CHAPTER FIVE

THERE IS A delicious anonymity that comes with being alone in a strange city. You can be anyone, anything. You can reinvent even the darkest corners of yourself, even if only for a little while.

With a plan now in place, I spend the balance of the evening roaming around the city, checking out obscure destinations I feel certain most visitors would miss. Among other things, I look over the restaurant where we will be meeting the following day, feeling lucky when I discover it to be a dark and romantic place at the side of a park. Both of these things will make my job easier in the end.

Back at my hotel, I prowl my room restlessly, a cat thinking about her prey. By now, I have forgotten/pushed away the details of his presence and am focusing on the things that I must do to finish the job at hand and the various ways in which my mission can be completed.

I don't spend much time on my personal darkness on this evening. I have other things to occupy my mind. The darkness will come, I know. It always does. But maybe it will let me do this job in peace. Maybe.

In the morning I go to an art museum, the best local one I can find. I spend the most time with the Impressionists, my heart soaring in recognition of the perfect clarity resulting from the indistinct lines; the order from apparent chaos and the sanity from visual madness, depending on where you stand; perspective being everything. Especially here. It's all about perspective.

I arrive at the restaurant early, order a drink; think about possibilities based on time and location. Think about getting home again. A flight out tonight? And my garden. And my forest. The dear dog. As well as all of the things not waiting for me that I don't have to do.

I am seated, so I see him before he sees me. I am taken aback—surprised anew—at his presence and about what it says to me, which is indistinct but moving. I find him attractive. There it is. Which is not a pleasant sensation in this instance. It is cumbersome, even irritating.

"There you are," he says as he joins me. "I had the feeling you wouldn't show."

"Really," I say. "Why?"

The simplicity of this seems to surprise him; that I would ask the question simply, no posturing. No pretense. Maybe it surprises me, too. I haven't always been this way.

* * *

I used to be a different way.

Once I had a whole life. A pretty regular existence, from what I can recall. But the recalling. That's the thing. Even the remembering of it now is laced in shadow. I think there are holes in my memory, but I can't be sure.

So I had a life. One that looks different from this one. There was a child. Mine. I can remember that. And a husband, but it seems to me I didn't like the husband very much, not in the end, anyway.

I know they're not alive anymore: child and husband. There's a haziness for me, looking back on it. Maybe there was an accident? At times it is more clear than others. And then there is now. In the meantime, a lot has transpired. It clouds everything else.

I know this: I am the sum of my experiences. That's true for all of us, I realize that. We have precedent. Proof. Raise a child without love or touch and he will be withdrawn. And unloving. He won't know how to love because he won't have experienced it: love will not be among his expectations. Raise a child with love and healthy touch and he will grow spiritually tall and strong; a vivid little flower growing toward the sun.

If your life brings you success and beauty, you learn to live with those things in your life. You come to expect them. But what if your life grows to be a black tar of broken dreams and bitter disappointments? What if everything you ever wanted or worked for turned not to dust but poison?

That's sounding very maudlin, I realize. I don't mean to pull things in that direction. Shorthand it: the sum of my life left me in a black hole. I was desperate, but I was also empty. Then life suddenly showed me the way to make sense of it. A certain kind of sense, anyway. That is, for a while, it made sense. I'm not at all sure of that now.

* * *

And then, you know: the date. The brief shot of companionship. Collapse into salsa. Yada, yada, yada: you know the drill.

And I end up alone. Again.

I try to put it all out of my mind.

I'm not particularly successful.

* * *

When I return to my forest home, the dog is insanely happy to see me. I don't blame him. Dogs aren't like people. Aren't like me. Dogs hate to be alone.

I've rigged this little system so I can leave the dog by himself for a number of days and nothing horrible will happen beyond him getting super sad. And I can't verify the sad part, but based on his reaction when I come back, he's probably blue for part of the time I am gone. You can't have that kind of happiness without some sort of tug on the other end.

But the system: he has the run of the house, and a dog door leads him into the large fenced yard area so he can get out when nature calls, or if he wants to weep sadly at the moon. He has an automatic waterer and I leave out a big bowl of water and the toilets open, just in case. I know he's resourceful. And I have this cool feeding machine I bought on Amazon that shoots the correct amount of kibble into his bowl three times a day. He can take himself outside. He can eat and drink when he likes. Theoretically, he could function for a long time without human interaction. Still. He seems to need me. I don't understand that, but I don't hate it either.

After the effusive greetings are done, I fire up the espresso machine and make myself a latte; carry that and a hastily made sandwich out to the backyard. It's slightly ahead of dusk, and somewhat peaceful. The hush that floats over the land before night falls.

The dog settles in at my feet, contentedly. He seems deeply asleep instantly, and I wonder if he slept at all while I was gone or if he hovered near the surface of consciousness always, prepared to make the excited leap of affection; the deeply felt greeting of the left behind.

The coffee is divine and the sandwich is serviceable. I munch and sip and reflect on my discontent, peering into the gathering darkness in the forest beyond my yard. Everything has gone very well. I should be happy; or what passes for happy with me these days. But I am not. I feel a disconnection. As though everything that has happened in the last few days has happened to someone else. I suspect I know the source. I had made a pact with myself and I hadn't kept it. It's not sitting well with me. I had told myself that things had occurred that would prohibit me from killing again without strong reason.

Killing for money. I thought I had moved beyond doing that. Yet here I am. The order came and I responded, like an eyelid that recoils when you poke a finger toward it. Instinct, is that what I'm suggesting? The order came and I jumped into motion. The order came and I moved. And now it's sitting in my stomach like a bad burger. The sandwich and coffee are helping with that, but not a lot.

I send the text without giving a lot of thought to what I'm going to say and why I'm doing it. I act. I know I'll think later.

The situation is changing, I text. *Need to reconsider.*

The reply comes more quickly than I would have expected. More quickly than it usually does.

Did something go wrong?

I shake my head as I thumb type.

No, nothing. Everything went perfectly. I think it's just me.

A pause. And then from their side, a surprising response: *An existential dilemma?*

It surprises me so much I sit and stare at my phone for a moment. And then I laugh out loud. Dry humor from the handler

I've never met or even spoken with. Dry humor or an observation so accurate I don't dare think about it.

In either case, it leaves me a bit speechless. I find I can't respond right away.

Maybe, I type finally. *Maybe that.*

I am surprised when my phone rings. No one ever calls me. When the call comes, I am examining my gun. Not for serviceability—it is in perfect condition, of course—but I am checking it for my current reality. If I go, who will care? The dog, of course. But perhaps a provision could be made for the dog. If a dog is your single tie to the earth, maybe you reconsider. That's what I'm thinking, with the feel of the familiar cold steel in my hands.

And then the call comes.

My phone shows the connection is from Ukraine, but I know that doesn't mean anything.

"Hello." I am tentative in my response. I figure I know who it is, but I haven't ever spoken with them, so I don't know what might be coming my way.

"What's different?" The voice surprises me. I hadn't known what to expect, but it wasn't this. It's a woman's voice. A woman of a certain age. And the voice is spidery. Light nails on a chalkboard. "What has occurred?"

Quickly, I debate how accurately to answer this. What's happened, really? Nothing. Everything. Nothing has altered. Everything has changed.

"It wasn't the job," I tell her, though I figure I probably don't need to. If there had been a mishap, she would have known. Even if I hadn't told her. It's her job to know everything.

"Oh-kay." I recognize the prompt and struggle for more words.

"I don't know how to tell it," and I find myself annoyingly close to tears. There is no one in my life. Everyone is either gone . . . or gone. And now this sympathetic voice on the phone. I recognize it is near to undoing me. And I don't want to be undone.

"Then maybe this isn't the moment. But, yes: I hear it in your voice. You're ready for things to be different. You're ready for a change."

A change. That sounds enough like it to be a thing. *Change.* It can have a lot of meanings. I think one of them might fit.

She doesn't wait for me to answer. "I have a thought. I'm going to . . . let's say, take you off active duty for now. You're okay for money, I guess?"

"Yeah. Sure." I figure that, whoever she is, she knows how much work I've done. A person would have a hard time spending as much as I've made in the last few years. Well, maybe not every kind of person. But someone who lives quietly at the edge of a forest—with a dog—and basically never goes out except to work. That person is already set for life.

"Okay, then. I won't call on you for now. Unless a mission comes along that would seem to require your . . . special touch. Unless a fit appears."

"Okay," I say. Floundering a bit. I don't know quite what is expected of me. "Thank you. Can I ask your name?"

She doesn't laugh in response, but I hear almost the echo of laughter there, just the same.

"No, dear. Who I am doesn't matter. If we were to have another call, I might be someone else. Take care of yourself." Then there is silence. I know she has disconnected. And once again, I'm alone.

CHAPTER SIX

HAD I BEEN expecting some kind of relief? Some kind of elevation? I think subconsciously I had. But I am disappointed. I have been "taken off active duty," yet nothing feels different at all. I personify ennui, which is such a concise, and elegant and useful word, it almost overwhelms me. But then again, *ennui*. So I sit down.

This, then, becomes my new reality. I am a couple of decades shy of any kind of retirement age, yet here I am, essentially retired.

I look back over all that I have been, all that I ever expected to be, and can't imagine what is left for me. As a result, I again spend some time with my gun near my hand, imagining what it would be to not imagine. To have that freedom. To finally make that choice: I have certainly danced closely enough to it more often than I can acknowledge as healthy.

The gun is a Bersa Thunder, a choice I made early on and have never regretted. The backstreet guy who sold me my first weapon out of the trunk of his car told me it was "a good gun for a woman." He has not been wrong. It is light and responsive, and when called upon, the thunder comes as promised. There's no going back.

So dances. And choices. But it's one I don't make, and I don't even know the reason. I don't quite go there. Why? There is the dog. There is the child, now lost, whose memory I hold. I am the only one who still holds it. That seems important, even though I know it doesn't count. Still. Also, there is possibility. I realize that last of all. Possibility. And with that, inevitably, comes hope. On that note, I sign up for an online course in becoming a nutritionist. The course is being offered by Cornell University. It isn't everything, but it's something. Something to begin. And, no: the irony of that choice is not lost on me. I who have made a late career out of killing people for money studying an art that helps people's lives be better. Different people, of course. But still.

It should be understood right at the outset that I have zero ambition in becoming a nutritionist. I am interested in nutrition. In the material that will lead me to the course, I read that I will learn about the transport of fat and the role of carbohydrates and other things that connect our health to the things we put in our body. These are topics that fascinate me, though I don't analyze why. They're so much about life, aren't they? And I haven't always been. And the diploma, when I've earned it, won't even be in my name, but in that of the fake ID on which I've built the forest part of my life. Still, ridiculously, the Ivy League nature of the association intrigues me. I—or whoever I have become—will have a degree in nutrition from Cornell. That's an accomplishment, no matter whose name is on the certificate. And maybe I'm ready for that, I think. Maybe I haven't had enough of accomplishment in a while. Or even ever. Maybe I want to raise my vibration. I think about the word for a while—*vibration*—and realize that it fits.

There are requirements to enroll in the course. Prerequisites. I meet them. Payment is of course required. I meet that, too. And though a lot of the material is online, some of it comes via snail mail—books, charts—and I am pleased at the tactile nature of them. In certain ways, it seems to make the whole thing more tangible. Things to touch and interact with. Non-electronic things. It makes everything—including me—feel more real.

As I settle into my classes, enjoying the feeling of learning and the expansion of mind that comes with it, a text comes in. For a moment, the sudden glow reminds me of the life I'd chosen, left behind, and the parts of that I had enjoyed. Not always the work itself, which has at times been awful. But the precision of it. And the feeling of accomplishment when it all comes together. Job well done, and so on. I savor that feeling for a moment now, before I look down at the text. Three words.

This one's special.

And I can't imagine what it means.

CHAPTER SEVEN

EVERYTHING IS SPECIAL, in its way, isn't it? Everyone and everything. We all have our place; the position where we fit, even if we don't recognize it in our everyday.

I'm pretty sure that isn't what the text means.

At first, I don't know what to do. I had cut off all connection. Closed, though not banged, the door. And it's not that I want back in, not at first. But I'm curious. What could be special enough to bring me out of retirement? To take me away from nutrition and Cornell?

I initiate a call to the Ukrainian number that had called me but there is, of course, no dice. Not even a wrong number. A recording. As though it had never been used at all.

Then the obvious answer comes to me and I return the text, thinking a while before I send it:

How so?

The answer takes long enough that I give up on it; thinking it will never come. I go back to my deep contemplation of saliva production and the body as a tube and other things I would never have thought of as being related to nutrition. Then two days later:

Something is rotten in Denmark.

And though I ponder for a while, the words make exactly no sense to me. Some connection with Copenhagen, maybe? Or cheese? Finally, I Google. It turns out it's from *Hamlet* and in modern terms means that some element isn't as it should be. Which, of course, is no more of an answer than continued deep silence would have been.

I think carefully before I reply, but nothing particularly brilliant comes to me. I go with a response that is weak, yet accurate:

I don't understand.

The reply comes much more quickly this time:

Of course you don't.

I'm still shrugging as the phone rings. I don't recognize the number, but I have to stifle a laugh when I note that it says the call is coming from Copenhagen.

Denmark.

Of course it is.

"Hello?" I say tentatively when I answer.

The voice. That first of all. I feel as though I would have recognized it anywhere. It is the same voice. Spidery chalk on glass. I am relieved.

"What makes it special?" I say without preamble once I've identified the caller.

A hesitation. And then: "It is opposite."

"Opposite?"

"Yes. Opposite of what we usually do. You will get a dossier with all the information you will need to complete your task. But the task this time is to keep the subject alive. Not kill her."

Her.

I scrunch my eyes up at the phone. Part of this isn't making sense.

"How did she even find us? There are people who are in the business of protecting people. Why call us?"

The hesitation is so long, I think maybe the connection has broken. Then the whispery voice is back. "She did not hire us. The client in this case is me."

"You?"

"Right. The subject is my daughter. She will not be aware you are on the job."

"Does she know she is in danger?"

"She knows she is in danger. She is not taking it seriously." A pause, and then: "She does not think it is serious and she will not know you are on the job."

There are so many possible questions that I don't know where to begin. I douse almost all of them, because I intuit my time on the phone with her will be limited.

"If you are, then, essentially the client, how will I be paid?"

She surprises me by laughing. It's not what she'd expected me to ask. For reasons I don't understand, that pleases me.

"You will be paid in the usual way. But the job won't be straight in and straight out, so there will be expenses. I'll cover those on this one."

"I'll be honest: I don't know where to begin."

"You will," she says.

"You're not making any sense."

"I know," she says without regret. "Not everything always makes sense from the very first."

I hesitate. Then: "I'm to trust you. That's what you're suggesting."

She laughs again. A warm yet whispery sound.

"I guess it could feel like that," she says. "Yet I understand that there are reasons for trust to be difficult between us." I think about that. About what it might mean: that we'd never spoken before that first, recent time. That she might be anyone. That I really don't know who she is, or if it had been her doing the handling of me all along, or someone else. Or it could be that the one thing I do know about her for sure is that she organizes people to kill other people. In polite society, none of these things would inspire trust. But here we are.

"And yet . . ." I prompt.

"Exactly," she says. And I smile into the phone despite myself. I can tell that even our sense of humor is similar. "And really," she continues, "I could explain myself, but even that wouldn't make sense. I guess, as you said, I'm suggesting you trust me."

And though it went against the agreement I'd made with myself, in the end, trust is what I do.

CHAPTER EIGHT

WHEN THE DOSSIER arrives the next day, some blanks are filled in, but not a lot. Not as many as I'd like.

The woman I am to protect is the CTO of a high-tech start-up with a billion dollar–plus valuation. She is chief technical officer of a unicorn start-up. That's a big deal.

She is around my age. And she is lovely—I can see that in the photographs. She is most often dressed in bright yellows and soft grays: both colors that look well with her complexion. She is possessed of thick chestnut hair and a bright, mischievous glint in lustrous eyes. Many would think her beautiful. And I think again about the handler's voice and wonder at the hints this gives about that woman on the phone. I check the CV: the daughter's name is Virginia Martin. She did her undergrad work at MIT, graduate work at Cambridge, then came back to the States to do her PhD at Stanford. All of that tells me that, in addition to everything else, she is brilliant. Brilliant and accomplished. Brilliant, accomplished, and beautiful. In case you've ever wondered: life is not fair.

Also, as it turns out, she is lucky. Or, at least, there are times when she has been. While in the Stanford Venture Technologies program, she developed tech for turning garbage into energy, though that had been her focus all along; even an award-winning science project in high school that seemed to start her trajectory along that vein. Saving the world by cleaning it up. It had always been her passion and is now her vocation, as well. It now appears to be her whole life.

As I research, I discover that what makes her technology different and better than all of the many who are barking at the edge of this field is that it is a completely green tech process—she'd won awards that said so, too. And five years ago, she'd been hired by a company called Greenmüll Energy to put into practice what she'd spent several years developing: a low-energy waste-to-energy system intended for home use. And not just any home—that was the key—for *all* homes. In the deck the CEO of Greenmüll prepared and had made available on the company's website, there was a device in every home in America. Hell: potentially every home in the world. That added up to a lot of devices.

In a carbon-starved world, it didn't take much for the potential of Virginia Martin's breakthrough technology to sink in. "Disruptive" was a word that got used a lot in the many articles written about her around the time Greenmüll brought her on board. She was a "disruptor" and her technology was "disruptive." It was going to change the world. Disruptively. And almost everyone wanted a piece of that action.

They raised a lot of money before they got anywhere near revenue. Early prototypes didn't work especially well. Coatings had to be upgraded and energy sources reconsidered. Then there was the matter of producing the devices. Martin was adamant that the energy of a technology meant to energetically save the world should not be manufactured in China.

"Does that even make sense to you?" an article in *Business Week* quoted her as saying. "What we're manufacturing will help to clean up the world . . . and we're going to schlep it all the way across the world from *China*? No. We have to manufacture in North America. It's not a discussion. North America is not ready for us? Well, get ready. I *know* there is an outfit here in the United States—or in a pinch Canada or Mexico, so it stays North American—that can make themselves ready to handle this. See, here's the thing: We're going to save the world? We're going to need all hands on deck."

That article was two years old, but as far as I could tell, the question of where the devices were going to be manufactured had still not been settled. Which meant they did not yet exist in the real world. Also, five years on, the company was still not in revenue. And they continued to raise money. It was an interesting setup, for sure. But none of it clued me in as to why someone might want her dead.

"Trust the process," I whisper to myself as I move ahead, not even fully sure what I mean.

I note that Virginia Martin lives and works in a largish city not far from me. In fact, it is close to my hometown. If I'm very careful and avert my eyes, I'll barely notice as I drive by. That will be my plan because I opt to drive to this assignment rather than fly. Social distancing has gotten to be a habit and I find I'm still not feeling comfortable in air-conditioned public spaces, especially when I'm trapped, as on a plane. There are days that I think I'll never have that easy travel comfort again.

It's early spring, and the days are cool. And since I'm driving, I decide to bring the dog along. He's always freakishly grateful for any ride in the car. And me: maybe I'm freakishly grateful for the company.

Once in her city, I decide to begin by getting a feel for Martin's routine and who might be watching. I think as I've been trained to think. If I were wanting to kill her, what would I look for? What would I do?

On first inspection I discover that she is not as easy a target as I had at first imagined. The company offices are in an industrial park at the edge of town. Fully high tech, but also low rise. It's a stretch for me to approach, which of course means that anyone wanting to kill her will also have a hard time getting close.

She lives in a townhouse in a gated community. Alone, as far as I can tell. To get close enough to her to fulfill an assignment, someone would have to get creative and wait for the right time.

Belatedly, I realize this is not going to be an easy in and out. I curse myself for bringing the dog when I try to book a hotel: not all hotels will take him. Many that do want assurance that he won't be in the room by himself at any time. Since I will be leaving him for a while by himself for sure, that's an obstacle.

I find a four-star hotel where check-in means an extra seventy-five bucks a night for the dog. The extra loot also buys us the special "canine guest pack" that includes a squeaky toy, a rawhide chew, and some cookies for him intended to be delicious and make his coat more shiny. He turns his nose up at the weird cookies, but goes batshit crazy for the squeaky toy. He's so happy with it, I feel like a bad mom for never having gotten him one before.

The rawhide chew I save for when I go out to take care of business. The way things are developing, it seems like he might be spending a fair amount of time alone. I may as well give him a project.

I know I need to look the situation over carefully, to see if I can determine the weak areas. Where would I begin, if the circumstances were normal? What would I be doing and considering if my goal was to kill her? And so I stalk her online, because isn't that always the best place to begin?

One thing I notice right away: the settings on her Facebook page are lax. They are so lax, I'm shocked that someone in high tech would not be more careful. Anyone can see anything she has said or is doing. Does that mean she doesn't get Facebook or that she is simply a very open person? Or maybe she doesn't care who is looking or can't imagine anyone would. I can't tell. But it affords me a glimpse of her life beyond her personal lockdown. She's a workaholic so there isn't much. I spend some time scanning through her photos to see if there is one of, or reference to, someone she calls "mom" but nothing turns up, so I get back to the business at hand: checking to see if she's left any clues to her schedule. It's a long shot, but I'm pleased when it plays out. That very morning, via Facebook, she had told her hairstylist she was looking forward to seeing her that afternoon. Her hairstylist has responded with a "likewise" and a bunch of heart emojis.

That presents an obvious beginning. Because it's Facebook, it is easy for me to determine the who and where of said hairstylist and then push myself in that direction so that I arrive ahead of the appointed hour. If I were going about my usual business, this would be the perfect opportunity: possibly from the car as she walked in. Then case closed and I'm gone before anyone even realizes what happened. But this is not business as usual. Still, getting my eyes on her at close range seems like a good starting point. Testing the waters, as it were.

Before I go in, I sit in my car for a while, checking the vicinity carefully. I see no place that would be ideal for a sniper to hide and no suspicious watchers or vehicles. We're in a posh neighborhood of low-rise condos. Taking her out from one of those would mean first having access to a private residence, but also—and maybe more importantly—it would be very easy to see where such a shot came from. It wouldn't be ideal for so many reasons. And this is not a usual stop for Virginia. She obviously does not head to her salon every day, plus I'm figuring that most people trying to kill her probably wouldn't first check her Facebook page, but I allow that I could be wrong.

CHAPTER NINE

THE SALON IS small and exclusive. Two stylists work in an airy space and you know instantly that this is not the sort of salon that has employees. Rather these are owner/operators and so they know their clients well and treat and protect them as friends. I can tell I'm going to have my work cut out for me because, in this environment, an outsider is detectable instantly. I have to work to be less outside. But that gives me an idea.

"Can I help you?"

The stylist who has approached me is an elegant woman with perfectly coifed blond hair. Movie star hair. The hair—color, style, everything—is perfect. I recognize her from her Facebook photo. It is she of the heart emojis.

"I . . . I was hoping for an appointment?" I say tentatively. After all, when in Rome.

The stylist looks at me appraisingly. Or rather she looks at my hair. At this point, that hair has not seen the inside of a salon for at least two years. It's possibly much longer than that, but I can't make myself think about it. I know it doesn't look crazy or wonky or anything, but to a practiced eye I'm certain the lack of expert care shows. Or maybe that's my own paranoia.

"Whadja have in mind?" she asks gently.

"I think it could use a trim," I say cautiously.

"You think?" she says sarcastically, and I decide not to feel offended at her prod.

Instead, I grin sheepishly. The look is genuine. "Yeah. Most probably. Maybe some expert advice, too. You know: recent breakup, blah, blah, blah."

She laughs at that, as she was meant to.

"Oh, I hear you, hon. 'Blah, blah, blah' indeed! I'm booked solid this morning. But I can fit you in for a trim and a consult while my next client is under the dryer. That might be a good start for you. Maybe forty-five minutes from now. You want to come back?"

"Okay if I chill here and read?" I ask, indicating a comfy waiting area not far from the stylist's chairs: recent magazines and a view of a charming street beyond the window.

"Suit yourself," she says. "Coffee?"

I say yes, and while she's making me a latte, Virginia Martin walks in.

In person she is even more beautiful than the photos had suggested. There is a sort of intense vibrance about her. I have a tough time imagining her entering anywhere and not turning heads. Even arriving at the salon, she looks as though she has just left a salon. I want to hate her, but find I don't have it in me. Especially when she shoots a smile in my direction. It lights the place up. "Hey, Minerva," she says to the stylist.

"Take a seat, hon. I'm finishing up here."

Martin sits down in a comfy chair across from me. She shoots an easy smile in my direction, exposing even white teeth. She looks at her phone for a minute or two, then grabs a magazine and settles in. I watch her surreptitiously for a moment and think I notice a strain at the jaw; maybe tiredness or worry around the eyes. I tell myself I might be imagining these things, but I don't think so.

Whatever the case, I realize this moment is a gift. Here she is: spitting distance. I can discover some things, maybe. I'll never have a chance like this again.

"She's good?" I say by way of a conversation opener, pushing my thumb in the direction of the stylist, finishing with a client.

She looks up from her magazine. Not enough time has passed for her to be truly immersed.

"Minerva?" she says. "Oh yes. She's wonderful."

"How long have you been coming to her?"

She pauses to think. "Six, seven years. You?"

"This is my first visit," and she doesn't comment on my unruly mane and she doesn't even look like she's thinking about it. She seems kind. Not critical.

"Oh, I get why you're asking then. Reassurance. Yeah: she's the best. She knows what to do with our kind of hair."

Our kind.

I touch my thick, raggedy locks. Compare what I feel with what I see. And I have a tough time imagining us—she and I—on the same plane of existence. She is exquisite. And I . . . I am not.

She sees my reaction and misreads it. An emotion floods her face. It isn't pity. Maybe understanding. I suddenly wish I was anywhere else.

"It's okay." She has spoken again, though I haven't said anything. She is reassuring me. Maybe thinking my lack of words stems from insecurity about my hair. I go with that.

"Yeah," I say. "Silly. I know. I once left a salon with a pixie cut when all I wanted was a trim."

"Pixie cut?"

"It's like . . ." I mime striking off all my hair with a chopping motion near my ears. We both laugh.

"How did you hear about her?" she asks and I spot an opening I hadn't considered.

"I walked in," I say, indicating the front door. "I thought the salon looked nice. You?"

I sense more than hear a hesitation. I don't understand it, but I wait. Listen. Feeling that whatever I'm seeing might make itself more clear.

"We go back a long way," Virginia Martin is saying. "Minerva and I have become friends. I'm not from here originally and I miss my mom a lot."

My ears perk up even more. I find myself wanting to ask about her mother, but I can't quite get the words out. I figure it is partly because I feel respectful of my handler's privacy, despite the situation. But also, I figure that any question in that direction might seem super weird. I content myself with a sort of sympathetic murmur, then guide the conversation in a different direction.

"I like to guess what people do for a living," I say. It's a lie. I don't usually care about the lives of strangers. Most of the time I have close to no interest at all. "And I'm usually pretty good at it. Indulge me, please. I am thinking you are a lawyer."

Her eyes go kind of wide and then she surprises me by laughing. "Oh, I'm sorry," she says. "But you're so far off."

"Really?" I sniff, as though lightly miffed.

"Yes. I'm in STEM."

I look at her questioningly and she replies to what I don't ask: "Science, technology, engineering, and mathematics."

"That's a lot."

She laughs. "Yeah. Truly. I never thought of it that way, but yeah. I guess it *is* a mouthful. It's shorthand, though. For the sciences. And all the stuff that goes with it."

"You're, like, a . . . mathematician?"

She laughs, like what I said was funny. But it's a kind laugh so I don't take offense.

"No. Nothing like that at all. I'm CTO of a high-tech company." I look at her blankly in order to keep her talking. I'm trying not to show how much I already know. Sometimes that's hard. "Chief technical officer. I developed a technology. And the company I work for is helping bring it to market."

"Cool," I say, meaning it. "That sounds super challenging and also satisfying."

A cloud passes over her face. A shadow. Gone so quickly, I'm not even sure I really saw it.

Minerva joins us then and the relief on my companion's face at her arrival is both comical and telling. If I hadn't sensed there was more to what was being said, I'd know now.

"You stay put," the stylist says to me cheerily, but you get the idea that she knows she will be obeyed. If she senses any tension, she gives no sign. "I'm going to get this one started, then settled under the dryer. Then I'll come back for you, okay?"

I thank her and pick up a magazine. Minerva's station is maybe sixteen feet from where I sit and it's not a busy salon. Still, I have to strain to hear what they say. They are situated at the farthest reaches of my hearing and another stylist and customer are in the range of what comes to me. And, despite the straining, most of what passes between them is banal.

And then the energy between Mineva and Virginia changes and it is more. I feel it as much in the energy of the room as anything else. I can see it, too, in their body language, catching glimpses from over the top of my magazine.

What I see is deep concern on the part of the stylist, the indication of emotion quite beyond the desire that the color she is applying be correct. And I think I see fear on the part of the client. The body language is clear. She is afraid. And not of Minerva.

And then it is my turn, while Virginia is under the dryer, and my hair is corrected and coerced and what has been wrong for a good long time is made right. Toward the end, when Minerva picks up her flat iron to finish my hair, I protest.

"Please. Not that."

"Sorry?" She asks.

"I . . . never mind. I would prefer if you didn't use that."

And she looks at me for a second like she might protest or insist, but then maybe at what she sees in my eyes, she relents. She uses a blow dryer and a brush to do the finishing instead.

When I leave the salon, I am beautiful. I can feel it. My hair bounces around me as though with a life of its own. Shampoo commercial pretty. A good cut. A salon treatment to finish it. I feel my hair springing around me as I walk out of the salon and all I want to do is cry, reminded of what was long lost.

CHAPTER TEN

I AM FINISHED hours before Virginia and so I get back in my car and sit outside the salon for a while and observe anything that seems to need observation. If she is in danger from anyone in the vicinity, I don't see it. Besides, seeing the salon connection was a lucky break on my part. If I'd looked at Facebook at any other time, I wouldn't have noted the exchange and known to be here. No: this salon would be an unlikely place for an assassin to even know about, let alone do the hit.

Still, I wait. And since the waiting doesn't require my close attention, I pull out my nutrition texts and give them my awareness. It's early days for me in the course and it's turning out to be a bit of a slog. I had thought I knew a lot about nutrition. I had thought this would be a skate, but it turns out there's a lot I don't know: like everything. And with my attention diverted as it is, it's often difficult for me to focus. At the moment, though, I can't imagine a time when I will be clear to simply focus again. And that's interesting, too. Being back in the world again is challenging me in ways I hadn't expected. It's like in my time in pain and isolation I've become a square peg and I don't fit in the round hole anymore.

I just don't fit.

After a while Virginia leaves the salon and gets into a Land Rover that is parked nearby. She drives away, but I don't follow. Instead, I sit there and watch, informed more by instinct than anything. I wait to see if elements of the scene change after she leaves.

Sure enough, almost as soon as Virginia is in motion, a dark blue sedan pulls into traffic behind her. And me? I pull out behind him. From my position, I can't see much. I balance my phone on the wheel while I drive and take a photo of his license plate. I'll run it later, but I'm reasonably sure the car will prove to be a rental. And how sure am I? There are factors of all of this that are stirringly familiar. Sure: it's a different package. And I know I've never met him before. Still: I recognize him. He is me and I am him. At some level, we are one. And I am certain he is here to kill Virginia Martin.

*   *   *

It doesn't help that I don't know the town. I don't know where we're going and I in no way understand the lay of the land. Still, I stick to him like glue. I know what it is to tail and be tailed. I do it carefully and am careful so that he does not detect me.

Virginia Martin pulls over at a Whole Foods and I see her prepare to go inside. I know it will be harder to tail her when she is in the store. Because of that, I wait for her to go inside, then I slip out of my car and begin to follow the follower. Before he enters the store, I approach him from behind and stick two fingers into his back. I smile, so that anyone observing would think it is a lover's joke, but to him I whisper, "One wrong move and I'll take you out right here," hoping like hell he doesn't realize that my fingers aren't loaded.

His reaction is instantaneous. My fingertips feel him tense up and he swings around as though to grab my gun. But the gun, of course, being my hand, puts me in a potentially dire predicament. I punch forward hard, directly into his solar plexus, and have the satisfaction of hearing him utter a sharp "Oof," as my fingers connect with soft flesh. It's a victory, but a tiny one. He is larger and heavier than I am and he recovers quickly. I see him pull himself together and I run back the way I'd come. I am unsure if he will chase me or go back after Virginia. I try to think what I would do in his place and realize, as I run, that I would likely go after my target, and never mind the pesky interloper: I'd have a job to do. Knowing that getting this wrong might cost me my life, I spin, half expecting to see him bearing down on me. When I discover that he is not, I'm both relieved and anxious because it means that I'm safe for the moment, but he has gone after Virginia. From the looks of this hombre, that means she is in serious trouble. What makes it worse is that she doesn't even know it.

In the store I have to guess where he went, because I see no sign of him. But, again, I try to think what I would do in his place were I on this job as I head back inside.

Reasoning that most people only do the perimeters of grocery stores anymore, that's where I head: I run the edges. It doesn't take long for me to come across both of them. She is in discussion with the butcher. And the follower is stalking her—a cat watching a bird—from the frozen food aisle. There is a store employee near me. "Excuse me," I say quietly, but catching her attention. "I know this will sound odd, but I'm pretty sure I saw that man stuff a pack of steaks down his pants a few minutes ago."

"What?"

"Yeah," I say.

"Ugh," she replies.

"Yeah," I say again, pulling a face this time. "That's what I thought and I figured I'd better report it."

"Yeah. Thanks. I'll alert security," she says as she hustles off.

I melt into the shampoo and vitamins aisle and hope for the best. Minutes later, a security guard does indeed show up and have a quiet chat with the follower. I can't hear what is said, but I see the follower shake his head repeatedly and gesture emphatically toward his pants. The security guard seems to insist that the follower come with him and they head off toward the back of the store. It's a break, but I know I don't have much time. I direct my attention back to where I last saw Virginia, but she is gone. Is it too much to hope for? I catch sight of her leaving the checkout and heading toward her car. There is no sign yet of the follower. He is likely still entangled with explaining how frozen foods are not in his pants. I can't help but smile to myself.

I get out to the parking lot with enough time to see Virginia pop her purchases onto the back seat and drive away. I watch her leave unfollowed, then I get in my own car and head in the opposite direction. Back to the hotel. I'm feeling lucky and a little bit smug. And it's only a little because I realize this was a reprieve. He is still out there, and from what I've seen, he is as deadly as can be.

CHAPTER ELEVEN

AFTER MY RUN-IN with the assassin, I find I am dog tired so I take my newly bouncy hair back to the hotel. Time to regroup. Time to try and understand whatever all of this is. Something more that the handler had said. But what?

Sitting with my computer at the small desk in my hotel room, the dog curled gratefully around my feet, I delve again into Virginia Martin's background. I poke at what I can reach of her life in the hope that aspects of it all will strike a chord and that things may begin to make sense.

She is in danger. Her mother has told me this. And, of course, I have no proof of anything, but sometimes one has to go with what one knows and if instinct plays a part, so much the better. If I've been fed things that are incorrect, I'll find that out soon enough.

I do more background research than is generally necessary. I have enough information on Virginia Martin's whereabouts and habits that I could devise an acceptable way to take her out if that was the assignment. But this is a different sort of gig. Someone else is trying to kill her, and now I've seen that for myself. I figure that I have to establish two things: Why would someone want to have her killed? And, if they did, what would be the best way to do it? If I can figure that out, maybe I can prevent what's been set in motion. And meanwhile, I must watch.

I find an online service where you can plug in a plate number and for ten bucks almost instantly discover who the plate is registered to. This astonishes me fiercely, especially since the day I try it, the service is on sale for $3.98. I realize that paying for it will trigger a membership that I will have to try and remember to cancel before the month is up, but still. It's all so easy, I can't decide if it's a good or bad thing. In a world where I can get the owner of a car's name from their license plate number, is there anything left I can't do? I shrug it off and move on. It's helping me on this day. I decide to leave it alone.

I use the service and am unsurprised when the assassin's car does indeed prove to be a rental. The bad part of all of this is that I have virtually nothing to go on in determining who this assailant is and that frustrates me. At the same time, I recognize that knowing his identity won't make any difference to the total picture. I know what he's here to do. Does anything else matter?

I can take him out. That comes to me in a single arrow-like shot. *I can take him out.* I suspect that if I do that, he will be replaced by someone else. Even so, I know that will buy me some time—maybe a few days—but that might be enough to figure out exactly what is going on. The thought sits in my stomach like a bad pancake. I had said I wouldn't kill anymore. Not without good reason, anyway. But I'm having a tough time figuring what else to do. Killing him is easy. Clean. It gets the job done. All the other alternatives seem like make-dos. And I need a few days to breathe and figure out what really needs to be done.

I rest for a while. The dog joins me and we catnap. I set an alarm for my phone to wake me at midnight, and it does. I dress quickly and slip out the hotel room door, trying hard to ignore the plaintive look the dog sends after me. He hates it when I leave him. He hates it even more when it's the middle of the night. How can he keep me safe? I can see the question on his face as plain as anything. How can he keep me safe if I won't stay out of harm's way?

But a choice has been made. A selection. I feel like Madam Fate or the minister of death. I feel like someone who can affect outcomes. And I am, I realize. I do.

I beeline for Virginia's condo, and my hunch is right: on my first drive by, I spy the same nondescript blue sedan with plates registered to a rental company. I park in the next block and walk back, my Bersa-weighted purse easy on my shoulder.

He doesn't hear me coming. He is sitting in his rental listening to tunes. Of all the things he suspects will happen, being blindsided by the woman with pokey fingers from Whole Foods is not one of them.

This time, the gun I threaten him with is real, and he knows it: he can feel the cold at his temple.

"We have the same job," I say. "I know why you are here. I'm here to protect her. Who wins?"

To my surprise, he laughs. "Well, hmmm. At the moment, I guess you do. Considering."

"Yes," I say. "Considering."

"But it could go either way."

"I don't think so," I say. The statement comes out sounding as confident as I feel. There is no way I anticipate he will answer my next question—he probably doesn't even know the answer himself—but I ask it anyway. It's the reason I've stopped by to chat. After all, it would have been easier to take him out from the other side of the street: he wouldn't even have seen it coming. With every muscle alert to movement, I ask it. "Who hired you?"

His answer is pure movement. He moves quickly, as he did in the Whole Foods parking lot. The difference this time is that I'm holding a loaded gun: not a couple of fingers pressed into his back. And he hasn't given me an option. I squeeze the trigger. He dies quickly. It makes a horrible mess.

CHAPTER TWELVE

AND AGAIN, IT makes a horrible mess. Blood and brain matter. At this moment, I feel there is not a shower hot enough in the world to erase what I feel. And I'm mad at myself. I'm mad as hell. There were certainly other ways this whole scene could have gone. I didn't *need* to take him out, did I?

Did I?

And if I *did*, in fact, need to do it, could I have not at least done it in a less messy way?

I'm annoyed with myself, that's the thing. And I realize at the same time that the annoyance I feel verges on the not quite sane.

I am surprised to find that by the time I get back to my hotel, I am crying. I am *crying*. The emotion is unexpected. I have taken many lives, most of them possibly less culpable than this target was. And yet, I am moved. I suppose it is because I had a different plan in mind, one that would keep me from killing anymore, maybe forever. And now I have compromised what I imagined for myself. That's how I feel. Not only that, I did the killing in such a way—messy—that I have to be careful getting to my room without being seen. I manage it, though, and once I'm in, I leave my clothes in a trail from the front door to the shower. I don't feel that the shower will make things better, but it won't make things worse, either, and at least I'll be clean.

I spend a lot of time under the hot water, willing my mind blank. Not thinking of my own personal goals or even desires. Thinking instead about what is required of me now. Moving ahead: one step at a time. I stood up, that's what I tell myself. When things were difficult, I did not sit idly by.

Out of the shower, I wrap myself in a fluffy hotel spa robe. It is much too large for me. The ends of my fingers emerge from the sleeves and the hemline sweeps almost to the ground. I am enveloped.

The dog sniffs around the brain-spattered clothes I have left behind me. "Shoo, shoo!" I tell him. "Leave it!" And I go behind him and pick them all up, trying to crush them into the bathroom garbage. When that doesn't prove to be large enough, I find a plastic bag intended for dirty laundry in the closet. I stuff the clothes in there and leave them on a console table by the door where I'll grab it next time I'm out and toss them in the trash. I take care to leave the bag up too high for the dog to sniff at it. The dog doesn't know what the mess is from, of course. But it upsets me to think about him snacking on it.

Yet another thing to upset me.

Beyond the mess, of course, I worry briefly about discovery and about what DNA—mine included—that the clothes might hold. I reason, though, that if I leave it in the hotel's garbage Dumpster, it is unlikely to be found and even less likely to be connected to me. One way or the other, throwing the clothes in the trash will make them disappear.

I know I have solved the problem, short term. Not the clothing, but the larger problem of my immediate assignment. That's the thing with a gun for hire. You could take him out—sure you could—but another will jump up to take his place. I feel certain of that. I realize that anything I did in that regard would be a stopgap measure. In order to get Virginia Martin out of danger, I have to figure out who hired the hit. And I have to take that person out, if necessary, or do some other thing to stop the problem. Or solve it. There will have been a reason for the hit order. I realize that if I can figure out the reason, maybe everything goes away.

It is that possible necessity that undoes me for a while. The possibility of an endless line of Matryoshka dolls of assassins, coming to try and take Virginia Martin out. I fall asleep thinking about it. See their wooden faces chomping at everything I propose in defense.

When I wake, the television is still on and it's a newscaster that is blaring: there has been a dire event in the Middle East. It's a terrible thing, but I can't make myself feel it. Instead, I become aware of the uncomfortable crick in my neck from sleeping half on and off two pillows. I feel also the weight of yet another death on my head and hands and I try to make it matter but I can't. It upsets me even more.

My eyes fall on the Bersa where I had dropped it on the coffee table in front of the television. It's blue-gray skin glints at me from across the room and I think again about what the gun is capable of. What I can do with it. Any time I want.

I could end all of this right now. I have that power. And with that I challenge myself. Truly: I could end things easily. To some minds, I know, I *should* end things. What cowardly instinct prevents me from doing it? And I think about some alternate future where my baby—my sweet lost baby—lies in my arms, laughs at my jokes, waits for my love. If I could believe in that future, I would end this all in a heartbeat. But I feel I know better. And that, too, breaks my heart.

I push endgames and exit strategies out of my mind and push off the tall bed and head for the bathroom. The dog doesn't get up as I pass, but his tail thumps the ground approvingly. I have given up trying to think his thoughts don't matter to me. *He is only a dog.* But he is everything to me now, so he counts. Sometimes that's enough of a reason to resist the call to see what lies beyond.

Sometimes that's enough.

In the bathroom my eyes widen at the sight of me. My beautiful, bouncy hair isn't beautiful or bouncy anymore. I had showered late and slept on it wet and now it springs from my head dementedly: no more beautiful salon finish. That seems a metaphor, but I'm not sure for what.

CHAPTER THIRTEEN

BUT I RECOVER. I breathe. I manage to get my hair under control and convince myself that I have a future that matters and I do these things all around the same time.

I take the dog out early. We walk to a local coffee place, taking the long route in both directions. It might be a long day and I want him empty and exercised. Not for the first time I regret my impulse in bringing him along. His company is welcome, of course. But I hate to leave him cooped up in the hotel. His placid face reassures me that he doesn't mind. He is a Labrador retriever: his single aim is to please. If that means he spends the day waiting for me in a hotel room, so be it. That is his lot. It's a dog's life.

On the other hand, what if I did not bring him? Where would that leave me? Where would I be? Would I survive? I'm not so sure of that at this point. I suspect—and sort of know—that he is strongly linked to my survival. That makes no sense, but I don't care. I know it as well as I know that I have two hands.

By seven in the morning, I am sitting outside Virginia Martin's townhouse complex in my pale gray Volvo, waiting for her to emerge. Wanting to see where she goes. My car is nondescript; indistinct. Chosen for its invisibility and customized to suit my needs. It is dependable. It is comfortable to sit or travel in for many hours at a time. It is not so luxurious as to invite attention. Nor is it so decrepit as to make people wonder what it is doing in their neighborhood. It is exactly right.

And so it is that when Virginia Martin leaves her townhouse complex at about eight fifteen in her two-toned black-on-black Land Rover Defender 110, she does not notice when I slide onto the road behind her.

She goes directly to her office. Of course she does. I'd argued with myself about where to begin the day: the possibility of a couple of extra hours of shut-eye almost too tempting to resist. But that was not the game; not what I'd told myself. I wanted the whole day; there's no part I wanted to miss in case something happened. As it had turned out, there'd been nothing to miss and nothing happened. But hindsight is twenty-twenty and, anyway, one never knows.

I sit for a long while outside of the low-slung building that is Virginia Martin's office. Greenmüll Technologies is housed in an industrial park near the airport. I'd learned a lot about the company from an article in a business magazine that came out right after they'd closed their Series B financing. In that first cash-flushed moment, the company had locked down the lease on this place. As far as I can tell, securing the 80,000-foot facility had been the first big expense for the newly solvent company. That and an IPO.

Before the fateful Series B that the article mentioned, they had enjoyed a very successful Series A, which had gotten them to the next stage after the classic first stage "friends and family" financing that had started everything on a shoestring. But with what they had on offer, Greenmüll was never going to stay on that shoestring for very long.

When word got out that Martin's technology was above and beyond anything anyone else had even imagined and was going to change the world, a big deal investment banker type had gotten hold of them. And once he'd done that, the investors had come flocking in. It wouldn't have been a hard sell. Greenmüll had all the right stuff. Green tech. A solution for environmental concerns. Disruption in the energy field. Boom. A trifecta in the finance world. After the close of the second big fundraising round, the Series B, they were rolling in it.

That had been five years ago. And a billion-dollar valuation sounds like it represents an endless amount of money, but I knew it represented the value of the company, not the cash on hand. Greenmüll wasn't in revenue yet, so they'd be going through what cash they had very quickly.

Looking at the impressive operation, albeit from the outside, it seemed possible to me that Greenmüll might have a burn rate as high as a half million dollars a month. Possibly more. And spending six million dollars a year on operations puts a lot of strain on any company, especially if it's all going out and none is coming in. Additionally, any time there's a lot of money involved in anything, the chances of people getting killed go up; that's what I've seen. High stakes increase the danger. Always.

From outside of Greenmüll, though, I can't see much. The 80,000 square feet are part of a larger complex. In the other units in the complex, different industrial things are made. Fancy furniture right next door. Some sort of plastic-based widgets farther down. It's all on one level and there are a lot of windows, but in keeping with being a place where high-tech stuff is carried on, the windows facing the streets are all mirrored: they don't want people looking in. And while I understand their reasoning, it's annoying because I can see virtually nothing of what is going on inside.

I park slightly down the street and across from the building, so they probably don't notice me sitting there, but there's no way for me to be sure. One thing I do know: there's not much I can see. I sit in the Volvo and wait. And wait.

In the time between, I try to study my Cornell nutrition stuff, but it's not easy. Every time I become immersed, I worry I'll miss some important detail and I pull myself back in order to observe what's going on. In any case, I'm finding it difficult to concentrate on epigenetics and gene expression when I also have to keep an eye on the exit of a parking lot.

After a few hours, I think about walking right in the front door and having an innocent look around. I think about telling reception I'm making a delivery and seeing what I can see. But there are a couple of reasons for me *not* to do that. If I do manage to get a glimpse of Virginia, she might then recognize me following her in the car, for one. Or she might spot me from the day before at the salon and I don't want that. Also, and maybe most importantly, I probably won't get near her anyway. I figure there are probably gatekeepers at the front door whose job it is to keep the riffraff out. And that would be me. Riffraff of the highest order.

Greenmüll is a unicorn. All of this makes me fairly certain that Virginia Martin will be deeply ensconced someplace in the building, doing whatever it is she does here. I don't imagine I'll be able to get near her.

And so I stay put. Waiting for I don't know what and I'm beginning to think it will never occur.

At eleven fifteen, a man in a Porsche Taycan 4S arrives. The car is noteworthy because of everything. For one thing, it is so distinctive it turns heads. I Google quickly and discover that this particular model is a two-hundred-thousand-dollar car. You don't drive a distinctive two-hundred-thousand-dollar car unless you want people to notice your arrival.

The man is distinctive, as well. He parks right in front of the building across two spots marked "HANDICAPPED," and strolls inside. I try not to think about what that says about him.

Aside from being arrogant in his parking moves, he is movie star handsome, though once he has unfolded himself out of the Taycan I can see he is not tall; perhaps my own height, which is average, at best. He is like a tiny movie star, and he moves with the self-awareness of the insecure: as though he is certain that everyone is looking at him. I am sitting in front of a building the size of a shopping mall. There could be hundreds of people inside. And yet I know—I just *know*—that this is what I've been waiting for. I feel it in my bones.

I jot down his license number. It seems likely that this car is not a rental. Then, because I also have nothing to do, while I sit in the car, one eye on the entrance, I put the plate into the service I had registered with the day before and am astonished all over again when I get the plate results within a few minutes, via e-mail. I am astonished, but also surprised with what I learn since the name that comes up for the badass Porsche doesn't belong to a person.

The car is owned by a company called Extreme Angels LLC. The name intrigues me. What about it is extreme? Anything with angels in it should be, of course. Or is it the alliance itself that invites extremity? I think about it a bit, then decide I won't be able to work it out. Before I can even hit Google, the Porsche driver emerges from the building, but now he has a folder under one arm. He jumps back into his car and makes to drive away. In one of those decisions so snap you later wonder if they were made for you, I start the Volvo and follow him, realizing that Virginia Martin might leave while I'm not watching, but knowing that I've made the right choice.

CHAPTER FOURTEEN

I FOLLOW THE Taycan out of the industrial park and then along a smooth business boulevard for a mile or two. I keep a few car lengths back; varying the distance, keeping it cool. At the same time, I second-guess my reasons for following him, hoping it isn't because I was bored. I know that he might have nothing at all to do with she who I had staked out. Yet even while I have this thought, I know that my instincts have not led me astray.

As I follow him into an older industrial neighborhood in a different part of town, I think about how it is that, left unfettered, my instincts seldom do head me in the wrong direction. That how while it's sometimes difficult to get myself to a place of solid listening to those instincts, when I get there—without the second-guessing and overriding of my conscious mind—I seldom head the wrong way. And is it that all of us have this additional information and knowledge inside us that we seldom have the skill to access? That's what I wonder. Are we all plugged into some universal neural network, and we're too stupid or dense or intentionally blind to see?

After a while, he pulls the car in front of a low-slung light industrial building, and I stop thinking about the existential. The street is quiet and I don't want him to notice me, even though he has no reason to care who I am. But I keep going, not parking until I turn the corner, out of his sight.

It is a neighborhood that I can tell was all gray industry not many years ago. Now it is in the process of revitalizing. I've pulled up in front of a nano brewery whose logo makes me think it is a place where beards and man buns would be in sharp evidence. The place is closed now, but it pulls the neighborhood into focus for me.

Over there remains a collision shop, "Graham and Sons, since 1972." It is right next to a fresh-looking furniture design shop that is next to a small film studio. The neighborhood is not yet what it will be, but neither is it what it was.

My target, he of the extreme angels, has gone into the building he stopped in front of. At a distance it could be a small paint factory or veterinary compound or a medical supply company. Up close I can see that elements of factory have been painted over and there is an air of elegant sophistication about the result. A small brass plaque at the door lettered in a stately, well-considered font announces that this is the home of Extreme Angels LLC. Though I can determine virtually nothing from outside of the building, everything I *can* tell leaves a sense of expense and no detail left to chance.

Farther down the block I find a chic café, as I expected I would. It is populated by young bearded men with alternate man buns and shaved heads—too much hair or not enough hair—all of them look as though they might work at the furniture place or the brewery or be hard at work at the next great American novel. The women with them are invariably petite and mostly have shorter hair than the men in the place: pert little bobs or cute and precise shag cuts. It makes them all look tidy and efficient. There is a certain uniformity for both genders. I don't think about it a lot, though. Social evaluation is not what I'm here for.

In the café, I order a latte. I'm not hungry, but I also order a cheese danish that looks as though it will be the best one ever conceived of, then settle at the one empty table in the place, at a window, yet farthest from the door.

The Danish, when I bite into it, is as earth shatteringly good as I'd anticipated. I wonder how I have survived this long without having tasted anything like it. It is so good that if I were in an emotional mood, I would be tempted to cry. I suspect it is possible I will never have anything so delicious again. Does it go without saying that the latte is perfect? As is the swan carefully sketched into the foam. Latte art. The perfection of the place makes me momentarily lament that there is nothing remotely like this in my everyday life, even though I have an espresso machine and I've recently learned to bake.

Once my awe at the near-perfect has subsided, I take out my phone and settle in to enjoy the rest of my coffee while I do a bit of research.

Extreme Angels LLC has a website. It is perfect, of course. Easy to navigate; clear to read. It looks very expensive. The website says a lot without saying much at all. We learn that Extreme Angels are a group of local businesspeople "intent on finding next year's best idea *now*." Which, of course, is exactly what every angel program ever thought of intends to do: they get together to pool money to lend to start-ups. On the surface, they are helping struggling young companies who lack whatever is needed to get bank financing. Below the surface, the angels are hoping to find the next big thing, because when that company hits it big, the angels will collectively own a piece of the action.

Though the language Extreme Angels uses on their website makes it sound like they are different from other angel groups, I don't see anything that confirms that.

The website *does* tell me that Extreme Angels LLC had been founded a decade before by Rance Carver. He is the managing partner. He's kind of the executive director of the thing: the face people see when they reach out to Extreme Angels. The voice on the phone.

There is a picture of Rance there. And I am unsurprised to see the man I had followed in the Taycan smiling out at me from the photo. He is classically handsome. A wide smile. Clear blue eyes. Fair, unblemished skin. That whole package and every other little thing makes me cautious about him from the start.

According to the website, Carver had started out as a teacher, but switched later to finance, landing a job at one of the major investment firms and successfully working with high-end clients over a number of years. "It was in this capacity that Rance came to understand the potential for greatness that all of us possess, as well as the connection to our inner selves that all of us can learn to speak with."

There was more of this: bullshit words intended to help people who feel they are missing essential pieces find the parts of themselves they don't have easy access to. "Everything you have dreamed about is possible. Everything desired can be yours."

I sit there for a minute, letting the words sink in.

Everything desired can be yours.

Not everything.

Inexplicably, I feel an old sadness choke my heart, but it doesn't last long. Then I push it aside. It's a feeling that can drown you if you let it. I know. I've nearly drowned here before.

I push myself on. I *swim* through it. I am so intent on the emotions I am trying to marshal that I don't at first notice the couple come in and take the table next to me, at the window, but closer to the door. She is willow thin, with a model's height and beauty. Her companion is not as tall as she is, yet his face is familiar to me. Having looked at his photo moments before, I don't recognize Rance Carver right away. When I do, I marvel at the coincidence of us being in the same coffee shop then realize, of course, that since his office is practically next door, the coincidence is slight.

The pair settle in with their coffees and I strain to hear what they say, but the ceilings in the café are high and the ambient noise is, too. I see them move their heads closer together in order to hear what is being said, and while I watch, I try to decipher the language of their bodies. Is an intimacy and mutual regard beyond the usual between them? Their heads are close together as they chat, but is it the noise or circumstance that forces them close? I wonder if they are lovers. Or maybe they are friends and he would like it to be more. This discerned from the slightest pulling away here and there—always her, never him. She doesn't want to offend, but absolute closeness is undesired. I chide myself on this narrative: it is me weaving this story, for sure. But I look over again, see him lean into her almost imperceptibly, then move back. I don't think that I'm wrong.

I lift my phone, pretending to examine and answer a message while surreptitiously taking a photo. Him I see only in profile, but it's really a photo of her. Why does her identity matter? I don't know. But I suddenly feel that it does.

CHAPTER FIFTEEN

WHEN I CHECK the Extreme Angels website, I discover that her name is Hattie Washington and she is from my hometown. Her name and face are not familiar to me though I know that, since she is probably several years younger than me and I haven't lived there for a while, not recognizing her doesn't mean I don't know her family or even her. Her beauty seems rare and exotic, but I'm guessing that, if I *did* know her, in memory I'd simply be seeing a cute kid.

I learn other things from the website. For instance, a bold link asks if I am interested in being an Extreme Angel. Following the link on the website lets me know that an introductory meeting is held every Wednesday evening at seven p.m. Business casual attire. Refreshments will be served. And when I consider, I realize that today is indeed that day.

I stay on in the café until after Hattie and Rance leave. I get into the Volvo, but I don't go straight back to the hotel. Instead, I follow a combination of instinct and tourist guides and find what I've been led to believe is the best shopping district in the city because I'd come for a simple job and now our third day will definitely stretch into a fourth. In addition to this, I have to go somewhere looking like I'm ready to do business. Supplies are needed.

I find a tony street; all chic boutiques. All too expensive, but for what? And I have a sense that fitting in with the crowd tonight will require straight hemlines and European-made shoes at the very least.

I buy an elegant outfit: black pants, gray t-shirt, black jacket. Altogether the ensemble costs roughly what I paid for my first car. I don't stress about it—and not because it was a cheap car, even though it was. I don't try to tell myself about how many times I'll wear these things in the future; I choose and then go. I buy, also, a casual outfit beyond anything I ever thought existed. The jogging pants and sweatshirt are gray and soft, like cashmere, but made to be athletic wear. I can't imagine sweating in them, but I know that I will try it, especially when teamed with the ridiculously expensive athletic shoes I buy to accompany them. Trail runners. Who even knew there was such a thing?

But the running shoes are so soft and light, I have to struggle to regret the purchase. In the same shop, I buy a signature bag and shoes that complement it, all in leather as supple as butter. The softness makes the shoes seem too delicate to walk in. I wonder about it. How can anyone walk in shoes so soft? And what is it about all this softness, anyway?

On the way back to the car, burdened by my packages, I pass a store selling elegant pet supplies. I pop in and buy a beautiful hand-tooled leather collar for the dog and a matching leash. And I get another squeaky toy while I'm at it. I'm not sure why, because he doesn't need a disguise, but it seems like stuff that he will like, and I seem to be in the mood to shop. I get the feeling and opportunity so seldom that I simply lean in and buy.

On the way back, to the hotel I stop at a drugstore and buy toiletries. Here again I buy beyond what I normally would. Lipstick in a dull plum shade. Eyeshadow. And BB Cream, though

I barely know what it is. Blush. Brushes with which to apply all this stuff. It is as though I am buying for someone else. Someone with more exacting and expensive tastes. Even though it's from a drugstore this time. I feel I have to draw some lines.

When I get back to the hotel, the dog is characteristically delighted to see me. It makes me feel like I've been gone for weeks. A month. As though he had doubted I would ever return. I don the smart cashmere-like tracksuit and put the dog's fancy new collar and leash on him and we head out for a walk. By now I think he must be beginning to miss our wild forest strolls, but he behaves very well on the leash in the city park. Memories from another life, maybe. Memories from a time when leashes and city walks were a normal part of everyday business for him.

"We'll get back to the forest," I tell him as we walk through a manicured section of park. But it's hard to imagine. Me in cashmere and with bouncy hair. Him in his rich dog attire. It's like we have transformed. It's as though we are no longer the creatures who began this journey.

We stroll in a nearby park. There are beautiful water features on either side of a long corridor of walkway. It is lovely, but it is not quite a forest; not quite the same. I imagine he looks at me hopefully, but I realize that is simply me being fanciful, even though the days do seem to be dragging on. We've been three days already, and I don't feel I've made any progress. I try to imagine the things at home that demand my attention, but realize there is nothing much. Even the small garden I've put in is self-sustaining, and the house locks up tight. We could stay a month—two—and nothing much would be different. There are things that are sad for me in that realization. I try to put it out of my mind, but it sticks.

I turn up at the Extreme Angels building slightly before seven. I find myself in an anteroom, face-to-face with Hattie

Washington. Even this close, I do not recognize her from our hometown, though I try. She is looking sleek and svelte in an outfit not unlike my own, but she's wearing dark brown slacks and a cream-colored blouse.

"Hello," she says, flashing me a high voltage smile. I look around, and though others have entered before and with me, her attention is on me. I wonder at that for a moment, then remember the bouncy, salon-fresh hair. The three-thousand-dollar purse. Shoes that match. All perfectly put together in a single outfit. And I'm certain it's perfect because that was the mandate I gave to the clerk in the shop: make it perfect, because I can't tell. Make it look as though I can be careless with money. The others in the clump I have entered with are more ordinary. Instinctively—though with help from the woman in the shop—I've managed to hit the right notes.

"Welcome to Extreme Angels," she says now. "We're happy to have you. What brings you to us tonight?"

"I run a family investment office," I say, to that point having given it next to no thought at all. Then I panic a little on the inside, because I'm not even certain what those words mean, having that afternoon read them for the first time in an article on investing. But it sounds fancy, and that's all I'm going for. I'm trying to sound like someone who is credible in these surroundings. Hopefully even desirable—someone who can potentially play at their level. I can tell it was the right answer, even though I'm pretty sure there isn't going to be a quiz.

"Oh, perfect," she says.

Emboldened, I embroider a bit. "And some of the opportunities you have been offering are of interest. It seems there are good eyes and instincts involved here." Flattery. "I thought I'd come and look around."

"Well, welcome," she says. She looks at me speculatively for a moment. Then looks a little longer before she rises and gestures for a young woman nearby to come and take her place at the table. "Come with me," she says to me when everyone is situated. "There's someone I'd like you to meet."

She leads me through an elegant warren of offices and conference rooms. It's an old building, built initially for industry, but everything here is charming. The sort of studied casual elegance that doesn't come without the input of a professional designer.

"Don't we have to be back there for the event?" I ask. "It begins soon, I think."

She smiles. "It can't start without us." The words mystify me until she opens a door at the end of a long room and Rance Carver is there, seated at a desk so big, his diminutive frame looks childlike behind it. Despite this, I can tell he is comfortable there, and in charge.

"Hey, Rance," my companion says. "I have someone here I thought you should meet."

Rance looks me over, up and down, in a way that would have made me wary of him even if I didn't know who he was. He is clearly used to female attention, and there is an energy about him that makes me think that two-hundred-thousand-dollar car is never very far from his mind.

But the way he looks at me puts my back up. The phrase comes to me. *Marked.* I am being marked for something, that is clear. I am a mark. Even the small talk we engage in tells me that. I'm not sure what is wanted or needed from me. Later I'll figure it out.

Our chat, with Hattie Washington present, is perfunctory. Even pleasant. Nothing beyond the most basic of welcomes and greetings. So short, really, I wonder why anyone bothered. Then, clearing his throat theatrically, he stands and excuses himself: he must prepare himself to speak. After he bustles out of the room, Hattie leads me back down the corridors we'd trudged through to the large room where chairs have been set out at proper intervals in order for us to hear Rance himself orate. The audience with Rance had been so brief, I'm not certain why Hattie brought me back there. Yet a part of me understands.

When he appears, the lights dim ever so slightly and everything stills in a theatrical moment. It is the stillness that draws us from our thoughts and conversations; the light that directs us to our focus: Rance Carver. And when he begins to speak, the room quiets in a way that is beyond polite: we hang on his every word.

Later, I will find out that there are roughly as many people in attendance from the existing Angels community as there are people new to the company and there to learn about it, like me. Perhaps forty people in all spend an hour listening to Rance speak with zealous fire. In between what feels like personal pep talks, he runs through various investment opportunities currently on offer to his Angels. Interestingly to me, dollar values are never discussed. The language he uses describes opportunities, with both spiritual and financial gain implied. It's made pretty clear to all of us sitting there: however happy we are in our life right now, we will be happier if we throw in our lots with the Extreme Angels. That is: what Rance is offering is beyond financial. With our investment, he says, we are building our own future. We are building what we want that future to look like. That can be a big job.

During this whole spiel, I feel as though he directs a disproportionate number of glances in my direction. I don't kid myself about this. I know it is not because of my suddenly more becoming hair. Hattie had cut me out from the pack for a reason: my purse, my shoes, and my shtick had identified me as a whale.

Rance is a good speaker. His voice is clear and resonant, and with him on a stage at a bit of a distance, you can't even tell how tall he isn't. He is very leader-like up there. I find myself becoming inspired despite myself. And I recognize the power in that. If I, who have come to do a job and have no actual interest in any of this, if *I* can find myself entranced, how much must he be able to affect people with able bank balances and actual holes in their lives or with problems that need fixing?

Afterwards there are refreshments. Iced green tea, delicate sandwiches, small and exquisite cookies. No alcohol, but everything is expensive, you can see that. No fast run to the local supermarket: this is the good stuff; both healthy *and* delicious.

"What did you think?"

Rance has caught me unawares while I contemplated spearing a cookie with the hand that wasn't busy holding tea.

"Impressive," I say truthfully. "You're a wonderful speaker."

"Well, thanks," he says. And I can tell the humbleness he displays is not quite real. *He* thinks he's a great speaker, too. "Would you like to be part of our group? I think you'd do very well with us."

I look at him for a moment, not quite sure what to say. I wasn't prepared to see him again so soon. I don't want to appear flummoxed at his words, yet I am flummoxed, all the same. He has made it sound like an invitation: and a rare privilege, at that. I hadn't known what to expect, but it wasn't this.

"What's the buy-in?" I say, hoping that is the right terminology.

"How much do you control?" he says, and I feel myself getting further and further out of my depth. I fake it and hope for the best.

"I control as much as is required," I say, aiming for the right touch of nonchalant confidence.

He looks at me speculatively, but I can't read anything from his expression. "I have a couple of special investments. Outside of the angel fund. Direct investments, you understand?" I nod, even though I don't understand at all. "One is right here in town. And it's pretty special. The moment might be perfect. Get in early, right? It's cleantech. Green tech. Gold chip. Maybe you'd like to see the operation?"

I look at him for a beat that seems so much longer to me. I can't believe my ears and it takes me a second to scratch out a response. Could it be that easy to get inside? It's possible he's talking about some other cleantech firm. Gold chip. But I don't think so.

"Sure," I say, trying to keep it cool; not show any part of my hand.

"Awesome, great. I know it's short notice, but how would day after tomorrow work for you? I already have a lunch scheduled with the CEO. You can join us. I'll let him know. We'll give you the full tour. Maybe the CTO can join us, too."

So that's how it happens. I feel like the fox entering the henhouse. I find that it's not a feeling I hate.

I don't stay at the Extreme Angels offices for long after that. He has other fish to fry. And me? I feel like I've accomplished everything I set out to do that evening. More. I exchange pleasantries with a few people, but mostly I am working my tea and cookies toward the door. When I get close enough, I put down my cup and saunter out. There is no need for stealth, of course, but it seems to have become a habit.

CHAPTER SIXTEEN

BY THE TIME I get back to the hotel, I am so tired I feel flattened. It's been a long day, and I'm not used to seeing people. I saw a whole lot of them this evening. Even interacted with a few. All of it has wiped me out.

I take the dog out to relieve himself, then we cuddle up on the king-size bed and watch some television. Rather, I watch, he cuddles, an activity I now realize I leave little enough time for in my everyday life. I vow to do better in the future. Every life, I decide, should allow enough time to cuddle a beautiful golden dog.

In the morning I do laps in the big pool in the hotel's courtyard, then I don the sporty gray outfit again, and the dog and I set out. Physical exertion, I have found, helps keep my demons at bay. I sweat when I can. There are times that it helps more than others. And, of course, there are times when it doesn't help at all.

On this walk today there isn't much to see, but we see it anyway. In any case, the dog mostly sees with his nose. In that regard, he finds plenty to amuse him.

But we round the fountain, walk through the gardens and by the water features, exchanging the wild beauty of the forest for the manicured loveliness to be found in the city.

Beyond helping with my sanity and orienting me perfectly, there is no professional benefit to these activities: swimming, walking. My hours on this job have turned silly enough that I have come full circle and am now glad I brought the dog: between odd bits of surveillance, he and I are on a high-class vacation. Things all might have turned out differently, I reflect, if I'd felt the need to hurry back to make sure he was okay.

Beyond walks and swims, I research. There are things not right with all of this, but that's pretty obvious: I wouldn't be here if that were not the case. And seeing it to fruition is not an option. I don't have that kind of time. I have to figure out who is trying to kill Virginia Martin. And why. I have to figure it out and put an end to it. One way or the other.

On the Extreme Angels front, I'm trying to figure out what the game is, and it seems that, at first glance, my guess is right: money. However flakey he seems, I know that Rance is the force that arranged all of Greenmüll's big deal financing and set them up for their IPO. And Greenmüll is a unicorn, which equates to a start-up with a valuation of over one billion dollars. And as much as that is a lot of value, it's also a lot of pressure. From what I have seen, Greenmüll has not delivered on what they promised early on. Now the company is back at the well: sniffing around for further investment. Which, considering the fact that Rance visited them this morning and left with a whack of papers, might indicate he is arranging the financing of a new round.

By their nature, unicorns with this sort of backing are start-ups. Part of what that means is that their value is based on their potential as well as expectation around their development. As I studied, I found that the valuation of a unicorn was not strongly related to their actual financial performance but rather against the heights they might achieve. And all of that is right. All of that is as it should be. But none of it added up to the company's CTO being a target for assassination.

With that in mind, I decide another round of following is in order, even though I hadn't done particularly well on the first bout.

It's the middle of a weekday, so I position myself near the industrial park again, pretty much in the spot I'd parked when I'd seen Rance and decided to follow him. From there I can see the Land Rover parked at the side of the building. Good. At least I know for sure Virginia is at her office.

Not long after I settle back into the Volvo for a long wait, I see a female form leave the building and head for the Land Rover. Virginia. I can't be sure at this distance, of course, but I do know that the car is hers so it seems a good enough guess.

The Land Rover leaves the parking lot, unfortunately heading in the direction opposite the one the nose of my car is pointed.

"Damn," I say, pulling a U-turn as surreptitiously as possible, then cautiously but efficiently catching, then pacing my target.

I'm focused on the Range Rover, but as I complete the U-turn, a motion in my rearview attracts my attention. A midsize silver sedan, even more nondescript than my Volvo, makes the turn, as well. Not sharply. Not so much as to be noticeable. But still: it was going one way and now is going another, and if I rack my brain, it seems to me, maybe it was sitting nearby when I was on my little stakeout? I think about it as I drive, but I can't be sure. All I can assume is that the soldier I already took out has been replaced very quickly. I stifle my disappointment. I had hoped for a few days' reprieve, at least, while I got my feet properly under me and tried to make a little headway.

I turn my mind back to following Virginia, knowing I must also keep an eye on he who is behind. It will be better for me if he does not figure out I am following her, too. That is, if I have not already been made.

Our little follow train progresses like this for a solid twenty minutes. I keep a few car lengths behind her; he stays a few car lengths behind me. I try to contain my patience as the urban landscape gradually melts into the suburbs, but it's difficult. The situation is untenable. Something's gotta give.

I keep driving.

Eventually, Virginia turns the big car into a posh neighborhood. I can't see where she's going, but I continue on straight. It's been miles. There's no doubt that he's been following. But what will he do now? To my surprise, rather than turning to follow Virginia, he continues to tail me, a move that makes me more nervous than I would have thought. Had I been that careless? I thought I had taken every precaution to avoid detection and protect Virginia from attack. Now I'm driving and he's following and I wonder if he's been watching me all along.

At this stage I know that the freeway is a faster way back to the hotel, so I head onto an on-ramp, thinking he'll flake off. He doesn't, though, and eight exits later when I take the ramp, he's tailing me by about four cars. I know what to do to lose a tail, but I spend a few hard minutes thinking about how to trap one.

With all that walking of the dog, I've gotten to know the vicinity of the hotel pretty well, and so I drive around the fountain we've walked past every day. I loop it once. He's still following me. I loop it again and I feel him slow. I turn the car into an alley I know ends in a bend. He's not right behind me, but before I make the bend, I see the car enter. I quickly tuck the car into an underground parking area, then exit on foot at the entrance to the alley. I know I'll have a few minutes. It takes him that long to realize he's lost me, then a few more minutes to turn his car around and emerge. When he does, I am standing at the entrance to the alley in a wide stance, the Bersa is in my hands, and I know that if he presses the point and does not stop, I am prepared to take him out right there. And my stance alone will probably make sure that he knows that, too.

And yes, it is broad daylight, but it's a quiet alley, and no one is around at the moment and, worst-case scenario, I feel pretty confident in my ability to run. But it doesn't come to that. I stand there, directly in front of his car, and realize I recognize him, though it takes me a few minutes to realize from where. When I do, there is a huge sense of déjà vu. All over again.

I lower the gun, realizing it's not Virginia Martin he's after. It's me.

CHAPTER SEVENTEEN

I HAD NOT instantly recognized him as the ball-capped follower from the airport, but it didn't take me long.

"Why all the drama?" I say to him. We have gotten his car out of the alley; he has parked it and we are sitting at a nearby café. I figured we'd been conspicuous enough already and I'm feeling lucky no one saw me, wide-stanced and with a gun in my hand out in broad daylight. It was an awful risk, I realize now. I'd panicked and handled things badly. Fortunately, the worst didn't happen and no one is bleeding or dead. Now I get the chance to redeem myself by finding out what the hell is going on.

Whatever the case, it's still morning and I am so ready for some caffeine. Most of all, though, I want to figure out why the guy who has been following me all this time—he of the paunch and ball cap—should still be following me now. For one thing, I have realized that if he's been following me the whole time I've been watching Virginia Martin, he has seen and knows too much.

"*You* are accusing *me* of drama?" Though he's lightly mocking me, I note he has kind eyes and a patient if tired-looking face. I don't want to like him, but I sorta can't help myself. "I'm the dramatic one. After you've been standing in the middle of an alley with a gun trained to my head."

I laugh. I can't seem to help it, even though I know it is not a laughing matter. But the absurdity of the situation, that's what's gotten to me.

"Okay," I say. "I'll concede that might have come off as dramatic, but—"

"I know, I know," he interrupts, "you would have done it. I've no doubt you would have taken me out."

"Correct," I say without inflection. "Now tell me why you're following me."

"Your family hired me."

The words take a full minute to sink in. Family. What family? I don't have a family. And not having a family is part of how I self-identify these days. And part of how I got on the journey I am currently on. And then I realize what he means.

"My mom?" It's a whisper. It's like I had forgotten she existed, so entirely does she belong to that former life. Until thoughts of her are evoked by his words. But it isn't that.

He shakes his head and his expression is so sad and sincere, I know what he is going to say before he opens his mouth.

"I'm sorry," he says, realizing fully that what he is about to say should never come from a stranger. "She died some time ago."

"Fuck," I say quietly. Thinking of clear blue eyes and a laughing mouth. "Fuck, fuck."

"I'm sorry," he says again.

"Do you know how?"

"Sorry," he says one more time, looking as though he means it. "I didn't know her. They only said she died."

"*They?*"

"Your brother and sister, I guess. Kenneth and Abigail?"

Pieces click into place. "Brother and sister-in-law. They hired you to . . . find me?"

He nods.

"Wow," I say, meaning it. "How on earth?" I'm nothing short of astonished. I had figured I was too deeply underground for anyone to ever find me. I'd worked at that.

"Facial recognition." He says it simply, but there's a note of pride in his voice.

"You did not."

"I did. Your family originally hired me a couple of years ago and I had, like, zero luck."

I nod. Pleased. That had been my intention: to not be found.

"Then I installed this new software a few weeks ago and here we are. A lot of airports are using it."

"But it's illegal for them to share footage."

He looks at me, his face neutral. He doesn't say anything.

"And you said you installed it a few weeks ago. I mean, how does it work? I'd been in that airport for a very few minutes. Before that I hadn't been there in months. Were you parked there every day?"

"No, ma'am," he says, and I feel like hitting him in the back of the head and snapping that "ma'am" right out of his kisser. "This is the closest airport to my office, that's all. I thought I'd come and check it out: see what I can see."

So he'd gotten lucky, that's what he was saying. He'd taken a shot and it had paid off. As unbelievable as it is, a part of me buys it entirely. There is, in the universe, this tendency to synchronize. It's eerie sometimes. But I've seen it often enough to know that it can be true.

"Okay," I say, letting it go. For now. "You've been looking for me for a few years." The deeper meaning to his words sinks in when I put some pieces together. "I guess you are telling me that my mom died a while ago."

"Yes, I'm sorry. Of course. This is all new to you. They hired me a couple of years ago, so yeah. She has been gone for a while."

Gone. Like maybe she's gone on a trip. Someplace pleasant. Someplace she always wanted to go.

It's still not sinking in. I have a feeling it won't, either. Not for a while.

"What are you supposed to do now?" I ask.

"Put you in contact with them."

"Yeah, no," I say. "I've been out of touch for a reason."

He looks at me without much expression, but there's a calm in his eyes. No judgment. But I know that he knows. I tell myself it's impossible. But I know.

"It's what they paid me to do."

"How do you know that I won't kill you now that you've found me? Before you get the chance to tell."

His eyes go wide at that, like he's seriously considering what I said. I like him for that: the considering. And then his pleasant face breaks into a smile. "You won't," he says. Then he calmly takes his card out of his wallet, puts it down in front of me. DALLYCE BAYSWATER. The letters are raised, but the result does not look expensive. And the name, of course, is ridiculous. Dallyce. I say none of these things. In fact, I don't say anything at all.

"Okay," he says, and I can see his air of nonchalance is real. "You call me when you're ready." Then he gets up. Turns his back to me. Walks away.

CHAPTER EIGHTEEN

I OBVIOUSLY DON'T kill him. I sit there for a bit and ponder. All of what I had and what is lost. The choices I've made. The things I could have done differently. And the things, also, that I had no control over.

My brother, Kenneth, made different choices. He met Abigail in high school. She became an ultrasound technician. He took up insurance. They decided early on not to have kids. A small, safe life. Tidy house. Predictable hours. Everything when and as it should be.

For a while, my life and my choices were similar. Not the childless part, but the safe, staid part. Do what is expected of you. Do as you are told. Responsible job. Appropriate mortgage. Money in the bank. All of that ended when my life came apart. I walked away from all of it—responsibility and connection— after my child and husband died. There was all of that pain, of course. I was swallowed in a sea of hurt. And I might have taken solace in my friends and family, but I couldn't stand the pity I would see in their eyes. All of their eyes.

Did I miss my mother and brother and my friends in the years between? In a way I had, of course. More than I can say. But also, it had been a relief. In those first dark days, no one knew what to say to me or how to act. They would avoid looking at me and would tell me my son was in heaven now. An angel waiting to do God's duty. Crap like that. I didn't want to hear it. And I knew better. My son had died a shitty, unnecessary death. He wasn't called home. He was quite plainly in the right place at the wrong time. And it had all gone downhill from there.

In a way, I had died then, too. The living dead. It maybe took a different form. One day I had packed up my minivan and driven away. I hadn't said goodbye to anyone. Hadn't left a forwarding address or even a note. And truth be told, as cold-hearted as it sounds, I hadn't looked back. Not really. There was so much I'd wanted to forget that I hadn't even tried to remember.

Now it was all back. With a vengeance, as though the suppression had made it all the more painful. My brother was looking for me. My mother was dead. After so much nothing, it was a lot to take. Almost more than I could bear.

It took me a while, after Dallyce, the PI, walked away, for me to get my mojo back. I sat there, a bit dazed and confused, trying to figure out what should come next. It was hard to get my head out of the past and back into the game, yet that was what I needed to do, for both my sanity and my job. Virginia Martin. Her safety. Not my broken past. That is what matters now. I realize that, with the diversion of having been followed while I was following, I have lost my subject.

I backtrack to where she turned off, then cruise up and down a few blocks of stately homes, but there is no sign of her Land Rover. She could be anywhere. Beaten by half a dozen cul-de-sacs and a few gated communities, I cruise back to Greenmüll, but the Land Rover hasn't returned and as it's getting toward five o'clock, I opt to throw in the towel for the day. And since tomorrow is going to get me into the building in any case, I figure the following day might provide me with some sort of edge or knowledge I don't yet have.

But I don't go straight back to the hotel. I've been at all of this long enough that I figure that more clothes for this part are in order, especially with a lunch looming. I wonder if my handler realizes she's going to be tapped to pay for a whole new wardrobe. I think about that briefly before I decide: of course she does.

I head back to the same tony shop. Once there, I am greeted effusively. I'd laid down a whole whack of cash last time. They won't be forgetting me quickly.

"Welcome, madam," the proprietress says in an accent so flawlessly Parisian it sounds fake. "It is so good to see you again. With what can I help you today?"

I tell her I've got a business meeting for which I want to dress-to-impress. Can she advise me? —It turns out she can. I tell her also that I'm in need of more workout stuff, too.

"I mean, I love that gray cashmere outfit I got from you, but I can't wear it every day."

"*Mais non!*" she exclaims, looking faintly horrified at the thought.

So I drop another couple grand on the clothes I figure I'll need to get through this gig. I get a plain but elegant business dress—just at the knee—and a dark but form-fitting blazer over a simple cream blouse, no collar.

"And this will make me look . . . affluent?" I ask timidly. I've never dressed this way before. I have no idea.

"The jacket is Alexander McQueen," she says archly. I don't know what that means, but she says it with so much confidence I understand that it's the only answer that is needed, even if I don't understand.

She guides me through buying two more track suit–type things—one in white, the other in a brighter shade of orange than I would usually wear. She assures me it is my *couleur*, then another pair of athletic shoes and another pair of dress shoes to go with the outfit. I put my foot down at another purse. Surely even rich ladies don't change purses every minute? I figure one super-expensive purse is enough for this gig.

Back at the hotel, I hesitate between the white track suit and the orange one, but don't put it on. Even if it *is* my *couleur* I figure I'll look like a safety cone wearing it. The white is a good fit and proves to be nearly as soft as the gray. I know I'm in good shape for a walk, with the dog.

We trek a good long way. I have a lot to think about. Not the least of it is the news that my mother no longer walks the earth. I feel like the news should bring real sadness. Tears, maybe. Or some deep new and mostly unexpected emptiness. Loss.

In reality, I don't feel anything at all. It's like there is a hole where the idea of my mother should be. She'd been lost to me so long ago, maybe that's it. As a result, this new and final loss is not new. I had never thought to see her again. She was dead to me already. My whole family had been, really. And not for anything they did, but for what I did. Or didn't do. Or whatever it was that had caused my life to end the way it did; the end that had given birth to this new life.

And then I find myself thinking about my brother, Kenneth, and what his life might look like now. His and Abigail's life. It has been so long since I thought of them as real and living entities. It's been so long since I thought of them at all.

And then I think about earliest Kenneth. The Kenny of our childhood. Freckled and with a cowlick, pestering his little sister. Building her a bike. Sucker punching her when he didn't get what he wanted. Defending her from bullies at school. All of those images are with me again. My brother. Lost to me. And now suddenly found. If, that is, I want to reach out. I'm not sure that I do.

I take out my cell phone. Call the number on the card.

"He have any kids?" I ask.

"Who?"

"Who? My brother, of course. Your client. Kenneth. He didn't have any kids last time I saw him." I don't know why it suddenly matters.

"I'm . . . I'm not sure," the PI says. "I can find out if you like."

"That's okay," I say. "Forget I asked. Please."

After our walk, I consider dinner. Mine, not the dog's, whose needs are easily met.

I vacillate a bit, then decide on room service. I'm sure I am missing some obvious thing, and I want to spend the balance of the evening doing research, without the distraction of having to sit nicely in a restaurant.

Though the truffled penne I order from the room service menu sounded exquisite, when it arrives it is limp and gummy. The scent of truffle is present, but the mushrooms themselves are not. Some recollection of truffles maybe. Truffles remembered but sparsely shared.

The research ends up being like that, too. It comes to me in incomplete pieces. It hints at possibility, then misses the mark. I am digesting all of this when my phone rings. My phone ringing happens so infrequently that I sit and look at the device stupidly for a moment before I pick it up. I note that the number is unknown to my phone, but since I don't know anyone in Belgium, I am able to buy a clue.

Her voice sounds dry yet welcome. I hadn't realized how much I had missed human connection until I had it again. It is nice, this has made me discover. It's pleasant to have in my life someone with whom I don't have to pretend anything. She knows all of the things that I usually have to be alert to keep covering up. I can be myself, whatever that means. It's a new feeling. I haven't had that for a long time. Maybe ever.

I can be myself.

"She still lives?" she asks conversationally and I smile. She said it in a tone one might also say, "Would you like another cookie?" I know that she must be more deeply concerned than her voice gives away. It's her daughter. But she is too much a professional to give a hint of any concern she might be feeling. This is not, after all, her first rodeo.

"She does," I answer. "I've been watching to make sure."

"And have you seen anything?"

"Well, I have and I haven't," I say honestly.

"I see." The words are so cryptic, I can't judge their meaning.

"Yes, well, she's alive. If you . . . if you had some kind of hint for me, that might help."

"Oh, I'd imagine," she replies without hesitation. "But then, what sort of fun would that be?"

I let that sink in for a moment. Fun. Is it all a game? An amusement? I try to feel incensed at that, but it doesn't take. If she has been honest with me, we are talking about her daughter's life. So, instead of losing my cool, I ask. No passion in my voice, because I don't feel anything beyond mild curiosity.

"Is this a game to you?"

The return pause is so long, I fear for a moment that she's hung up. I'm surprised at the feeling that comes up for me when I think that. What I feel is surprisingly like loss.

When she finally speaks again, I can tell her voice is careful, but I can't tell if she's holding back or protecting herself.

"No, dear. It's not a game. It's an unusual situation, that's all."

And I could tell it was an unusual situation. I'd never been phoned before, until recently. And I'd certainly never been called while on a job. The opposite really. Once I got the assignment, I was always completely autonomous, then a very impersonal check-in upon completion to let them know the job was done, a notification that would be answered with a deposit to my Bitcoin account, never any actual words. So this? Yeah, it was different for sure. It was all new territory.

"Can I ask a few questions?"

"While you've got me, you mean?" I could hear the smile in her voice. It didn't sound unkind. "Sure. Ask away. I'm not saying I'll answer. It will depend."

I returned the smile into the phone. I couldn't help myself: I liked her. I lobbed a difficult one at her anyway.

"How did you know a hit was ordered on her?" I ask it even though I figure from the start that I won't get an answer. I'm not wrong.

"You know I can't tell you that."

"I do. I thought I'd try. I thought I'd know anyway."

"Really?" The handler sounds skeptical.

"Yeah. What I can't figure is exactly why."

"At this point, who do you think?"

"Rance Carver. Do you know who I'm talking about?"

"I do," she replies.

"I'm pretty sure it's him. Not totally but pretty. He honestly seems like he'd be good for it," I say, realizing how lame that sounds. Though I'm not yet sure why.

She surprises me by laughing. It's a gentle sound. And the laughter puts something else in my mind. I've been running around thinking I am the single game piece she has put into play.

But am I? If I were her, would I have left it at that? I think maybe I would not. This thought fills my brain so completely for a moment that I almost can't continue. Almost. I know I can't function that way, though. Wondering. I push the thought out of my head and force myself to listen to her words.

"Your instinct, that's what you're saying. That's what makes you think Rance. Well, they're well honed by now, those instincts. But don't take it as read." I gauge the voice to see if I can tell that means yes or no or even if she knows anything at all, but then I give it up. She is being careful to be neutral, as I always am with her. She continues. "What else do you see?"

"There isn't anything else. I've brought you completely up to date." I consider telling her I'm being brought in under the guise of possibly making an investment, but I hold myself back. And it isn't any one thing. Maybe only that I'm used to playing my cards close to my chest. You have to, if you want to get out of this sort of work alive.

She doesn't buy the act, though. Even though I'm not sure why. "Not quite, I think. You're not telling me what you think."

I reflect before answering because she's right, of course. There's what I've seen, but then there are the conclusions I've been drawing, and I'm not even fiercely sure, on a conscious level, what those conclusions are.

"I'm out of the loop on this one, I'm afraid. What I've seen: Virginia is a star and everybody I've met so far likes her."

"Your instincts are good, dear. Go with those."

And maybe it is because I flush with pleasure at her words that I don't hear her disconnect. And it is then, with dead silence buzzing in my ear, that I realize I have no idea if she was agreeing with me. Or not.

CHAPTER NINETEEN

ON THE MORNING of my lunch with the Greenmüll CEO, I don my new finery. The Alexander McQueen jacket fits like it was made for me, which, considering the cost, isn't a leap. And with the jacket and new shoes in place, I figure I look every inch the part I'm supposed to be playing, even with the same purse I'd used with the other outfit. It conveys the look of ease and wealth I'm after. The dog watches me with interest, but offers no opinion on the getup. He observes me sadly as I head to the door. Without him.

It feels funny to drive right up to the Greenmüll offices and park rather than skulking around across and down the street. It's a high-tech company, so reception looks like a tech cubicle. The guy whose desk is closest to the door looks up distractedly as I enter, the look on his face telling me it has taken him a minute to call himself back from whatever he's been working on. I don't even have to announce myself before Rance comes in right behind me.

"Hey, Archie," he says to the kid. "We're meeting Himself for lunch."

"Oh, yeah," Archie says. "He mentioned. He told me to tell you he's had a call come up. Has to take it. Said to get Lisa to start the plant tour and he'll join up with you guys when he's clear."

"Sounds good," Rance says, but he's already in motion, down a long hallway. I follow. "Lisa is head of PR," he tells me as we move. "Nice kid. Knows her stuff."

We barge into an office and are met with a sweet grin. Lisa, the PR manager, is waiting right inside the door when we arrive. She's wearing a grin that looks like it's part of her normal expression.

"Thank you so much for coming!" She appears open and friendly and is awash in the sort of enthusiasm communications professionals always have an abundance of. Who knows? Maybe it's even a prerequisite for the programs that churn them out.

Rance introduces me to Lisa, but I have the feeling she doesn't even need to know who I am. Doesn't care. She's done this tour lots of times. It's apparent as soon as she starts talking. It's not that she has the words all memorized; more like she lives and breathes every aspect of the business she is promoting.

I wonder about the missing CEO. Maybe there even is no call for him to be on. Maybe Ethan is bored with this part of the show. Yet another investor. He'll save himself for when he is needed to reel the whale in. I'm thinking that before I even meet him even though I know very little about him. Maybe that's even *why* I'm thinking that: in this moment I am wondering how I don't know more.

"You're okay with signing an NDA?" Lisa asks, pushing the document in front of me. Even asking is a formality. I've done some research on this part, as well. In this sort of tour, it's pretty normal for no one to get past the front door without signing a nondisclosure agreement. I sign it and then we're off. She points Evan Hollingsworth out as we pass his office door and, beyond the window, I can see he does indeed seem to be fully engaged with whoever he is talking with. At a glance, he looks like you'd expect with that name. The blue blazer, chinos, and perfectly cut hair cement the idea of Ivy League and old money: prep school uniform.

"Evan is the CEO," Lisa says, already starting her tour. I know from my reading that Evan was the person responsible for connecting Virginia Martin with Greenmüll. Lisa tells me the story behind what I'd read: how Greenmüll had been a company with a cause, but lacking the technology to truly do what they wanted to do before Evan had connected with Martin and her methods.

"See, a lot of people are making fuel out of trash these days. But they are doing it at least partly using incineration. While that can work on the commercial level, it is not practical putting incinerators that burn at temperatures in excess of 1500 degrees Fahrenheit. into people's homes."

As she's been talking, we've moved into what she calls the plant area of the operation. I have no idea what I'm looking at, but it's impressive. Lots of shiny machines with various types of technologists making them all do different things.

"Fifteen hundred degrees would consume a lot of energy," I offer.

"Correct," she says, nodding. "Also, let's face it, it's dangerous. *And*, as you pointed out, it uses a lot of energy. That's the thing that is so revolutionary about the technology Dr. Martin has developed. It uses a proprietary blend of gases—benign and green—and water combined with specially prepared trash to make a high-grade fuel. We've had competitors tell us our methodology makes no sense," she says, smiling, "and yet here we are."

"That all makes tremendous sense," I say, deliberately echoing her word choice. Like I have any idea of what I'm talking about and hoping I sound more clued-in than I feel. I reassure myself with the fact that I'm not pretending to know anything about science: I am simply someone with access to a lot of money. Knowledge about what they do to or for the money is unnecessary. "It all sounds perfectly logical. Where are you in the process?"

"Well, our commercial scale aspect is producing as it always has been. That portion of our operation is more, let's call it, conventional. High temperature incineration and the energy we are creating at ever higher volume. There are buyers for that, which means at that end of the business, we're in revenue. And it is a respectable amount of revenue—you'll have seen the numbers in our deck," which I had recently discovered was what start-ups like to call a pretty and public version of their business plan. "Those numbers are good, but they don't support the whole operation." She makes a sweeping motion with her hand that I take to mean the offices, the overhead, all of the technologists and support people, all of the research: the whole ball of wax. "But we hope that, once the consumer level aspect has rolled out, we will work toward a time when we shut down those energy consuming incinerators."

I think about that for a minute before answering. Then, "Let me see if I have this straight: if everything goes according to plan, there won't be enough garbage available to keep the plant running."

She laughs. "I guess you could put it that way, but yes, I suppose that's it. What we're hoping, essentially, is that we put that part of Greenmüll out of business." I've done some reading. I know she's pitching the company's green line. It is fact that there is enough garbage in the world to keep Greenmüll's green machines functioning into a far-foreseeable future. It's a big planet. And we have a lot of trash. But imagine the picture they are building: a beautiful green future, and every American household doing their part. It's a lovely image, and they've been milking it to the tune of millions in investments for the past several years. Still, if it works, it will be a gamechanger. It truly will change the world.

Everything I see at Greenmüll supports this idea. The "plant" is dead impressive. Everything about it is interesting, and since all of it is over my head, I realize I could have skipped the tour. Except I learn a lot. And it's also interesting to see all the things they have been doing and saying to impress investors. On the tour, nothing seems less than what it should be. It's everything you ever thought a high-tech plant could be. And more.

There are a lot of machines whose purpose I can't even imagine. I know I could ask Lisa or even Rance, but I figure the answers will confuse me still further. Mounds of garbage are heaped on conveyors that feed them right into the gaping maws of the waiting incinerators. The smell is not overpowering, but it's present.

"I'm imagining that is not a smell a consumer would want to have in their home."

Lisa laughs. "You thought of it. Not everyone does. But the consumer product is odorless. The process is very different. You'll see it in the lab. Next stop."

The "lab" is part of the cavernous main building, off to one side but clearly distinct and going about its own business. It is presided over by Virginia Martin herself, a pristine white lab coat designating her as the boss of the space even if nothing else would. And there are things that would.

More and different machines of various types are arranged around. I don't know what I'm looking at and have a feeling I still won't know after they are explained. Virginia approaches us, obviously having been warned of a potential investor visit, and I am glad to see she still breathes. I haven't missed my window, then. It's been concerning me.

Virginia looks at me as though she's trying to place me: as though she's seen my face but can't quite make the connection. I don't offer any help.

Lisa introduces me and, even though I feel like she recognizes me, Martin doesn't say anything. Rather, she throws herself into showing-off mode. You can tell she's done this many, many times. She's a pro and she gives me a tour of the place that manages to be both interesting and slightly over my head. I don't mind. I'm paying close attention, not only to her but trying to feel the nuance of the things she is showing me. Energy created from garbage at the consumer level, that's the thing I'm meant to take away. And it's all impressive. And it's all high tech. But here in the lab, I don't see it happening at this consumer level.

I watch very closely on the tour: What am I hearing? Am I being misdirected? Are there things that are overstated? Am I able to imagine that the process she is describing is ready to work in the American home? That is, after all, what the big-bucks investors have signed on for. Martin's process will do nothing short of revolutionizing the energy industry. And playing big-deal investor, as I watch I gather the information I need to ask the trenchant questions. I hope. She handles the questions easily. But what else had I expected?

"How will homeowners be able to manage the process on their own?"

"The version we are doing here at present will be streamlined in the extreme. We have a whole team on that. Working out, for instance, how is the technology brought into the home? Is, for instance, the chemical element hardwired rather than consumer applied?"

"Chemical element?"

She shifts her weight from one foot to the other as she answers. Clearly, she is anxious to be done with this time away from her work and probably would prefer no interruptions. As a potential investor, I and my ilk are a necessary evil: without loads of incoming loot, the research stops. It's an expensive business, but the potential for profit is immense.

"Yes: the proprietary green cocktail that runs this thing."

"Gotcha."

"And how does it get into the home?" I can tell by the way she has said it that this is one of the usual questions and so her spiel is intended to preempt where she figures it's all going to go. Not her first rodeo. "By way of example, think about the internet and how it is delivered to homes. Think fiber optics. It doesn't work if you don't have whole neighborhoods or apartment buildings signing up so that the infrastructure can be installed. We're talking about replacing garbage pickup with a system that turns that same garbage into a positive: fuel! Putting in infrastructure that accommodates that is actually possible. "Just think"—her eyes shine as she warms to her subject—"all of the plastic in the ocean? What if it could be made to be a commodity? If garbage was so rare we had to pay for it to make energy. What would happen then? It changes everything. Do you see?"

I hesitate for a minute. Is the question rhetorical or does she want an answer? I think about it, as she has asked me, and: yes. Absolutely. It would be earth-changing. If people could get paid for trash, the oceans would be clean in no time, that's what I think. And all of the world's problems would be so very different. I play all of this out internally, thinking about what it might mean for everyone on the planet if this were to happen. But then I see that she is peering at me intently, so I scratch an answer out.

"That . . ." I begin hesitantly, ". . . that would be wonderful."

She nods but doesn't say anything, like she's waiting for it all to sink in. It's a theatrical moment and she works it. She knows what she's doing and she's very, very good. I hadn't seen this part of her when I'd met her at the salon. There she had seemed like any other human: even if particularly lovely and especially nice. Here, though, she is in her element. The lioness in her own jungle. She is both completely at home here and entirely in charge. I figure she is a big reason of why they've been able to raise so much money. Sure: the technology is special. But to stand next to Virginia Martin waxing poetic about her technology is almost like standing next to a prophet. She is compelling, yes. But also, she galvanizes you. I feel a little better and cleaner and ready to change the world by simply standing next to her. Who wouldn't give money for all of that?

CHAPTER TWENTY

"It will change everything," she says. And I can see that she means it. And I figure also that she's right: a lot of the world's problems would look very different if pollution was turned on its head: trash to treasure, as it were. Everything would be upside down. "It will change the world."

I think for a minute before I speak again. "But the energy then. Where does that go?"

The question is naive enough that Rance chortles. Lisa shushes him and Virginia looks at me blankly for a minute. All of this reaction lets me know that I've missed some salient bit. When Virginia speaks again, that impression is confirmed.

"Where does it go? Why, we are powering people's houses, of course. Or rather, helping them to power their homes themselves."

A light dawns. I wonder if, in that moment, I look as clueless as I feel. "Oh," I say lamely. "You're saying they are using the power they themselves are creating with their own garbage to heat their homes and their water and to drive their air-conditioning and so on?"

"Yes," is all she says. But there is depth to that single word. And her eyes glow with . . . what? Accomplishment? Possibility?

All of that and more. As she herself has said, this is technology that will change the world. "In the near future, I imagine we will also be able to power our cars with it. Imagine: every home, every individual with the ability to power all of their devices, modes of transport, and the needs of their home."

I don't say anything. There is nothing to say. As the reality sinks in, the enormity of it blows my mind, in a way. She is doing important work here, I realize. If everything goes the way she plans, she will win all of the prizes, and deserve them, too. The idea, fully revealed to me nearly in action, is more radical than I had imagined. It's like a scene from a science fiction movie. And in those movies isn't there always some bad guy trying to put the kibosh on whatever good is being done? I shake off the image. In that scenario, I become the hero, and I've never seen myself that way. At all.

I'm still marveling as Martin walks me over to another part of the lab, talking while she moves. "There is more than one possibility. We are working on all of them. What would be ideal?" She gestures toward the sky. The sky is the limit, that's what I understand her to mean. Since she's been talking about her vision, she has come to seem warmer and more present than she had before and, as she speaks, she seems more alive. The feeling is confirmed when color floods her cheeks. She continues, "Anything is possible." She points across the lab toward a setup that makes little visual sense to me. I see a silver appliance that looks like a trash compactor. She opens it up into a place where trash might go as well as a couple of canisters. "This is the version of the system that is independent of infrastructure. Obviously, it is the more expensive of the options." She points. "See here? This is a canister that the homeowner pops in when empty."

"Pops in?" It seems disingenuous to me.

"Yes, for sure. That's the chemical portion. Think Sodastream. To make fizzy water? A canister. Clean and easy. A child can do it."

"Okay," I say. "What about the fuel or energy that is created? Where does that go?"

I don't see the discomfort on Martin's face when I ask that, but I feel it anyway. Or maybe I'm making it up. I can't be sure.

"We covered that," she says, and I notice her subtly shifting her weight from one foot to the other.

"Right. Yes. I got that: powering the home. But what about any excess they might create. I'm guessing potentially there could be some?"

"Well, that's the million-dollar question, isn't it?"

"Or billion," I say.

"Yeah. Okay," she says, but there is some sort of reservation in her voice. "Fair enough." And I realize she's taken it as a shot about the company's unicorn status. And fair enough, as she said. There's that. "It's an issue, for sure," she says. "Storage has always been the challenge for alternate forms of energy, including solar. What to do with what you create?"

"Can you feed it back into the system? I know with solar you can do that in some places."

"It all works better if the infrastructure is in place. But we have a limited amount of control over that." We are interrupted by an immense clattering from near one of the machines. One of the technologists has dropped a metal tray. It lands on the concrete lab floor, scattering implements in every direction. The young man responsible looks at us as though he would like to sink through that concrete floor: disappear. He has straw-like hair and a yellow cowlick. The lab coat seems incongruous. He has a small-town hayseed look about him. I follow her glance and see him duck backwards, as though avoiding her laser vision is possible by getting out of the trajectory of that look. I doubt that it is. His scrambles for the exit are almost comical, and I'm not sure if it's because he's afraid of her response to his clumsiness or because he has to clean chemicals off his hands and shoes.

"Forgive me," she says, not taking her eyes off the place where he disappeared. She is moving before she has finished speaking. "I need to have a word with someone."

She isn't gone long, but it's an uncomfortable break, and I can't even quite place why. While she's gone, Lisa, Rance, and I shift our feet a little bit. None of us mention what just happened but Rance, showman that he is, makes some attempts at conversation.

"Did I mention the plant is at technology readiness level six?" He's asked it in a way that implies I should know what that is. I don't, but I fake it.

"Oh. Wow. Really. I did not know that. That's great. Umm . . . when does it get to seven?"

"When the betas are out in the field," Lisa supplies. "Level seven is when the tech is out of the lab and in an operational setting."

We probably would have gone on in that way, discussing the various technology readiness levels, but fortunately we are spared that when Virginia rejoins us.

"Sorry about that, guys. I had to go and set someone straight. We're at such a time of details." She shoots a big smile in my direction, and it looks genuine enough, but I don't think I'm imagining the tension I also hear in her voice. Also, the blond kid hasn't come back. I tell myself that tension is natural enough at this stage. She has a lot riding on outcomes. "Remind me if you can: Where were we?"

I think for a moment, but Lisa jumps in before I have to come up with an answer. She's obviously been taking notes. After all, this is her job. Virginia breaking off in the middle of a tour might even be business as usual.

"You were talking about having the infrastructure in place," Lisa supplies effortlessly. "In the event that the household units are too successful, and more energy is created than what is required."

"Great. Yes. Thanks, Lisa." She sends the younger woman a grateful look. Lisa glows under her approval. "You'd asked about solar, I think. And storage systems."

"Yes," I reply. "As I understand it, that has always been the sticking point for alternative energy: storage."

"Right. Yes. Okay," she says, and it's clear she is gathering her thoughts. "First, the idea of 'alternate' energy. I know you can build an argument for this being called that, but I'm not certain I agree. If a few things break right for us, this will not be an *alternate* source of energy. It will be the *main* source."

She pauses. As though letting the enormity of what she is sharing sink in. It does.

"But you're right," she says, continuing as though she hadn't interrupted herself, "storage has often been the sticking point. You can create it or harvest it, but if you can't store the energy once you have it in hand, you're answering half a question and you'll have to end up back talking to some giant power company. As you pointed out, some states buy it back from people who have created an excess of electricity—more than they need—but it is always at a wholesale price and, when the consumer has none available, they're paying full retail to buy it back."

"Wait—what? If you make excess power—say windmill, solar, whatever—you have to sell it cheaply to the power company, then if you need some, you buy it back at full price? Is that what you're saying?"

She beams at me. I feel like a student getting an A.

"Yes. That's it exactly. And it is unacceptable. That is, we are not accepting it. The Greenmüll system demands that each household be independent of their local grid."

"Like, completely independent? No connection at all?"

She smiles, pleased to see I've understood the nuance of that, as well.

"Yes. Completely."

"Wow. Okay. That's huge. But what is the alternative?"

"Well, we've been playing with a few very solid options." She moves us toward another trash compactor–looking thing. "In option one, the homeowner uses all of what they create. Maybe they even control the garbage they feed into the system based on their needs."

I look at her skeptically. It seems far-fetched. She seems to think so, too, because she shrugs.

"Yes: asking the modern consumer to hold back their garbage for a rainy day, as it were, is a big ask. So we're working on that part. But collection," she continues. "There is a cylinder, not unlike the type attached to a home propane barbecue, that collects the energy. Once full, it is either stored in the home—in pretty much exactly the same way a home propane tank is stored—or taken to a depot for reclamation. Maybe even sale."

"How often?"

"That depends on the parties involved. How much trash do they generate? How much power are they using? This is a stopgap measure, remember. The first line is actual usage. That's why we're doing all of this. And anyway, what is the nature of the trash? That's one of the things we are thinking about. And these are the variables that make it difficult to share absolute numbers."

"You'll need those numbers to begin marketing."

"Of course," she says, waving my words away impatiently. I see Lisa look back and forth from me to Virginia. I think she is trying to see how Virginia's curt words land. Virginia doesn't notice and my skin is tough. I know that what she is saying has nothing to do with me. She has a vision and it's all she can see. "We'll definitely have those numbers before we get to that stage."

I think for a minute. And then, "So if there is infrastructure, it gets whisked away. The energy, I mean. Is it collected for either use or resale?"

"Correct. It's a tidier solution. But then if your infrastructured community is generating insufficient trash, the system breaks down again. You need enough people making enough garbage for the whole thing to make dollars and sense, but not so much that the system is overloaded. It's all a matter of balance. At least until you get to full scale."

"Full scale?"

Her eyes glow again. Apparently it's another favored area of discussion. "Everyone in the United States using the system." A beat, and then, "Everyone in the *world*. In that scenario, we *are* the infrastructure."

CHAPTER TWENTY-ONE

I THINK FOR a while, breathing in the quiet in the wake of the flash and fire generated by the person who had given birth to all of this. She has a lot at stake. Everything. And she's not quiet about it. I'm not quite sure what to think.

"But it works, right? In either instance? Once installed it makes the garbage go away?"

Martin looks at me sharply. I can tell she does not like the question and maybe hadn't expected it. But she's a pro: she doesn't back away.

"Yes. Of course. I mean making the garbage 'go away' is certainly an oversimplification, but it all works as described."

There is more, but I find after a bit that I've checked out. It's been a lot to take in and, in any case, I feel as though I've learned everything I can and observed everything available to me. Really, I've learned a lot. More than I need to know for my particular mission.

I signal to Martin that I'm ready to go and I don't know if the look she gives me is one of disappointment or relief. I'm prevented from probing at it to see if I can tell which it is by the arrival of Evan Hollingsworth. It seems apparent he'd timed his arrival. How else could he appear at exactly the correct moment right at the end of the tour?

"Impressive stuff," I remark as we are introduced. It seems the right thing to say. And it *is* impressive. We are back in the most vibrant part of the plant now, with all of the big machines humming and buzzing and turning the garbage they bring into some sort of fuel. Standing there, with it happening all around us, it is easy to believe in a trash-free future. It's impossible to think that so much energy and money could have been put into technology that does not work.

"We're setting out to revolutionize the energy industry," Evan says with confidence. There is a smoothness about him. A practiced art. At first meeting, I'm not sure quite what to make of him. He will require watching, that much I'm sure about.

"We covered the part about changing the world already," Rance says in a voice of feigned boredom. Everybody laughs.

"When do you think you'll have models in homes?"

"Technology Readiness Level Seven," Lisa says smiling. But it's an aside. And she hasn't directed her comment to anyone in particular.

"We will have beta versions of the consumer device in selected homes by the fourth quarter," Hollingsworth says.

"That soon?"

"God willing."

"How many beta units will there be?"

"Lisa, you have those numbers, don't you?"

Lisa nods, then begins reciting. "We have 500 test families prepared, in selected areas across the country."

"Wow," I say. "That's hugely impressive."

Lisa nods and continues.

"But there won't be 500 beta units. Not right away," Lisa says.

"And maybe not ever," Hollingsworth interjects.

"Right," says Lisa. "That would be very expensive. And probably not necessary. But we have the families lined up and prepped. We figure as few as the first 100 installs will give us our baseline."

"And you'll turn the other 400 into customers?" I ask it lightly, but I'm only half kidding.

"Possibly," Hollingsworth says. "But it will let us know what we're dealing with on several levels."

I nod. It all sounds very sensical to me. As you'd expect it to. Obviously, a lot of thought has gone into every aspect.

"But that 100 homes doesn't put you in revenue," I point out.

Lisa looks at Hollingsworth for an answer. I think he looks uncomfortable at the deferment, but it's gone so quickly, I figure maybe I was wrong.

"Well, not right away. We'll absorb the cost of the units," he says quickly.

"Because," Lisa picks up the thread, perhaps sensing his discomfort at being put on the spot, "we're building a problem-solving period into that first 100. We are aware everything will not go as planned right from the get-go."

"The get-go," Rance repeats, nodding, which I find idiotic but I don't say anything. Parroting for the sake of hearing his own voice, it seems. Ever the showman.

"Right," Hollingsworth says, as though what Rance had said should be paid attention to. "We are anticipating there will be problems we haven't even imagined yet once the units are functioning in homes. We will essentially be putting the finishing layer on our testing in the field."

"Wouldn't it be cheaper to do that in the lab?" I ask. It seems to me a question that a proper investor would ask, but when I ask it, I'm not even sure it's a valid question.

"Oh yes," he answers right away and I feel relieved. Whatever the answer, the question itself does not seem to have been off the mark. "For sure. But in this case the field is the right answer. And Dr. Martin insisted. Until real people are using the system, we won't see all of the problems."

"And when will that be?" I ask, fully aware that I'd asked Lisa minutes before. "When will the system be in real and non-beta use?"

"Fourth quarter next year," Rance answers quickly. It strikes me that he has jammed the reply in before Ethan could get a chance to give a different answer, but I can't be sure.

"Dr. Martin was talking about the challenges of infrastructure. Is that a threat to investment?"

Did Rance and Hollingsworth exchange a glance? I wouldn't have thought so. I would have thought they would be pro enough to avoid a move like that. So maybe it is more of an intuition on my part. Or maybe it was nothing at all. But the feeling, that was the thing.

It is Hollingsworth who answers. "There are always challenges at every level of development *and* investing. I'm sure you're not hearing this for the first time."

"True," I go along. "'The biggest risk of all is not taking one,'" I say, quoting and hoping it is the right quote.

His rakish smile tells me it is. "Without risk there is no reason to invest. That's the game."

And that's the thing I've come to understand. This is all a game, at least to some of them. Oh yes, by all means, change the world. And play with a lot of money: it's all the more fun if the stakes are high. But make no mistake: to the suits in all of this, it is high-level play. The worker bees likely have a different idea, but no one is asking for their opinions.

"Well, that's enough work for the morning," Rance announces as though he had been waiting for the opportunity. "My stomach is growling. Let's go eat."

"You guys go ahead," Martin says, already disengaged and looking slightly relieved to be done with us. "I'm heading back to the lab."

Rance looks as though he might object, but he stops himself just short of speaking, obviously torn between being polite and getting what he needs. Hollingsworth sees the exchange and interjects.

"Virginia is busy. She is always poised on the verge of a breakthrough," Evan is moving us toward the front office and the parking lot. He doesn't touch, so I understand we are being moved by the sheer force of his will. "And really, we don't need to take any more of her time. We can give you anything you need in terms of numbers and expectations and so on. Virginia is bored by all that stuff anyway." He pauses, as though gauging our reaction before completing his lunch thoughts. When he reads no objections from us, he goes on. "We can continue all of this over lunch. There's a great French place downtown. We'll take my car." He indicates a giant-sized SUV that looks like what a Russian oligarch might drive.

"Actually, let me follow," I say, unsure of why I hesitate. "I've got a thing after." Which, of course, is a lie. But I find I want to be under my own power.

Hollingsworth at first looks as though he might object, but then he acquiesces. And, to his credit, Rance doesn't seem to care either way.

"How well do you know the town?" he asks me.

"Not very," I say.

"Okay then. Follow me," seemingly contenting himself with the control of the path to the eatery.

When we get to the restaurant, it is clear they know Hollingsworth. Maybe that's even why he chose it. The staff fusses over us, finding us a good table and generally making sure everything is exactly as it should be. And I get that it is more than all show. The place is as excellent as promised, a stereotypical bistro as might be found in a small town in the French countryside. And I understand that is why we are here. Everything is perfect, yes. But also everything is executed with respect for Hollingsworth who is treated like every inch of a big deal. I imagine he thinks it matters to investors. I doubt that it does. Why would they care what sort of respect is accorded him by a maître d? Yet that's part of the game. I come away from it all partly admiring and partly sickened, and I suppose that is part of the game, as well.

I order a Salad Niçoise. I order it in part because I like it and you hardly ever see it on the menues. And I order it in other part because I can nibble it without taking much attention away from whatever conversation might engage us. Olives, baby potatoes, green beans, a cleverly cut hard-boiled egg, rare tuna, and lightly dressed salad greens: I can happily spear and munch throughout whatever time we end up spending at the bistro.

It doesn't take long for the boys to get down to business after we've ordered. I realize they've been doing this for a number of years and have their patter down. Not their first rodeo. And I can view it all with the detachment of someone who is truly detached because I am: anything else is a sham. From the distance of my subterfuge, I feel I see gentle avarice on Rance. I am guessing it is his normal way of being. But Hollingsworth is a different story. I can smell a sort of deep hunger on him. But whether it's desperation fed by actual need or simply how he is,

I can't tell. Always hungry, that's what I think. Always going in for the latest bit of fresh meat.

I find myself going from liking him a lot to feeling he is distant and superior; putting on a nice act to bag yet another investor. It's an uncomfortable feeling. Maybe those who do this for a living get used to being coveted for what they hold. For me it is new and unusual and I don't like it because it makes it hard to know exactly where you are. And I chide myself for that, too. I have spent too long at the edge of the forest, conversing with a dog and not much else. I have invested a lot of time into not interacting. How do I imagine I will be a good judge of human interactions now that I've invested a good chunk of time into having so few?

"Family office I think you said." He says it as though he hadn't memorized every interesting tidbit from my—entirely bogus—CV.

"That's right," I say, offering nothing. This is a thing I've learned, too: to keep my yap shut and let others fill in the blanks. They mostly don't notice because everyone likes to hear themselves talk. What they don't seem to realize: while I'm busily saying as close to nothing as I can get away with, they're talking hard to fill in the spaces. At least, that's what Hollingsworth does, his smooth face animated with all sorts of talk of his—and Greenmüll's—successes. Rance, I note, hangs back from this. Observing. But whether that's because he's letting Hollingsworth do all the talking or he himself is playing a waiting game I can't tell. I suspect that no matter how casual any move looks, Rance always knows what he's doing. And why.

"Fourth quarter, you said," I remark when there is a break in Hollingsworth's stream of consciousness. "Ideally I would bring my investors a *fait accompli.* Not a ghost of a possibility that is more or less half-baked."

That "half-baked" shuts him up solid, I note with satisfaction. It was, after all, my intention.

"What do you mean?" Rance says when it becomes obvious that Hollingsworth and all his chatter have been stymied.

"Well, that's not far in the future at all. A few months away. I'm thinking we draw up the papers for an investment for my firm now, based on getting those beta units out as promised and anticipated."

They both look at me. Hard. They are not open-mouthed, but I feel it, nonetheless.

"It doesn't work that way." Rance is the first to speak.

I raise both eyebrows at him. I don't know what I'm talking about, of course. But I know what I know.

"It'll work any way I want it to."

Hollingsworth laughs. It isn't an unkind sound. While he laughs I notice him look at me with new respect. As though he's seeing me for the first time. And maybe the look is deeper. It takes me a minute or two to recognize it for what it is: desire. Apparently, he likes a girl who takes charge. That makes me wonder if there has been a connection between him and Virginia, or if there had been at some point because, in the taking charge department, Martin is a queen.

"You're not wrong," he says, warm laughter still full in his voice. I notice Rance has his arms crossed and is scowling. But Hollingsworth keeps talking and I get the feeling he has amped up the charm. "You can wait until the next quarter if you want, but we're doing the Series C now. It'll be closed out in the time you are describing." I start to speak, but he cuts me off. "And, sure—you want to invest then? We'll find a piece of the pie for you, you know we will. But it will be a smaller piece and it will cost you more. The numbers we've been discussing? That's for now. Based on our current valuation."

I nod. I'm trying not to look like too big a goof—like I don't know what I'm doing—but Hollingsworth is either being kind or he's hungry. Maybe both. And then there's that extra that I think I see in his eyes.

"It's all been very interesting. I'm going to take this opportunity to my . . . my board. See what they say. It's a risk, of course."

Rance snorts, but offers no explanation for the sound. Hollingsworth smiles.

"Of course it's a risk," and his smile is warm and seems to touch his eyes. "I promise you: it wouldn't be worth doing if it wasn't."

CHAPTER TWENTY-TWO

THERE'S MORE TALK after that, but none of it is on point. We have played out all of the investment possibilities, that's what I think. So we talk about the weather, the food, the local sports teams. After a while Rance leaves, claiming a meeting he must get to. Evan and I sit for a few minutes longer, but he wastes no time into getting to what is now on his mind.

"Have dinner with me?"

The question is a big enough lane change that I'm flat out shocked. I had sensed maybe a *frisson* but from that small spark to a *date* seems like a big walk.

I struggle for a reply, but he's looking at me expecting an answer and I know that, under the circumstances, I'm not going to turn him down.

"Is that a conflict of interest?" I've got to start somewhere.

"No. I'm certain that it's not. We have to eat!"

I laugh out loud—I *LOL*—and he sees it. "I can't argue with that logic," I say.

We agree to meet the following evening. He'll pick me up at my hotel. He says he is taking me to an innovative Japanese restaurant that opened recently in town. I'm not sure if I should feel flattered or stalked as an investor. He hasn't made it clear to me which this is—business or pleasure—and I'm suspecting this is someone who could easily travel in both lanes. He is a gamer, that's what I think. Someone who plays life for advantage and, one way or the other, he thinks he sees one in me. I don't know how I feel about that, but spending more time with him will at least put me in a better position to judge his part in all of this.

"What you've built is an incredible accomplishment," I say, trying to steer things back to business.

"Am building," he corrects gently. But he's right, of course. Much has been built, but the future of the business is what's going to make them all stars: if everything goes as it's meant to and, at the moment there is no reason in sight why it should not.

For the balance of our time together over the remnants of lunch, I try to get a stronger sense of Evan, especially since—but not entirely because—he has asked me to dinner. It's funny, you know: you can have an instant connection with someone. A real and immediate rapport. This isn't like that. I'm not even entirely sure I'm attracted to him. Not because he's unattractive—he's not—but because to me he is unreadable. Oddly maybe, considering my recent history, I have most often been attracted to people with a warmth and openness about them. Evan has neither of those things, at least on first meeting. I determine to try to reserve judgment on that aspect of him, but it's not easy.

As I am thinking these things my phone rings. I glance over and am surprised when I see that the call is from someone I hadn't thought I would hear from again.

"You have to take that?" Evan asks, following my glance.

"No. Sorry. I'm good," I say, but I am curious about why this particular blast from the past might be calling me and I am a little astonished about the timing. Just as I was thinking about a man who seems closed off and not particularly warm, I get a call from one of the most open and warm people I've ever met. It is almost as though my assessment had summoned him, which, of course, is silly.

I don't stay long after that. My curiosity about the call is piqued and, anyway, it seems as though everything that can come from lunch has occurred. By the time I say goodbye to Evan, I'm wondering why I ever agreed to have dinner with him and then I remind myself that, of course, he is high on the list of those who might wish Virginia ill. I don't have an idea of what his specific motivation might be. Yet. But it has occurred to me in a sort of distant way that it might be him who has become a threat to her, if by proximity as much as anything else.

Once in my car, I listen to my voicemail. Curtis Diamond has left a brief message that says nothing. His newscaster voice says hello and asks me to call him and even that manages to whet my curiosity even further.

I put my car in motion toward no place in particular and return his call. When I get him on the phone, he sounds happier to hear from me than I would have imagined.

"I didn't even think I ever gave you my number," I say, perplexed.

He laughs. "You didn't. Your phone did. When you called me."

"Oh duh," I say, remembering. "Of course. Why are you calling, anyway?"

He laughs again. "Ever to the point, aren't you? I was thinking about you. It occurred to me to pick up my phone and dial. See how everything turned out."

"That's really sweet," I say—meanwhile I'm wondering what else is going on. Has life made me cynical? Possibly. But Curtis is a top reporter with a big LA station. It strikes me odd that he would call me out of the blue like this. "You know better than me how everything turned out," I say. There had been a bad man. Some would have said I killed him, but Curtis was holding the gun. Maybe that was enough. Maybe that was the thing that would tie us together. Always. I get a funny lump in my gut when I think that.

"You anywhere near LA right now? I figured maybe we could get dinner."

And what's with everyone wanting to break bread with me all of a sudden? This too is new.

"Sorry, no. I am nowhere near LA," I say, with no intention of giving away anything about where I am in real time. I am about to hang up when I remember. "Wait. Am I right in thinking that you started out your career reporting on the financial side?"

"You are," he says.

"Cool. Well, hmmm . . . since I've got you, can I ask you a technical question?"

"Working on another book?"

"You could say that. Sorta."

"Okay. Shoot."

"Let's say you had a big publicly traded company. A unicorn . . ."

"Nice."

"And you're the CEO. And all of a sudden you come to understand that the tech everyone has invested in is not working. Would there be any benefit in killing the CTO?"

"Excuse me?"

"You heard."

"I know. It wasn't where I thought you were going."

"Anyway . . ."

"Right. Okay. Beleaguered CEO. And the CTO is who developed the tech, I take it?"

"Correct."

"Geez. Sounds like I should do a story on whatever it is you're working on."

"We could get there. Please answer the question. If a story emerges, I'll holler."

"I'll hold you to that. But okay, yeah, in a situation as described there are a couple of scenarios I can imagine where the CEO would be better off with the CTO out of the picture."

"Shoot."

I hear Curtis hesitate. This is not what he'd expected when he called me. But then he plunges in. I figure he knows there is more here than meets the eye.

"Well, okay, one," Curtis says, "if he's about to be large-scale embarrassed by an all-out tech failure, it might be better to get him out of the picture."

"Him who?"

"The CTO."

"Right. Gotcha. Go on."

"You could fire him, I guess. But definitely him dead would make it more definitive."

"Okay." I think Curtis might be enjoying all of this a little too much. I remind myself that he's a journalist, after all. Wherever they end up, they start out as creative types, and Curtis is certainly that.

"Also, if everything is riding on the CTO's tech, the company might feasibly have insurance on him."

"On the CTO?"

"Yeah. Like, you know, insurance on the legs of movie stars because that's what brings in the box office?"

"What?"

"Never mind. But, yeah: insurance on the critical element in a publicly traded company is not unheard of."

"Geez." It opened up a whole new realm of possibility. And investigation. "I hadn't thought of that at all. Thanks, Curtis. You've been super helpful."

"You're welcome. But remember what I said: I meant it. If there's a story there, I'd love in on it."

"I'll keep you posted," I say as I ring off. As I do, I have absolutely zero intention of keeping my word.

CHAPTER TWENTY-THREE

ONCE I GET off the phone, I find I have wandered far off course, blabbing and driving. I am unconcerned, though, because I didn't have a destination in mind anyway and the Volvo is super good on gas, relative to its size.

When I get my bearings, I realize that instinct has guided me because I'm not far from Greenmüll once again. I set my course to cruise past, where I see that Martin's Land Rover is still in the parking lot. The giant SUV the guys took to lunch is not. The Taycan is still in place, making me think Rance must have grabbed an Uber or otherwise found his way back to his own office. But everything seems still. I toy with the idea of settling in and watching for a bit—staking things out—but I decide to keep going for now, and maybe circle back later and peek in. The thought of spending more hours in the car waiting and sitting doesn't appeal at the moment and the horizon looks so quiet, it seems pointless to hang around.

I cruise through the rest of the industrial park keeping a sharp eye out for whatever I might see. A few blocks from the Green-müll offices, I come to the sort of watering hole business districts tend to breed. It looks reputable. Like the kind of place you could get a good sandwich *and* a decent beer without the expectation of getting either hassled or in trouble. I'm still full of lunch, so I'm not looking for food, but the idea of working in a neutral space for a while appeals. I take my notebook and laptop inside, intending to camp out for a while and to do some thinking while partaking of refreshments. It'll be good to stop moving for a while.

I'm by myself, so the hostess shows me to a small table near the bar. The people watching is great. There are a few warehouse types, putting back cold ones and probably complaining about partners and bosses, but it's early yet. I figure there will be more of them later. There are office workers clad in cheap clothes fashioned to look expensive: shoes, bags, and haircuts that match. Michael Kors and Tory Burch everywhere. The largest percentage, though—unsurprising due to the address—are tech workers. They're easy to spot. Their nonconformity ties them together. They would think it ironic—maybe absurd—to see themselves as being connected by what they feel sets them apart. Exactly the same. Only different. But that's pretty much how it looks: the singularity of teenagers carried over to adulthood.

The people watching is good, but that's not what I'm here for. I want the space to pause and consider. The pieces I've been gathering aren't quite coming together. There's a lot that I'm missing. It's like I'm mired in quicksand or some other viscous material that's holding me back from seeing what I need to see.

Virginia Martin is about to change the world. Half of America's tech industry is—heck! The whole world's collectively holding their breath, waiting for her to do it. Smart investors have shelled out millions because they figure they're going to make money from her ideas. Yet not everything feels quite right, though I can't quite put my finger on it. Do I think I'm smarter than all of those investors? No. It's not that. But maybe some time has passed since they handed over that loot. Maybe it's as simple as the fact that there is more for me to see.

At the lunch I'd shared with Rance and Hollingsworth, I felt as though I'd gained insight into each of the men and how they work together. I don't have a full picture, of course. But, as with anyone, when you spend time with people, you begin to get a sense of them and how they fit within their worlds.

It seems clear to me that Hollingsworth is hungry. I mean, in every possible way, but for investment especially. I allow that it might be the way he's geared, but maybe it's deeper than that. As CEO he will have the best handle on Greenmüll's burn rate. Despite the millions already invested into the company, I sense a desperation beyond just that burn rate. I am guessing the company needs, not to only to finish its plans, but to make sure that it can keep going. And, as Curtis had suggested, there might be more ways—those that are not patently obvious—for a CEO to make sure the company's balance sheet ends up on the right side of red.

As I sit, with various tech and business dramas playing out nearby, I find myself taking notes—mental and otherwise—building timelines, trying to figure out the pieces I can't see. I'm so deeply engrossed in all of these thoughts and doodlings that when I glance up and see a familiar face across the room, I can't place it right away. I have to pull myself back. Focus. Before I can place him. For one thing, he is out of context. When I had last seen him, late this very morning, he had been wearing a lab coat and an expression of fear and apprehension. Now the expression is similar, but it's a more relaxed version. He is sitting on his own, staring morosely into a beer, pushing his shock of yellow hair off his face in a way that makes him look even more pathetically young and sad.

I flag down my server and tell her I want to send the young man at the bar another of what he is drinking. She looks at me sharply but doesn't say anything. It seems possible she is thinking he is not my type, but she keeps the opinion to herself.

When the server delivers his drink, I see her explaining where it came from, pointing across the room in my direction. He squints at me, reaching for recognition. I smile and wave lightly and see him look sharply away. This is going to be more difficult than I thought.

I give it a few minutes and can see him pointedly avoiding looking over at me. I open one more button on my blouse and head over to where he is.

"Hiya," I say, taking the empty stool next to him. "We met earlier today. Sort of. You work at Greenmüll, right?" He is avoiding looking at me, but I can see that his ears have turned a sort of bright crimson, which makes me figure that my first assessment was right: he isn't avoiding me because he doesn't want to talk to me. Necessarily. He's avoiding me because he's super shy. And in this case the second reason is definitely easier to deal with than the first.

"Yuh," he answers without looking at me. And I realize that he is shy enough that the loosened blouse button might have been a step too far.

"You recognize me? I was there, on a tour today."

He nods but doesn't say anything. Truly, I think, it's like pulling teeth.

"I was there when . . . um . . . when . . . you dropped something."

Again, I realize I've chosen the wrong thing to say. I can tell when his ears go back to that vivid shade of red.

"It was awful," he says, but he's speaking so quietly, I have to strain to catch the words.

"Can I join you?"

He looks at me and I read panic in his eyes and his ears turn even more red, which is not something I would have thought possible. All of that, but he doesn't answer me, so I hop onto the chair next to him and motion for the server to bring another round, even though he's barely touched the drink I bought him.

"What's your name?" I ask when some time has passed and his ears seem to have returned to a more normal color.

"I'm Matt Sundstrom," he says without looking directly at me.

"Nice to meet you, Matt," I say. "Thanks for letting me sit. I think we have things to talk about."

He shoots a look at me, but he doesn't say anything. And the ears. They float between rosé and burgundy. It's getting to be kind of frightening.

"Well," I begin as though he commented, "I'm a potential investor, so I'm looking for as much information as possible. And it seemed—from what I saw of your interaction this morning—that you might know more about the situation at Greenmüll than I do."

"The situation?" He says it so quietly I can barely hear, and I find it odd that he has broken his silence with this comment.

"Well, you know, what's really going on there."

"I don't think it's much different than you saw," he says. His voice is barely above a whisper and I have to strain to hear, but it's clear that loyalty comes to him naturally.

"Your exchange with Dr. Martin was . . . riveting."

And I feel badly having said it, because his ears turn bright crimson again, and just when they had gotten back to a relatively normal color.

"There was nothing to it," he insists. "She was well within her rights to take me to task."

I look at him for a minute, and his ears turn red once more under my scrutiny. I'm beginning to feel sorry for him, though I don't do anything about it.

"It didn't look like nothing," I say at length, this time ignoring his ears. I don't want to feel sorry for him. "It looked like she humiliated you. In front of all of your colleagues, too."

Pure misery appears on his face. I feel a bit sorry for him. And I fear, in a way, that I've gone too far. Still, I press on, telling myself there are larger matters at stake.

"These are critical times." He says it so quietly, I have to strain again to hear.

"Yes, yes, of course. But they are all critical times right now. I don't think she had to embarrass you in that way."

And this time the ears don't get quite as red, I notice. And I see one hand curl into a fist. I'm imagining it is involuntary. Imagining also that I'm getting very close to the core of the matter.

"It wasn't the first time," he says, his voice barely above a whisper.

"The first time for what?"

"My carelessness. It's become a problem for her, I know."

"I'm sure you're exaggerating it. Or she is. I don't think it's as big a deal as we're making it. And I saw your face. I'm figuring that careless wouldn't even approach it."

He looks at me plaintively. Shifts his eyes.

"She was hard on you," I say again. And I say it without preamble or by finishing the thought. A simple fact. I'm trying to get him to talk.

He nods and there is nothing accusatory in it. Vindicated. It's a big outfit and he has some responsibility in it. I can tell from his body language that her demanding way with him is business as usual. Nothing personal. And yet. The fact that he is still here when I have invaded his table makes me think he has more to say, else why wouldn't he have taken his ears to a different part of the bar or fled altogether?

"She's not mean, really," he says, and I don't offer anything but a nod. He seems so ready to talk, and I don't want to break the spell. He moves his hands for a moment and no sounds come out. I can see he is struggling for the right words. "She has a lot on her plate."

"Yes," I agree. "She certainly does. I've been learning about what she's trying to do there. She's got her hands full."

"I'm pretty sure I'm not telling you anything you don't already know when I say that we've already missed some deadlines." He stops abruptly, like he thinks it's possible he's said too much, but I can tell there is more he wants to say and so I push a little bit. Maybe he has even invited that push. It doesn't take very much.

"How many? Deadlines missed, I mean." I ask as a starting point. There is more that I could say, but a gentle beginning feels like the right course.

"More than a few," he says without meeting my eyes.

I think a bit before I say anything more. He's skittish, I can feel it. A feral cat or a wild horse. If I move too quickly—say the wrong thing—he will sidle away and run back into the wild. And so I take my time. Feel him out. He wants to talk, but he also doesn't want to think of himself as telling tales. I can feel all of that. And it's a fine line. I still feel a little sorry for him, but I also feel I don't want to let this opportunity slide. I'm sure I'll never get a chance like this again.

"Do you know why?" I breathe the question out gently, then watch it land.

"Why what?" he asks, but I figure he already knows.

"The deadlines. Why she missed them."

"It could be a lot of things," he says. But he doesn't meet my eyes.

"It could," I breathe back with the same gentle air.

"There are whispers," he starts, his voice hardly more than a whisper, too.

Our server reappears then, and I curse and thank her in the same thought because while she's interrupted the conversation and I've barely touched my drink, he has drained his. He orders another, and I order one back, a light beer this time, and when the new drinks arrive, I send my barely touched martini away. So engaged is he with his thoughts, he doesn't seem to register my drink maneuvering. I breathe.

"Whispers," I repeat, prompting him. "People talk. Things aren't always true." And I also know but don't add that less than fifty percent of company rumors are ever true and that's a statistic. I'm taking everything here with a grain of salt. Many grains.

"Are you saying I'm making things up?" There, I'm pretty sure I heard what I've been waiting for. A definite slur to his words. That slight loss of clarity when the booze is starting to kick in. And the eyes: not quite as sharp or focused. And his ears are turning red a lot less now. I keep my face neutral though. I don't let him see that I'm pleased.

"I am not saying that, no. I'm suggesting that maybe your sources are imperfect. Or just talking, or whatever."

"I've seen it with my own eyes." It's clear that it's important to him that I believe him. Not because it's me, but because maybe people usually don't.

I gesture almost invisibly for the server to bring another round. And the bar is not busy yet, so she's fast and stealthy, and

I figure she's invested in making our tab larger because that will bring in a bigger tip. He has just finished his drink when she brings the new one and, at a sign from me, she whisks both my barely touched one and his empty glass away. We are complicit in this, she and I. We don't have to discuss things to know that men have done this to each of us: conspired to get us to drink more. She doesn't mind being part of this turning of the tables. She plays her part with aplomb.

"What have you seen?" Once he's settled again with his drink, I say it quietly. Even coquettishly. I've leaned toward him, too, trying to give him something additional to think about. I see his eyes fall to the vee in my blouse, see also the bead of perspiration on his brow. All of these things—plus booze—are contributing to him feeling a little off balance, though I can see he is not uncomfortable. He has forgotten to be mesmerized by shyness and is now moving smoothly into the role of disgruntled employee.

"I guess it isn't so much what I have seen, as what I haven't."

I look at him, not quite taking his meaning. At least not right away. He obviously wants another prompt, so I comply.

"What do you mean?"

"Well, the results. They haven't exactly been there. They haven't been what was anticipated."

"Results?" Another prompt. They seem to be necessary to keep him moving. Another drink shows up then. That will keep him moving, too.

"Lab results. The markers we're to have hit. We haven't done a lot of that. And that's the problem, really. She knows I know."

I try not to show my frustration. It's difficult.

"What do you know?"

"She's secretive about that." He has kept talking as though I hadn't asked a question. "And she is careful to do some of the rest of the work when no one is around. But I would have thought . . . all this time and all these markers later . . . we would have actually seen—some sort of activity."

I look at him carefully, wondering how much of this is real and how much is sour grapes. It's hard to tell. But it sounds to me as though what he is implying is beyond disgruntled employee.

"Tell me what you mean," I say.

"I feel she is close to putting it all together, but maybe not close enough. And she knows I know."

I shake my head involuntarily, as though trying to make all of the words make sense.

"Wait: What do you know? And why does it matter?"

"I don't know," he says. And then again. "I don't know. I think I've said enough."

I try to get him to talk more, but he has clammed up, and I can't tell if it's because he's had so much to drink, he's now feeling queasy or if he's had a sudden bout of loyalty to his master. I suspect maybe both. Whatever it is, once he decides not to talk anymore, it's like a drawbridge has gone up.

We exchange phone numbers, but even that is a stretch. He is no longer trusting me, or maybe he is no longer trusting himself. Whatever the case, the result is the same: he has stopped talking, and I'm pretty sure nothing I say or do will change that. I say goodbye to him, getting almost nothing in response. Then I go back to my own table and my long-abandoned stuff, settle my rather large bill, and head out.

CHAPTER TWENTY-FOUR

When I am alone, I think about what I've been told. Even more, the information he has given me—or maybe nearly given me—dominates every aspect of the situation. He'd had a lot to drink, it was true. But I did not get the sense that he was beyond himself. The booze he had consumed might have lightened his load of responsibility, but it did not relieve him of it. I was certain he had known what he was saying. So the question remains: why? Was what he had told me a given within the company? That things weren't happening quite as they should be? Were these the things those working in the lab were seeing and feeling? Or did he have additional information and was wanting to send an alert further afield? Or was everything he was feeling pure sour grapes? I had no way of knowing.

Also, I had sensed that he was frightened, though I don't know of what. In fairness, he had seemed frightened of everything. I think again about those red ears. But was he exhibiting fright beyond shyness? I can't be sure.

When I think about it, though, what, really, had he said? Pulled apart and stripped to bare essentials, it had seemed to me at the time that he was implying that the core technology on which Greenmüll's unicorn financing had been based might not work. That was huge. As well, it changed the picture and confirmed what I'd learned from Curtis. The danger to Virginia may not be a rival company wanting to take Greenmüll down, which was the theory I had been leaning toward before this day. But possibly it was someone with a vested interest in covering up the fact that Martin's technology was further away from fruition, and therefore revenue, than what had previously been thought. Not ready for primetime. And who would have the most to lose if that were the case? It seemed to me to be ever more clear: the one I needed to be watching most closely was Evan Hollingsworth.

*   *   *

Before I return to the hotel, I head back to Greenmüll. It's after six and the Taycan is gone now, though Virginia's car is still there, of course. From what I've learned, she has a lot of problems to solve. The only place to do that would be the lab. I settle in to my spot across the street, intending to do some watching. After a while, though, as the small amount of booze I drank begins to leave my system, I start to feel kind of sleepy and ready for another meal.

Sitting and watching Greenmüll is producing a big fat zero tonight. There aren't even any workers or delivery people to watch coming and going. Finally, I talk myself into letting it be and I roll back to the hotel where I take the dog for a long walk and ponder as I prowl.

I have answers to none of the questions I have been asking, yet I feel pretty good about having the sense to pose all of them.

Something is afoot and no one is sure where it is all going. But I feel like I now have a picture. As perfect as it all looks, is it possible that the world-changing technology Martin has conceived and has been trying to execute doesn't work? I hadn't thought about it in that way before, but I think it through now. Isn't that what yellow-haired Matt Sundstrom had been saying? I'm thinking now that it was.

If that were the case, though, it would be a catastrophe for everyone involved. What if you do everything right your whole life and the thing you've hinged it all on doesn't function as it's supposed to? What happens then? And though I am inexpert on anything that is scientific, having spent some time in her world, I can see the places where everything might not be quite what they seem. What if she had told people: "Everything will be this," and instead, it had turned out that "everything was that." If the technology didn't work, the whole dream would dry up. The whole infrastructure—the big lifestyle, the unicorn valuation, the magazine articles and esteem from peers and fans— would prove to be a house of cards. Bring in a big wind? The whole thing comes tumbling down.

Back at the hotel after our walk, I contemplate other disguises, other things to infiltrate and get yet another view. Then I realize I probably don't have to. What Matt had said resonated: that was why I had kept him talking. It had fit with everything I had seen. If the tech doesn't work, there will be hell to pay. Greenmüll is a unicorn because of Virginia Martin's vision. If three years on, that vision is faltering, who will suffer? I know the answer before I ask the question: there are a whole complement of players involved now. It has all moved far beyond Martin's purview. The implications are so far reaching, I know I can't even fully grasp the whole thing.

I grab a notebook and sketch it out: Who will be implicated if Martin's vision does not develop as planned? The answer to that question might give me the answer I need for mine. The cast of characters seems too large. I start at the top. Obviously, Ethan Hollingsworth will be implicated in everything, no matter how small. Beyond Martin herself, plus Hollingsworth, Rance would seem to have the most to lose. He had arranged the financing that had brought unicorn status to Greenmüll. There would have been an expectation that he had done all of his due diligence before recommending that those who depended on his good opinion should invest. After all, someone in Rance's position is only as good as his most recent deal. If it came out that Greenmüll was still years away from a goal that might ultimately prove unattainable, Rance's reputation would suffer. In any case, he probably had skin in the game: anything that hit the stock price would likely hit him personally, as well.

Which, again, leads us back to Hollingsworth. What if the CTO he had staked everything on was not capable of delivering? Would removing her from the picture before it was known that he had backed a bad horse reduce his culpability?

It was the investment aspect of this whole thing that was producing danger, that much I was certain of. And yes: investment is always a risk. If it were a sure thing, everyone would do it. You invest to make the possibility of the big bucks come alive. That is, if you keep your money in your sock drawer, where it most probably belongs, it will not multiply. For sure. But if you invest in a thing that is big and sexy and probably unattainable, you might lose it, you might break even, but you might also—and this is the smallest of the mights—you might make a fortune. And people take that risk because, well, if they win, they won't have been the only one and they'll be able to buy larger sock drawers.

These are the thoughts I am thinking while I fall asleep. What is possible? That's what I think about. Is it more than I have been led to believe? Or less?

CHAPTER TWENTY-FIVE

IN THE MORNING things are different again. I find I can't get out of bed. There seems no earthly reason why I should. Sure, I have a job to do, but what possible good can come of it? And who cares anyway? Who cares about what I do or do not do?

Suddenly, this warm bed, fitted with crisp hotel sheets, is as far as I want to go. Ever. I might be curled up there still, arms twined around my legs, but the dog makes a good case for me getting up. First he looks at me from the edge of the bed with deep concern. This isn't the first time he has encountered this challenge. And the way he looks at me I understand: he is worried that this might be the time he is unsuccessful in his efforts.

"You don't get it, though," I say to his patient golden eyes. "You think you do, but you don't. Sometimes it's too much."

He waves his tail at me then. Not ecstatically: a gentle there and back. Reassuring me. Or maybe it is a prod. *Please*, he seems to be saying, *don't let this be the time you don't get up.*

"I'm sorry." I'm crying now. I couldn't explain it if you made me. If he made me. If anyone made me. "I'm just . . . I can't."

I roll over—away from those probing amber eyes—and pull the covers over my head.

At first there is nothing. He gives me a solid few minutes to wallow. Maybe he's contemplating his next move.

And wallow is what I do. Deeply and beyond reason. After a while there is a surprisingly light *thump* onto the bed. Surprising because he has grown to be a big dog, yet that *thump* is careful and delicate. The covers are still over my head—over all of me— but I feel him rest his head gently on the blanket-covered s-curve of my hip.

I'm here. He doesn't say it, of course, but I feel it anyway. *I'm here and I care. You aren't alone.*

Somehow that undoes me completely, and I indulge in an additional half an hour of sobs I can't rightly track the source of. They are for those I have lost; I suspect that. They are for those whose shapes and scents I can barely remember. Those who took up all of my heart and consciousness, but who have now slipped away.

How did I let them slip away?

And the sobs wrack me again.

He lets me sob, that beautiful golden dog. He leaves me to my sobbing. But not for very long. After he's given me my half an hour or so he prods his cold, wet nose under the covers and pokes it into the small of my back. I scream at the shock of it and then I laugh because I know what he is really telling me is that the time that he will be indulgent with this behavior has passed. There is a day out there waiting for us and it must begin with him getting outside to pee.

I dress hurriedly to take him out, knowing that he's indulged me for so long that his need has become urgent. On my way out the door, I catch a glimpse of my face in the hall mirror. I look wan and pale. My skin is blotchy and my eyelids are fat and red from all the crying. I look like hell, but I have survived once again. Miraculously—again—I have survived.

Once we get back from our walk, I clean myself up, cool myself down, then get back to work. It's a better option for this moment, I decide. My eyes run over the hotel safe where I stored the Bersa before I went out. Thinking about the gun reminds me that my exit strategy continues to be available to me should I decide to take it.

On the business at hand, I still don't have a handle on who might be out to kill Virginia Martin. I know she is alive—or was the evening before—and I'm starting to get a picture of why someone might benefit from her being dead. It's a start.

I read articles. Watch interviews and speeches on YouTube. There is a lot riding on the success of her technology. More, probably, than I even know. Still, for whatever reason, the things Martin had promised early on are not coming true. What my source didn't say: a company with a billion-dollar-plus valuation had bet everything on one horse and that horse appears to be coming up lame. Should one shoot the horse? Well. There was that possibility, too.

There is a lot at stake and the numbers are high. And I realize a piece I have been missing: with a unicorn company, there are investors. A lot of them. Was it possible one of them was disgruntled or afraid? If Martin were to die, would their lives or outlooks be improved? Who would benefit?—that was the question. And, more important to me right now, was there a way I could find out who they were? If I could talk with the investors with the most at stake, maybe I could get an idea of who, if anyone, is disgruntled. That might give me a lead on who was angry enough to wish Martin dead. And though I start out thinking that it would be difficult to find a way to find out who those investors were, I suddenly realize it is not: Rance would have a handle on all of this because he was the one who had put the investors together in the first place. Figuratively, if anyone knew where the bodies were buried, it would be Rance. I need to find a way to know the things that he knows.

I sigh deeply and suck it up: I will need to talk with him again the following day. I am not looking forward to that.

It is in this spirit that I set out for another stakeout session. I push my hair under a ball cap to thinly disguise my look, then sit in front of the Greenmüll offices again. It's all I can think of in that moment and it's an activity that provides even less satisfaction than it did previously. Delivery people and employees come and go and I watch in frustration, knowing that all of this is getting me exactly nowhere: any one of those people could be taking her out and I'd never know until the arrival of an ambulance. I start to feel a little frantic until, finally, I've had enough. There has to be some better, more fruitful activity. I put the car in gear and head to Martin's townhouse. Watching her place of business, I've decided belatedly, isn't going to do anything other than either break my last nerve or help me see her die. And neither of those things will do: too little too late. If I'm going to get a break in this situation, I'll have to try and make it myself.

The townhouse is exactly what one would expect under the circumstances. A residence that seems artfully sketched for a successful and busy science type who works nonstop, has a lot of loot, and needs a place to live.

It is in a community that is gated, but there is no gatekeeper. So I wait for someone to be leaving, then slip in before the gate closes. It's a legit move that I don't fear will arouse concern: so many people do things like that because they've forgotten their clicker or they're visiting their mom or whatever little domestic drama has occurred. People don't usually bat an eye when it happens, especially if you happen to look like me, which is basically unremarkable and vanilla and therefore invisible, especially when driving a nice enough car. Most of the time, no one sees me. That's not a bad thing. That's not always a bad thing.

I pull my car into visitor parking, then stroll over to number nine like I look like I know what I'm doing: like I belong. The townhomes are identical. If there were no numbers outside, even the residents probably wouldn't be able to find their way home.

When I figure out which one it is, I don't try the front door. No one leaves their front door unlocked, and in any case, a watching device would put my whole operation into the toilet. It's a townhouse, so there is no side door—neighbors on either side—and there is no easy way to figure out which is which in back. I walk to the neighboring property, a mixed-use commercial development that covers several acres. From there I can see that number nine is second from the end. Scaling the wall isn't difficult—it's not that high—but I'm very aware that someone might see me and think it's out of the ordinary. Here again, my invisibility shield of middle-aged woman holds. I am well dressed. I don't look as though I am trying to hide anything. I don't see anyone, and if anyone sees me, they do not stop me.

Behind the complex, I perform a kind of inelegant stop, drop and roll, and find myself in a tiny but perfect back garden. A fountain is running, there are two sets of French doors and a small personal swimming pool: a "cocktail" pool. This is the home of someone who could easily afford a beautiful house, but has opted for a luxury townhouse for ease and also security, though I guess I've put a lie to the security part. So much for that.

A large, fluffy gray cat is regarding me with interest. Apparently, people don't come over the wall every day.

"Hey, old son," I say. A risky move, I know, because I can't even be sure it's a male.

"Meh," the cat says, all nonchalant, and heads toward the door.

The wall is not that high—sufficiently so to discourage casual access, and keep the cat in. The result: no further security is required, apparently. One of the sets of French doors is open, presumably to allow the cat and fresh air inside. I follow my fuzzy host into his lair. A scratch under the chin brings rich purrs. He is glad of the extra company, even if it has arrived from an unexpected source. Not a watch-cat, then. So much the better.

The house is more comfortable than I would have expected, from the little I know of its owner. Is it the STEM thing? I don't know, but the furniture is comfortable and oversized and it's all perfectly elegant and probably expensive—that's how it all looks. A big TV. A kitchen island with two breakfast plates left on it. I wonder at that, but not for long.

The plates are in a chef's kitchen replete with every appliance ever conceived, and the dishes are undone. It's all describing Virginia Martin's personality in ways that are new to me, but I can't quite nail down how. Ordered visual cacophony and probably someone comes in once a week to clean to keep whatever mess might grow under control. That seems to be how she rolls. Everything is perfect. And everything is right on the edge.

Upstairs it is exactly the same, only different. There is a guest bedroom/office configuration that looks as though someone was working there right now but had perhaps gone out for a run. I've recently seen her car at the office, so I know that is not the case, but still. That is the impression one gets. As though everything in her home is always ready and waiting for her to go straight to work. I'm guessing even the cleaner doesn't get access to this space: maybe only to do the floors, which look perfect. But they leave everything as they find it so that Virginia can drop into work mode at any moment.

The master bedroom is not the same. It is pristine, as though no one has ever lived here. The king-sized bed is made. No clothes are strewn around. The generous shower stall is scrubbed and perfect and ready for use. In contrast with the rest of the home, the master bedroom seems over the top, as though it is meant for show. Again, I wonder what this says about Martin's personality. Or maybe it is not her personality at all we are talking about and reflects the tastes of some unseen designer. But it is clear that her personal space has to be perfect. That need is reflected in every bit of gleaming oak. Every spotless mirror. Every pair of perfectly spaced shoes.

In the large walk-in closest, there are definitely two distinct sides to the closet. One side looks as one would expect: different types of clothing and colors hung in what I imagine is a normal way. There are dresses and pants and tops, grouped roughly by type and maybe slightly by color, but mostly simply put away. Tidy but nothing remarkable in the organization.

On the other side of the closet, clothing seems organized by type and color. There is a whole section of good gray pants and surprisingly similar yellow blouses. A few lab coats, hung together. A few smart but simple dresses, all in sober grays and yellows. I'm imagining this is the business side of her closet—and maybe her personality. I have seen interviews with Virginia Martin. And photographs. And I have of course met her, as well. The clothes she wears are a uniform: it might be that the colors she has chosen to highlight her wardrobe—gray and yellow—are a nod to femininity, but I don't think that. I figure that, like a lot of other brilliant minds, the similarity of the clothes allows her to dress consistently sharply without the need to give it much thought. The shoes are also similarly uniform. Several pairs of very good Chelsea boots: elegant, practical, comfortable—story told. There are a few pairs of trainers and some very good heels, but the Chelseas are numerous and perfectly maintained: what she wears to work. Other than this whisper to her inner workings, there is nothing of interest to me in either the closet or the bedroom and I've left the office for last because I suspect that's where I'm most likely to find things that will be useful to me.

Virginia's desk is properly old school, a vast acreage of oak. There is a catchall drawer filled with pens and a pencil sharpener and paper clips: nothing of interest. Below is a file drawer, everything neatly labeled. It will take some time to go through. On the desk itself is a vertical file where half a dozen folders are stacked, though I have no way of telling if they're waiting for attention or to be refiled. I start there. I look through the folders. Unsurprisingly, everything seems to relate to either the procurement of appropriate trash—for a moment, I think about a future where trash has become an asset: the thought amuses me—and notes on what I imagine might be the refinement of the formula for the cocktail of gases used to break the garbage down. At least, that's what I think it is: I who barely has any idea of what I'm looking at. Science. Math. Algebra. Not my world, yet the themes seem familiar, based on what I have been learning about Virginia Martin's work.

An unlabeled file lays where you might place a laptop. I flip it open, expecting more formulations and notations and am surprised, instead, to see printouts from an online forum, with some of the entries highlighted in yellow, presumably by Martin herself. I read the first entry that has been marked and recoil. The note, by a user who calls himself Daddy McPhee, is dated from three months ago and it is so venomous and vitriolic, reading the words alone make me feel queasy.

"This stupid bitch is deliberately stringing us along. If I told you how much money I have sunk into GML you'd puke. It seems like every time she goes on the rag, the stock tanks. I'd be happy to see this cunt swing."

The words are vile, but not in isolation. Pure poison spewed right into a public forum seems to be how he rolls. Anyone reading them about themselves would have been alarmed, even frightened, and Martin has been no exception. I imagined that, somewhere in all of this, I might be the reason she called her mom in the first place.

The most recent entry is dated the week before. The date, I note, is the one just before the handler contacted me.

"I am past the point where I will trust the fuckwads in charge at GML to take care of business. They have been given every chance. This should be considered a warning—or promise!—that I am going to take matters into my own hands."

What doesn't make sense to me the most—in a field of a lot of things that don't make sense—is why a stockholder would be threatening the CTO, which is what he is essentially doing. He'd said he wanted to see her swing. It was a pretty obvious threat. I felt a small surge of triumph: this then was the reason I had been brought on. It was this loser. So stupid. I wish that they had let me know this earlier—I could have saved a lot of time. I had been imagining worthwhile foes. This guy sounded like I'd be able to take him out in an hour. If what I'm thinking now is true, I'll be home in a couple of days, tops.

There is another folder on the desk. It is marked "Performance Review." At the top of the pile is a familiar name: Matt Sundstrom. I scan Virginia's notes. It's difficult, because it turns out her handwriting is like that of a physician: dense but almost illegible. As near as I can make out, she wants him fired. She feels he is incompetent and not to be trusted around her tech. The next page is a printout of a correspondence between her and Evan. First Virginia writing to Evan and telling him that Matt is a detriment to the project. Evan responding. Telling Virginia that, basically, Matt is untouchable. Matt's father is an investor. The job is a favor. "Feel free to assign him someplace where he'll be out of your way, but he can't be terminated. I've promised his father he'd have a job and maybe a career with us."

I think about some of what Matt had told me. Sour grapes? Bad blood? A feeling, certainly, of being unwanted and him pushing back. I don't know any of these things, of course, but all seem possible.

I photograph the various printouts, then replace them carefully, pretty sure I've gotten what I came for. More.

I am enjoying that triumphant feeling and trying to determine what to do with it when I hear a key in the front door, then the click and tumble of the lock. Martin has left the office early? I've been watching her carefully for several days—her leaving early doesn't seem to happen. And yet.

CHAPTER TWENTY-SIX

I GO OVER the floorplan in my head. Front door. Back door. Cat. I am trapped and I don't have a lot of options. I take the Bersa from my purse, check the safety, then hold it by the muzzle. I tuck myself behind the office door, then I listen and wait.

It takes a long time, but eventually I hear a light tread on the stairs. There is a longer wait, and then I hear footsteps toward the other room, movement there. My body aches with the strain of taut waiting and I think about taking my chances and making a run for it while she's in the other room. It doesn't seem like a good option, though. It seems like a loser's game.

Eventually, I hear her head toward the office where I am hidden behind the door. I tighten up even further, easing one muscle, then another. The light tread gets closer. In the dim light I see her smooth, dark hair right in front of me. I aim carefully, but she's moving and I'm afraid of detection. I bring the butt of the gun down on her temple with what I hope is the right amount of force, but not too much. She buckles at my feet like a crumpled flower. I hope I have not killed her, but I can't be sure.

I bend down. Turn her over. And realize it isn't Martin at all.

I study the beautiful features—the smooth dark hair. I struggle with the name that belongs to these things: she who is very like Virginia, yet not her. She's not someone I know well. Then it comes to me: the oddly elegant, archaic name that goes with this extreme beauty not at all.

Hattie, whom I had met that first evening at the Extreme Angels office. The lovely young woman who had accompanied Rance to coffee.

She is as still as death and I find it interesting that I, who have taken so many lives, should feel such a deep concern at the potential loss of this one.

I feel one thin wrist. It seems cool, but her pulse is distinct. Not dead, then.

I think about what to do with her. Since she is nearly my own size, taking her anywhere is out of the question: I'll be physically unable to hoist her around without help. I think about trying to revive her and asking her what she is doing there, but I discard the idea instantly. I have no idea why she is here, but whatever the reason, she is an enemy, not an ally. I feel fairly confident in that assumption and I'm not even sure why. I mean, after all, she and Virginia might be friends. Or Hattie might be here, doing her a favor; like feeding the cat. All of these and other possibilities. But none of these things seems likely. My best guess is that she is here as I am, though with a different motivation. But she is here, invading Virginia's privacy in the hope of either discovering something or leaving something behind. I need to determine which.

When she fell, Hattie had dropped a backpack. I use gloved hands to scoop it up, keeping one eye on her at all times, even though at present there is no sign of her rousing.

The backpack holds the usual sort of things. Lipstick. Hand sanitizer. A mask. A hair brush and hair products. Usual pretty girl things. But in the part of the pack that might usually hold a laptop, I hit pay dirt. There is a thick file and it is labeled with a single word: Greenmüll. When I pull the file out, I am surprised to find a small handgun beneath it. It seems odd to me that Hattie would feel the need to carry a gun, but it's not unthinkable. She works in a newly gentrifying part of town. It seems entirely possible she does not always feel secure there. Some people respond to that by walking faster. Others get a permit to carry.

I check the thick file. Inside there are press releases, schematics, and other things relating to the business. None of what she is carrying makes any sense to me. Lots of financial stuff, which is not surprising, considering Rance has been arranging financing for Greenmüll since the beginning and Hattie works for Extreme Angels.

I keep an eye on Hattie—still out cold—and move more deeply into the room. I'm going to have to work fast to get through the parts of the office I haven't gotten to yet. Faster than I had planned.

There is a sheaf of files in a stand intended for them on the desk. The first two don't turn up anything. The third are Martin's tax returns. They are signed. I photograph her signature and put the file, returns inside, back to the spot on the desk where I found them.

Returning to Hattie's fallen form, I quickly photograph the documents Hattie was carrying. This all smells bad to me. Something, as the handler had said, rotten in Denmark. I reason that, if this had been an expected visit, Hattie wouldn't have been skulking around at a time when Virginia was clearly going to be at the office.

Hattie groans and stirs a bit. She is beginning to wake. I don't hang around long enough to see her eyes open. Rather I stuff the contents of her pack back inside, then pop the Bersa back into my own purse while I head for the door.

Downstairs, I go back out the way I came in. The cat watches me, his tail slashing back and forth angrily. I think he looks like he'd like to clobber me, though I'm pretty sure that can't be true.

* * *

Back at my hotel, I do some yoga stretches and work at calming my breathing. If I were at home, I'd light a candle and maybe some incense, but I don't have that luxury today. There are things I need to think about. I need my wits about me. I need clarity and am not sure where that will come from.

Was Hattie's visit to Virginia's home expected, or was it part of an attack? Since Virginia wasn't home when the other woman arrived, I am inclined to believe the latter. And though I have nothing to base it on, my first thought when seeing them together was to think that Hattie and Rance were lovers. That doesn't explain why Hattie would be carrying Greenmüll paperwork, and to whom. And what did it mean?

But pondering things won't get me very far, and I have other fish to fry. And even the things that are right in front of me that I'd like to deal with have to be put on hold. For instance, I have to stop myself from jumping up and taking action on finding out about the abusive forum stalker who calls himself Daddy McPhee. It takes almost everything I have to stop myself from digging in to try and find out more about him. I have to bargain with myself. Just *one* internet search? But no. I don't have time.

CHAPTER TWENTY-SEVEN

THE REASON I don't have time seems ridiculous to me: I have a date. I have an outfit to put on. Unfamiliar makeup to put on my face. I do a credible job, though. And by the time I go to the lobby to meet my date at the appointed time, I figure I don't look bad at all. Brand-new me.

When Evan pulls up in his long black SUV, I'm standing right there. He hops out and opens the door for me, and we are congenial as he drives to the restaurant, though I'm still unsure if this meeting is meant to be business or pleasure. I do entertain the thought that, as with a lot of very successful men, there is never a moment when he is not prepared to be either. Or both. Or even more.

Koi Izakaya is precisely as promised and as the name implies: hip, fun, chic, and not so quiet as to promote intimate conversation. I'm relieved about that.

I end up liking the place very much and, despite myself, I start out right away liking the company very much, too. Away from the office or business influences, Evan seems warmer, though it's possible he's working at that, too. Over cocktails it strikes me again that he is flirting with me, though I tell myself I can't be right about that: I don't imagine myself to be his type. And is he mine? Well, I don't know that at all. Not the type of woman who lives alone at the edge of a forest, no. But the well-dressed and coiffed creature I've become? I allow that it is possible that she might be the kind of person who would partner with an Evan Hollingsworth and be comfortable with things like beautiful clothes and nice cars and doors that are opened for you when you walk toward them.

I don't feel like myself anymore.

I don't know who myself is.

"You seem far away," he remarks. His voice is warm. Teasing. He is trying to be charming, not invasive. "It's like you're not with me here at all. Where are you, lovely one?"

I smile at him. "Ha! I was kind of wondering that myself. The place and certainly the company are both very good. But I have a lot on my mind."

He nods and indicates to our server that we should be brought another round. "I understand," he says. "It's the danger of our work. It can be captivating. But then where does that leave us?"

"I'm not sure I follow."

"I've dropped myself into my work so completely for the last decade or so. It engages you, you know." He looks at me properly, then, "I *know* you know. I can smell it on you. You're a hard worker, too. And then you wake up one day. You look around. And what? Why do I keep doing all of this?" He gestures toward the room, but I know the restaurant is not what he means, rather the wider world into which he has poured his adult working life. "I've put everything in, and for what?"

I look at him and grin. "You're kidding, right? I mean, I had not thought we'd have such a thoroughly existential conversation over dinner."

I wonder for a moment if I've said the wrong thing, but he grins back. "I knew my instincts were right about you," he says, somewhat mysteriously, I think. "I like you. You're no bullshit."

"It's true," I say, also grinning. "I've got a pretty sensitive meter in that department."

"Fair enough." He nods. "I've seen it."

"Anyway," I continue, "it's all bullshit, isn't it?" I've surprised myself, saying this out loud. I watch him to see if I've pushed too far this time, but he nods, agreeing.

"It is," he says.

"We're born. We work. We die."

"That's cheery."

"No. Seriously. We make a lot of noise about everything in our lives, but we're simply passing time." These aren't things I've thought of in this way before. But once I've said them, they seem to make sense to me. "It's the things between all of that that sets us apart. How we marshal all of what happens to us between those key events."

"The birth of character," he says, nodding, and I'm startled enough by his words to look at him closely again. It was not a comment I had expected from him, though I chide myself instantly for underestimating him. But if not that, what was it that had been expected?

By now our food has arrived. Interesting-looking concoctions deliciously rendered and beautifully served.

"That's an interesting way of putting it," I say. "The idea that character is born in the space that comes between."

"Right?" he says, nodding, looking pleased that I'd remarked. That I'd noticed.

"There's more to you than meets the eye," I say.

He looks at me speculatively before answering. "I would say that's going around."

And to my horror, I feel myself blush at the comment because, of course, it is much more true than he knows.

We eat companionably. We could be two people who met under normal circumstances: mutual friends or an online service, it is as comfortable and explorative. Easy. After a while, he says as much. "I'm enjoying myself rather a lot," he says with the air of someone making an admission. "It's been all business lately. I can't remember the last time I went on a date."

"Is that what this is?"

When he smiles, his nose wrinkles slightly and his eyes pick up a mischievous glint. "I think so, yes. There's the business connection, of course. But it's not like we're coworkers. We could get over the business stuff."

"To date, you mean?"

"Well, kinda that ship has already sailed. Because we're dating."

I look at him blankly for a moment, then grin.

"We're on a *date*. That's not quite the same as *dating*."

He shrugs. "Tom-ay-toe tom-ah-toh."

"Oh, it's like that, is it?" I say it sternly, but we're both grinning now and that feels good, too. That feels surprisingly good, a feeling forgotten, now remembered.

Flirting.

And it comes to me then that while I can enjoy this moment, it can never become anything. Everything about me is a lie. Everything he thinks he sees is untrue. It surprises me when I find that makes me sad. It's made me realize I can never have a real relationship with anyone, probably ever again. The things that are true are things that aren't part of me anymore. And the things about me that are true are things I dare not share.

By way of diverting myself as much as any desire to see what he knows, I change the subject so abruptly I notice him notice. He answers though. And likely puts the source down to other reasons.

"I have a question. I have no good reason for asking it, though. I'm simply curious."

"Shoot," he says. "Ask away."

"Did you and Virginia ever date?"

To my surprise, he looks at me incredulously, as though I'd asked if he'd ever walked on the moon.

"Virginia Martin, you mean?"

"Of course I mean Virginia Martin. Who else would I be talking about?"

"Have you heard anything?"

"No."

"Why did you ask then?"

"It makes sense to me. And I thought maybe you guys had a, you know, *frisson*."

"*Frisson*, is it?" He's teasing me and I don't like it. If there was warmth to it, I wouldn't mind. But he's retreated at my question. I regret asking it, but I can't pull it back.

"Forgive me. It's not my business. And it doesn't matter anyway. I was making conversation."

"I'm sorry you felt the need for hollow talk. I thought the conversation was going fine. Without aid."

I feel that I've blown away some of the smokescreen my dinner partner had created around himself. I'm now seeing him in a whole new light.

"No, I'm sorry," I say again. "I obviously hit a nerve. My apologies. I wasn't aware. I just blundered in. Let's forget it, okay?"

And even as I say these words, I know he's not going to forget and the words aren't going to fix anything. Maybe they'll even make things worse. And it makes no sense to me, but the easy camaraderie Evan and I had shared ten minutes before may as well never have been.

"It's not a sensitive issue. At all. We were never lovers. There: I've spelled it out. Even if I'd ever wanted to, it wouldn't have happened."

"Because you work together," I say.

Inexplicably, he grins mirthlessly. "Something like that. Anyway, it's entirely moot. She's involved with someone."

"She is?" This is news to me. If she had a boyfriend, why had that not been part of the dossier I'd been given? And why had I never seen any indication of an intimate connection? Was it possible she'd make up a relationship in order to ward off Evan's advances? Spending time with him now, it sure seemed possible to me.

"Yeah. And it's been going on for some time."

Our conversation is interrupted by the arrival of our server who comes bearing more tiny and delicious offerings in the seemingly never-ending supply of things we have ordered.

Both of us dig in, maybe anxious to be able to think about a topic beyond the one I'd blundered into. The tension eases somewhat as we eat, and I decide to change the subject completely.

"I've come across some online forums. Discussing GML. Do you track them?"

He looks at me carefully for a minute. I can see him wondering if he should be candid. Or not.

"There's some whack job out there saying crazy things about Virginia."

I nod. "You ever think about responding?"

His head goes up, but he doesn't say anything right away so I blunder on. "You know: taking action."

"What are you saying?"

The question and the tone catch me off-guard.

"Saying? I'm not saying anything. Wondering is all. Some of what is being said is pretty nutty. It can't be good for investor confidence."

"Every company has to deal with things like this," he says, a note that is new and stiff in his voice. And now I have felt him withdraw from me completely. He's chosen to take offense, and I can't help but think it's still a reflection of what I'd asked earlier about him and Virginia. And a part of me is saddened by that. But another part is relieved. It's not a good idea for me to like people on a personal level. To get involved with them. It hasn't proven healthy for anyone. Seeing him for what he is will prevent that. That's what I tell myself. I tell myself a lot of things.

"Well, maybe not all companies. I mean, I can't imagine that's true. But a lot."

"Success breeds whackos."

"Okay . . ." I reply. Now I'm trying to placate him. The sudden animosity in his tone is distressing. Now I simply need to get through what's left of the evening.

"I don't know why you would feel the need to imply we're not doing everything we can."

"Whoa, whoa, what? That's way too big. I didn't imply anything." I think for a moment, then, "I *don't* imply things. It isn't how I operate. If I'd wanted to say that, I would have said it."

He looks as though he's not even hearing me or has come to a conclusion about me that doesn't require my input.

"And yet you said what you said," but he's not looking at me as he speaks. Instead, he has caught the waiter's eye and indicated that it's time for the check.

I look at him with one eyebrow raised, deciding my next move but, really, he's left me only one. I move to get up.

"Oh, you're leaving?" he says archly. "Sticking me with the check, too?" He's needling me now, I'm sure of it. He'd invited me to dinner and also I'm a company guest. On both personal and professional levels, I'm fine with him buying dinner.

"There are circumstances where I might have offered to pay half, but this isn't one of them."

And then I leave, cloaked in my drama. I call an Uber and am still waiting for it when he passes me wordlessly and hands his ticket to the valet to get his car. We shoot sidelong glances at each other, but no one says anything. It's pretty bad. Fortunately, my Uber arrives before the valet shows up with his car. I climb in back and give the driver the name of the hotel. The Uber driver must sense my mood, because he doesn't say anything all the way there, giving me time to fume and also think about how this whole deal moves forward under the circumstances, forgetting for a moment that there is no actual deal being made.

CHAPTER TWENTY-EIGHT

AND THEN I realize what's really bothering me about the whole incident: it has me wondering if he was at all who I had thought he was. Ever. Everything I liked about him seems to have been some kind of put-on. What else was put on about him? Seeing the sudden change in him has me wondering about his sanity. Wondering also if it really might be Evan who is a danger to Virginia. His responses to me in the latter part of our time together had seemed at least somewhat irrational. Why else all the drama if he didn't have something to hide?

By the time I get back to the hotel, it is late but not ridiculously so. I had intended to follow Virginia this evening, and I figure that since it's ten p.m. and so still pretty early, I might catch up with her at some point. Then I realize I now have some new data to process: Daddy McPhee and the whole issue of the online forum, as well as Evan's reaction to it. It confirms to me that it's an avenue that needs investigation.

First, though, I want to talk with Matt Sundstrom again. The personnel evaluation I had gotten a look at while I was in Virginia's home office had me thinking that there was more to the situation with the yellow-haired technologist than I'd previously thought. What had Virginia said in her notes? That Matt was

incompetent and she wanted him fired. And Evan had replied
that Matt was untouchable since his father was an investor. Any
of those things taken on their own might not have added up to
anything, but with so many questions swirling around Greenmüll at present, the cocktail of incompetence mixed with an
untouchable employee seemed to need looking into.

When I call the number I had for Matt, I hear it ring several
times before it goes to voicemail. I think about leaving a message, but decide against it. What, in any case, would I say? It's
not even as though I have a specific concern; just a vague
uneasiness.

Then I put all thoughts of Matt Sundstrom out of my head
and refocus on this business at hand: Daddy McPhee. I plunk
myself down in front of my computer and begin.

From the first, the stock-dedicated forums strike me as
uniquely dumb. I had known that, but looking at them closely
hammers it all home.

In the forums, anonymous users connect under the guise of
sharing knowledge and information while commenting on
stocks they have purchased or are thinking about buying or
maybe that they are holding in their portfolio. The people commenting are not industry professionals. At least, none seem to
be in any way connected with the companies they are commenting on. Rather they seem to be investors—large but most probably small—and their comments range from the insightful to
the inane to the inflammatory, as is the case with "Daddy
McPhee."

Since the forums *are* anonymous, it's an easy place to hide. It
strikes me that people trying to promote a stock might lie about
who they are. Likewise, people who would like to damage the
stock—competitors, for instance, or someone plotting some

sort of takeover—could also use the anonymous nature of the forums to try and wreak havoc. To a layperson, anyway, there's nothing good about the forum. It seems almost designed to make trouble in an already tenuous system. At a glance, too, there is no way to figure out the real identity of any user and so I begin my research, as I often do, with a Google search. I want to see what comes up.

"Daddy McPhee" ends up being a completely disconnected pseudonym. That is: I can find nothing to do with the company that might produce a connection. That's not conclusive, I know. But it's a start.

When I click on the forum bio for Daddy McPhee, it shows that he has also commented on several other securities. It doesn't give me enough to begin to try and figure out his identity, but again it's a start.

By the very nature of these things, Daddy McPhee's identity is hidden. I should, by rights, not be able to figure out who he is. Yet by the simple act of registering himself on the site, he has left a trail and I know where to begin with that. That is: I know who has the resources, and it isn't me.

I cannot call the handler: I've already observed that. But I do know how to reach out to her. It's not the fastest route, but I figure I'll end up with her on the phone.

I start with a text.

I need to determine the identity of an abusive stock forum user. Possible?

The response is not instantaneous, but when it comes it is conclusive: *You had doubts?* And I can't help but smile. I hadn't doubted even for a second. But knowing those resources are, for the moment at least, at my disposal, is comforting. A light hand in the small of my back.

And then I wait. Or rather, I engage in an activity I anticipate will be as unproductive as sitting there doing nothing, but that is still an activity that might move things ahead: I search some directories.

It seems astonishing to me now, but when I was a kid, a book was published every year that listed the names and addresses of everyone in every city. In big cities, it was a big, fat book. In small cities, it was more slender. The front of the book had pages that were white. In the back of the book, the pages were yellow and listed businesses. It was called the phone book and you got a fresh one every year.

By the end of the year there would be pages missing and, in my house anyway, it was dog-eared and doodled on and generally messed up. Not only were a lot of the phone numbers and addresses out of date by then, but the book was a big ol' mess. Twelve months in, you needed a new one.

I hadn't thought about—or missed—a city phone book for a long, long time, or even thought about one or how I might use it. But tonight, I craved that simplicity: a master list of everyone in the city, along with their phone number. The very thought of that now seemed luxurious and impossible. But the idea of putting my hands on a physical book and rifling through it until I found the McPhees. I was certain there would be no "Daddy" listed, but it might still give me some thoughts or ideas. As it was, I was coming up dry.

I bring my challenge to Google and right away, I'm making better connections.

It turns out there are over a hundred people with the name McPhee in the city I am in. The number goes up when you include the outlying areas. There is, of course, no "Daddy" McPhee, but I hadn't expected there to be. He does exist on a couple of forums, and I explore these now: reading his posts on different securities. He sounds like the worst kind of sore loser. The other thing I realize while reading his puerile notes: a part of me had been thinking he was possibly someone who knew Virginia personally, masquerading as a disgruntled stockholder. But his appearance on a number of forums being equally disagreeable would seem to rule this out. If he's simply out there—randomly mean to people at companies he feels he has some kind of beef with—then maybe he is not the threat he appeared to be at first.

The person I am drawing in my head now—this caricature of Daddy McPhee—is not fearsome. He is pathetic. And not someone likely to have either the knowledge or the resources to hire a hit person. For instance, he does not strike me as the possible employer of the guy I took out that first day. And he wouldn't have made professionals, such as my handler, as nervous as whoever I was after had obviously done. Still, it's a lead, and I haven't had a lot of those.

I'm chewing on that, and getting ready to figure out my next move, when my phone rings.

"I have a name for you," she says without preamble.

"That was fast."

"It was easy." I smile because she sounds smug. It seems I like her better and better.

"Nice."

The name she gives me isn't McPhee at all, and I smile at that, too. I could have spent a lot of time chasing down people with that last name. And while the name she gives me doesn't resonate at all, the location does. Bryce Donegan. I'm not surprised that it rings no bells.

"He isn't in the city where you are, though," the handler tells me. "Somewhere nearby. A burg called Tressbury."

I don't say anything right away because too many things are rolling around in my head. Tressbury. What were the odds that he'd be from my hometown? I mean, the odds are not bad, considering we're in the same part of the country. But still.

"You're sure?"

"Of course I'm sure. How often have you known me to joke about things like this?"

And of course, the correct answer is zero: the handler was many things. Jovial is not one of them. Warm, sometimes. But never jovial.

So I have a name. And I have an address. Now I have to figure out what to do with both of those things. I go to sleep thinking about it, not yet knowing the outcome to this particular mission, but feeling a little closer to it in any case.

CHAPTER TWENTY-NINE

SOMETIMES WHEN I wake up it is like I have been swimming underwater. I come slamming to the surface, shattering the calm all around me as I break away from the deep. I never know if sea creatures have been chasing me or the water itself has been pulling me back, but it leaves me feeling drained, that dream. Spent before I even begin the day.

This morning when I wake from that dream, I lie there in the dark, realizing that the covers are drenched in my sweat and my breathing is heavy. I don't move for a dozen or so beats of my heart, waiting to catch my breath.

I wait while the calm shatters in the corners, and I think about what it is that chased me out of sleep. The dog sits and watches me, concerned, while I collect myself. He never understands my invisible dangers, but he doesn't bring doubt to them, either. He always believes in me. One of the many sterling qualities of the golden dog.

With the dog calmed, I think about what it is I left behind me in the underwater deep, dark peace. What, if anything, was I supposed to be learning/picking up? After a while, of course, it all fades, as these things do, and I am left feeling vaguely foolish and entirely unfulfilled, and I am forced to begin my day without an answer.

I know one thing for sure: I want to go home. I am tired of living in a hotel room with a mission that at the moment seems vague and undoable. I am jousting with ghosts. Even if I am beginning to think I know why someone might want Virginia Martin dead, protecting her from this distance is super difficult if not impossible. It seems like a mission without end. I might even stop an attempt on her life—or several attempts—but unless the source is removed, whoever has orchestrated the danger against her might keep trying forever. And I might remove an immediate threat, only to have whatever foot soldier I take out replaced with another. It could be an endless game.

And I have another reason for wanting to go home, even if briefly: I am worried about the dog. That reason sounds silly, even to me, but that doesn't stop it from being true. He is a golden retriever. He is not meant to spend most of his hours confined to a hotel room, even if it's a super fancy one. This gig has already gone on much longer than I imagined it would. I should never have brought the dog with me. But I did. And now I want to take him home.

I know I have a lot to do, but I don't spring into action right away. I force the morning into a place of leisureliness, even though it is the last thing I feel. I walk the dog, of course. We have a long, pleasant walk around the fountain and back. And then I have room service deliver a carefully chosen breakfast. Oatmeal, OJ, coffee. Everything is soft. No hard edges. That's what I'm feeling this morning.

When enough of the morning has passed that I feel it's late enough to make a call, I shake off the last echoes of the ocean deep and settle in to do some recon work.

Bryce Donegan. That's the name the handler had given me. Despite the hometown connection, it doesn't resonate with me at all. It also does not seem to have a connection to the user name he chose. From what I can tell, the single reason to have chosen it was that it was not his real name, but I concede there might be elements I don't see.

With his name in hand, I'm able to find a phone number. I figure: what the hell? And I call him up. With the call I'm not trying to do anything other than size him up a bit in advance.

It rings a long time before anyone answers, and then I figure I must have the wrong person: the voice is vibrant and young. For what I had read from him on the forum, I had expected to hear someone old and crotchety sounding. Downtrodden. But the minute I hear Bryce Donegan's voice I realize my expectation was built on nothing beyond my own preconception of who or what we were dealing with.

"Hey there," I say in my chirpiest voice. "My name is Brandee and I'm calling from Corporate Data, Inc. I was wondering if you had time to take part in a brief survey?"

"Well, not really," he says hesitantly.

"Oh, if you possibly could, it would mean a lot," I lie. "I'm a student and we get extra credit when we get a certain number of people to talk with us."

Honestly, I don't know where I come up with this stuff sometimes, but it comes out sounding smooth and believable: the college student asking for help. And I feel him bite. He hedges a bit, but I know I can push him over.

"Well, I mean . . . if it doesn't take too long . . . ?"

"Oh, thank you! That means so much. And it's super easy. It's a quiz about your internet usage."

"Internet usage?" His objections have stopped. And he's willing to be helpful. I can hear it in his voice.

"Yuh," I say. "Like how do you use the internet and is your speed fast enough and all that kind of thing."

"Umm. Well. Okay. Like I said, as long as it doesn't take too long. I guess I can help you out."

"Oh, thank you," I enthuse again, a touch of a gush in my voice. "That makes me ever so happy. Thank you!"

He grunts.

"Okay. Let's get started. How many hours a day do you spend on the internet?"

"Like, me? How much time do I spend?"

"Well, your household, I guess is what they mean."

"It's just me."

"Um. Well. Okay," I say, filing the information away. Point one: he lives alone.

"How many hours a day do you spend on the internet?"

A hesitation. Then a very reasonable comment.

"That's difficult to quantify."

Quantify. Even the choice of that word gives me information about him. Not everyone would have put it that way.

"Go on," I prompt.

"Like, there are times when I'm using the internet when I don't even think of it that way. Streaming, for instance. Music or TV shows. Or when my phone is doing things."

"That's true," I say, realizing that the question I had spitballed might be kind of dated.

"But, yeah. I guess if I boil it all down to internet, I spend a lot of time using it. When I think about it, I mean."

"I think I have to go back to my professor," I say apologetically. "His question might not be perfectly current."

To my surprise, he laughs. "I can see why. No worries, though. Really. I heard what you asked. I can reply to your question with whatever it brings up in me."

"Really?" I am disingenuous. Butter would not melt.

"Yuh. Like, you know, I do some social media. Like everyone."

"Like everyone. Yes."

"I also do some online stock trading."

"Oh yes."

"Yeah," he says, managing to infuse the single syllable with the music of pride. "And, you know, sites that are focused on stock education."

I feel heroic. I hear him say these words and I don't laugh out loud.

"Oh," I say instead. "How interesting. Like . . . umm . . . university websites?"

"What? No. There's nothing like that that I know of." Though I feel like I hear him take a mental note. "I mean like stock-focused websites. Some of them are very informative."

"Oh yes?"

"Yes. Informative articles and things like that."

"Right. And I guess also interaction with others with like interests?"

The hesitation is real this time. I don't have to guess why either.

"Yeah," he says. "Yeah, I guess. That would be right."

By the time I get off the phone I have a different picture of Bryce Donegan than I had going in. His forum messages, while threatening, had a buffoonish quality. On the phone, though, Donegan had sounded very much in control. The more I think about it, the more I figure that writing him off might be a mistake. Having spoken with him, would I say he's trying to kill Virginia Martin? I wouldn't go that far. But what do the police say? Suddenly, he is a person of interest. I know that I'll pursue the lead.

CHAPTER THIRTY

I FEEL MYSELF pulled in several different directions at one time. I have a lot of half-leads and maybes, nothing solid and certainly nothing as concrete as I would have expected by this time.

Whatever else is true, I know that I need to get out of Dodge for a few days. The various layers of *home* play around in my heart and brain. The word means so many things to so many people, but right now the nuances of all of those meanings seem to be fighting inside me. I realize that part of that might be coming from the recent reminder that I still do have some family in the world, but whatever the case, there has been a shift. I can feel it.

Going home.

Without giving it too much additional thought—or the chance to talk myself out of it—I collect my things and the dog and we check out.

It's only a few hours' drive, but once we are home, I feel surprisingly happy. It's a feeling you don't recognize right away if it's been absent for a while. A feeling of buoyancy. Lightness. Clarity. As it comes, it's like my muscles for happiness have atrophied. It feels like when you take an advanced yoga class when you've been away from it for a while. You know you've done these moves before, but your muscles don't remember it anymore and you can't stretch that way. That's what happiness feels like to me now. It has been absent in me for so long, I almost don't know how to do it. But the vestiges. They are there. The ability for happy might be there, too. If I reach for it.

And being home is so welcoming, that's part of it, I think. You don't know how much you miss your own bed until you're sleeping in a different place. Your own way of making coffee. Your own smell. Your own clean laundry. The way your own toilet seat fits under your butt.

There are elements about the job—incomplete—that bother me, but I push myself past them. I need this space to pause and rethink. There will be time enough to deal with it all later. I'm not sure if I'm glad about that. Or not. But since no one has made a move on Virginia Martin for a while, I am optimistic she will be safe until I get done with some business. I have to be optimistic about that, anyway. I can't clone myself so I have no choice.

I observe that the dog is happy to be home, too. He had been spending a lot of time in a hotel room, and he doesn't have a particular feeling for sports or old movies on television. That is, he does not have the disposition or inclination to appreciate the nice things about staying in a four-star hotel. It had been a lot of sitting around. And now, in a few hours, we're back to "normal." Whatever "normal" is for us. We're back to our life and business as usual. For a little while anyway.

We do the things that we usually do when we are home. I take the dog on walks. I collect some berries; make a pie. Weed a garden that seems to have done better with me gone for a while. Is that possible? But it has sprouted beyond the amount of time we'd been gone. Regrout my bathtub. I do other domestic stuff. All of the things that have come to make up the passing days of my life: no extreme pleasures, but no searing pain, either. The texture of the day-to-day. I am content, like a cow. And for a little while anyway, the darkness is at bay.

While I'm home, I get the idea to try to get ahold of Matt Sundstrom again, but when I call the number the yellow-haired technologist had given me, it rings and rings and this time it does not go off to voicemail. Instead, a voice comes on telling me that "the voice mailbox you are calling is full." And that happens often enough in life that it should not be a cause for concern. Still. It makes me wonder. I make a mental note to call him again in a few days.

On my third day back, I know it is time. Nothing is different. Exactly. But I am recharged and renewed by my time home in the forest. I don't have a better idea of what is wrong, but I know things aren't right, either. I know also that there are a few things I need to do before I go back. And they're not here.

I leave the dog behind this time, though it wrenches at me to do it. I know he will be fine and likely happier here with his automated food and easy water and his at-will strolls of the yard.

And then I realize: Who am I kidding? He is a dog. He only ever seems truly happy when he is with me in whatever activity—or lack of activity—I choose. And while I know that's true, I leave him behind anyway. I know that this time he will be safer, if not happier, alone. And most of all, I want him to be safe.

CHAPTER THIRTY-ONE

THE DAY THAT I didn't kill him in an alley and then we had coffee, the private eye had given me his business card. I take it out now. It has an address on it. That address is in my hometown, and I can pretty much tell exactly which strip mall the storefront is sitting in from those coordinates.

It's not a posh address, not that there are a lot of those in my hometown. I'm not even exactly sure why I begin there, rather than with Bryce Donegan/Daddy McPhee. But I have business with the PI. Personal business. And you have to start somewhere. Sometimes you simply have to begin.

It isn't until I've staked out the office that I wonder why I'm doing it. What am I hoping to see or to gain? Not only do I not have a clear vision, it doesn't take long before I get a whiff of how fun this self-assignment is not going to be. If you imagine that there is an activity more boring than following a PI, you're wrong.

It doesn't take at all that long to figure out that the PI's paunchy ball-capped life is mundane in the extreme, even though he has a pretty cool name. I realize that is probably different when he is on a case, but he doesn't seem to be on one now, and so I watch him in his strip mall storefront waiting for I'm-not-sure-what.

But it is as though, between him and my handler on the phone, memories and echoes and longing for family have been awakened in me. And maybe also news of the death of my mother has shaken me more than I had anticipated it would. It had been one thing, not seeing her, just subconsciously imagining her safe some place. But the knowledge of her death tears at my heart. And it's hard, even, to define what I feel. Grief isn't quite right, though I feel wisps of guilt whirling around in there, too. And guilt, certainly, though I know it wasn't my fault. There is even additional guilt at the grief I don't feel and a sort of hollow sorrow at the place in my heart where my mom used to be.

So I imagine I have taken all of this useless emotion and channeled it toward Dallyce Bayswater instead.

And why don't I call the PI up, like a normal person, and ask him the things I want to know? Well, one reason is that I'm not sure I know what I want to know. I have some partly formed thoughts and ideas, but I'm not quite ready to know what to ask. Also, the habit of hiding has grown in me. I have become unused to being seen, especially without disguise. I discover that the thought of it frightens me.

There are other things that scare me. For instance, my brother. Would he even want to see me? The fact that he'd hired a PI to find me makes me think he does. But the thing inside me that is broken shies back from the contact, even while following the PI he hired to find me puts a lie to that.

From across the street, I can see Bayswater perfectly. The PI sits in his office, occasionally sneaking a bottle out of a drawer and pouring a few inches of amber liquid into the coffee cup on his desk. A cliché, I think. He's watched too many PI shows. Read too many books. He has become who he thinks he's supposed to be. Does he think no one can see him through the plate glass storefront window at the front of his office? Or does he imagine no one would ever watch him? Considering his occupation, he should know better.

To pass the time, I go back to nutrition. The sensible, logical reading soothes me. And the even, well-thought-out tests after each section. It all makes me feel as though it is possible for the world to be right again.

It should be understood that there is a difference between a dietician and a nutritionist. I had to figure that all out before I signed up for anything. Because dietician is not what I wanted to do or learn about.

It turns out that dieticians are also often clinicians in that they are certified to diagnose eating disorders and other maladies that appear around food. A nutritionist, on the other hand, helps people be their very best. And themselves, too, that's what I'm thinking. At least as I understand it. They know all about food and what goes with what to help you live the longest and healthiest life possible.

There is also more certification required to become a dietician, but I didn't care about that. After all, what did I have in the world but time? But, no: I was more interested in the science of, for instance, the role carbohydrates play when they interact with fats than I was about how to help others. I had no intention of ever practicing, after all.

I have immersed myself in reading about boosting immunity with medicinal plants when I see Bayswater take a call. After he rings off, he takes the bottle out of the desk and pours what appears to be another couple fingers of amber liquid into the glass on his desk before heading out.

When he leaves the office, he climbs into the same silver car he'd followed me in a few days before. Now it is me doing the prowling. That turnaround doesn't feel bad. At all.

I follow him until he parks near a seedy-looking motel and proceeds to sit and watch it. Now I am the watcher watching the watcher and it amuses me to think that, in the space of a few days, our situation has reversed. It amuses me and it also makes me feel sad for myself. Is this what I've become? He was watching me and now I am watching him. The rub, though: he had an assignment. I don't even have a reason.

In a few minutes a young woman emerges from a second-floor room. He takes out a camera, conspicuous by its long lens, and photographs her progress to a car. More shadows from a movie.

When she drives away, he follows, but I've decided I've seen enough. I can put the picture together from here and realize it's not one I need to see. Someone's wife/daughter/lover having spent an illicit afternoon; the low-rent PI following her to gather evidence for some distasteful proceeding.

The PI points his car south; I point mine toward the old part of downtown, the part where I'd spent my childhood, before the mall came and sucked away the hamlet's heart and teenagers. I know I will connect with him later and, having watched him for several hours, I now feel I have the makings of a plan.

Though I now know my mom is gone, I have a sudden urge to be close to her. To be in a spot where I can see what she saw and breathe what she breathed. I haven't felt that way in a long time. And it's my hometown. They say you can't go back, yet here I am.

It's an odd feeling, driving through the town. I've been living an anonymous life for so long, back in my hometown I feel exposed. Like any second someone might see and recognize me and everything I am and have been in the time between will come out, as though it is written on my face or in some cloud of odor or energy all around me. And I am both afraid it will happen, and afraid that it won't. It makes no sense, but I feel nothing but duality. I move forward anyway.

I feel like I've been away for decades. And also like I never left. As I drive through a downtown core that is both familiar and entirely new, reality and unreality float over my head. Like I don't know what's true anymore.

None of the people walking on Main Street are familiar to me and suddenly, despite everything, I want to be seen. I park and stroll into the general store, miraculously still intact and as I remember it on Main Street. I don't know the girl behind the counter. She looks maybe Indian and her voice resonates with Southeast Asia. This exotic element in my previously entirely non-exotic hometown updates me somewhat. Time has, in fact, not stood still. And here we are.

"Can I help you?" she asks politely.

"I don't think so," I say and she looks at me searchingly, as though what I said was off the mark, and I realize that, of course I have missed it. And I am from outside. Now I am the one who has become exotic: an outlander. The reality of that buzzes around in my head.

With a mumbled apology, I back out of the store. I know that it probably looks weird, but I don't care anymore and, in any case, I can't do anything about it. Too much time has passed. I know I don't fit here anymore. Too much life has passed this way. Too much everything.

I'm getting back into my car, resolved that I won't see anyone I know, when I hear a voice.

"Oh. My. God," the woman says. "Is it really you?"

I fight the urge to ignore her and just keep going and maybe I should, but I don't.

"It is," I say. And I stand to my full height, as though standing my ground is important. As though there will be a contest and my performance here will count toward an unseen goal.

"I'm surprised to see you here," she says. "After everything. I'm surprised."

"Me, too," I say, which I realize is so ambiguous as to be nearly meaningless.

I am looking at someone both completely foreign to me and intimately familiar. It's like I am looking at someone who was in my posse in high school, but now they're old. Now we're old. Well, not old as in . . . old. But old as in the age our moms would have been when we were friends. Old. It's like I'm looking at her mom. I wonder if she thinks the same, looking at me.

"Lucinda?" I say, sure but not sure.

"Yeah. 'Course. I was sorry." She is hesitant. It's how people are, I've discovered, when faced with the unthinkable. They don't know what to say. "When I heard . . . I'm sorry. I could have been a better friend to you."

I shake my head. "It wasn't your fault, Luc." The childhood diminutive of her name comes to me so easily, I don't choke on it until it's out. Then I can't bring it back. "I didn't let anyone get close enough. Not ever."

"And then you went away. And I felt, you know, it was my fault." The way she says it sounds both regretful and accusing. I've come to understand that, too. It's how people feel. If I had been better at letting them in, they feel that on a certain level. They could have helped me then. But I didn't let them. I've gotten over feeling badly about that. People feel what they need to feel. Even if the feelings are tied up in my reality, what they feel has nothing to do with me. I can't let it have anything to do with me.

"What do you think was your fault? Not the accident." I have this moment of sheer panic; afraid that what she will say will break me. Break my heart. Her words ease that fear, at least.

"No, no. Of course not. Not that. But that you felt so unloved or abandoned or whatever that you had to leave. I thought if I'd been able to reach out . . ."

"Oh, Luc, no. Let that go, okay? There was nothing you could have done." She looks dubious, so I push it home. "No, really. There was nothing anyone could have done. It was . . . what it was."

And I see reflected on her face such a profound sadness I almost can't bear it. And I remember yet another layer of why I went away. She would hate to know that the sympathy that greeted me everywhere I had gone in this town after my child died had driven me away. It was not their fault. It was an impossible situation. People want to help. But my child and all of my hopes and dreams were dead. I was beyond help.

I understand that they wanted to. But still. Seeing what I see on her now brings it all rushing back. I feel like finding a rock. Crawling under. And it all comes back to me, in perfect color. I feel, again, as though I want to die.

"I was sorry to hear about your mom," she says. Both of us knew the subject had to be changed. And I try to forgive her for pushing it in this particular direction. After all, after so many years, it's not like we have a bunch to talk about. How many topics are left to discuss? She has kids. She won't bring those up. Because me? I don't. I have a beautiful golden dog, but even he is tough to explain.

"Thanks," I mumble. "It's kind of why I'm here. I heard a few days ago."

"Really?" She looks at me in disbelief. "But it happened two years ago. How can you just have heard now?"

"Listen," I say, heading in the direction of the car, "it was amazing running into you. So good to hear your voice, see your face."

I know she replies something, but I don't hear the words. I'm already gone. No doubt what she said was appropriate. Sympathetic. But what I see on her face seems more on point. There is pity and doubt and maybe even a little fear. Who knows what to do in the face of real grief? Who knows who to be. Most people, I've found, do not. I do, of course, but that's a different kind of knowledge. Sometimes you saddle up. Put your head down. Move on.

Move on.

CHAPTER THIRTY-TWO

By the time I park the car on the street outside of my brother's house, I have lost my appetite for the whole expedition. In truth, I don't know what I am doing here. Trying, maybe, to go back to a past that doesn't even exist anymore. Or not back to it—even I know you can't go back—but maybe it's possible to catch up a little. Possibly even claim some of the love I know I have coming. Does that represent the beginning of some kind of recovery? That I have returned, at least, that much?

Maybe not.

A part of me had wanted to reach out—reach back? —though fully another part hadn't been at all sure what I was doing here. But after talking with Lucinda, I realize that I don't have whatever is required inside me anymore. Maybe the family part of me has died? Whatever the case, I feel the need to get as far away from here as possible.

And yet here I am.

I am putting the car into gear to get myself away when a late model Honda slides into the driveway. I put my car back into park and wait it out. My sister-in-law gets out of the passenger side and smiles back into the car at the driver. She grabs her purse and some packages, and heads into the house. She is softer than I remember. Rounder. But something in her gait and her face brings back all of my memories of her, and they are warm memories. I recall her being a lovely person with a beautiful heart. A memory of her holding my son as an infant comes rushing back as I watch her and it is all I can do to stop the tears. How are those tears so close today? I can't explain it. But it is so good to see her face.

Once his wife has gone inside, Kenny sits in the car for another few minutes. I can make out that he is on the phone, possibly tied into a call he took on his car system and doesn't want to break off. After a while he unfolds himself out of the car, and I see his dear form. He stretches, as though he's been in the car for a while, and I can see he, too, is softer than I remember. And maybe a little grayer. More tired. And though he looks very different, there is so much about him that is as familiar to me as my own hand.

He looks as though he might head into the house, but stops and unwinds a hose in order to water the plants that grow alongside the foundation. He is intent as he does it: giving it a focus so full, I can picture the corner of his tongue sticking out of the edge of his mouth as it always did. And the expression is so dear and familiar to me and so easy to imagine, I feel tears stand in my eyes. I don't know my hand is on the door handle until I feel my heart race with the thing I am suddenly preparing—unplanned—to do. And I can imagine his reaction. Shock. And maybe joy. Mixed with relief? And then a bear hug that envelops me in acceptance and love. And my heart aches for that.

The vision is so vivid that my hands are shaking with it as I start to open the car door and I am walking toward him as he turns off the hose and goes into the house. And I stand there for what feels like a long time, but I know it takes me a half score of seconds to consider what to do now. It would, of course, be an easy thing to keep moving. Go to the door. Knock. See Brenda's face. See Ken. Ignite a reunion. But I don't. I don't do any of that. Instead, I turn around and settle back into the welcoming and unquestioning embrace of my Volvo. And I'm not sure what it is that has held me back.

Once back in my car, I sit for a while, calming my breath. While I sit, I grip the wheel until my knuckles turn white. Then I start the car and head back toward town. Love was right there and I could have claimed it. My family, what is left of it, was right there. And I decided again to turn away. Me. I have to make sure I own that. The first time, after everything happened, when I drove away, I was raw and broken. And now, all this time later, what is my excuse?

CHAPTER THIRTY-THREE

But I don't think about any of those things. I turn off that part of my head/my heart and drive. I don't know that part of town, but I have an address and so it is easy to find.

Bryce Donegan lives in a decrepit old trailer at the end of a long driveway. Like me, he also lives at the edge of a forest, but I'm guessing his reasons are different than mine.

I park the car down the road a piece then skulk through the trees toward the trailer as darkness falls completely. I am relieved to see that I am hidden by night. Also relieved when no dogs start barking to warn of my approach. It usually presents a problem when there are dogs and I can never bring myself to do what is reasonable and just take them out. They are dogs. Faithful. Loyal. Doing their job. Nothing is ever their fault.

When I get my first glimpse of the trailer, I think it looks like it's on its actual last legs. It's not that it bows in the middle, but it gives that appearance: of the center sinking lower than either end, as though some terrible weight is pulling it down. Maybe the nature of the weight is the passing of time.

There is an incredibly shiny red pickup truck sitting in front of the trailer. It looks brand new. It appears so new, in fact, it should be sitting in front of some other, nicer, better trailer, some other place. It is the car of someone who cares about appearances . . . and never invites anyone to his home.

It is dusk and, as I watch, lights pop on in the trailer. One, then two. And I notice, also, smoke coming out of a chimney, which in this area makes sense, even for a trailer: if you live in the forest, heating with wood is a no-brainer. For me, though, it adds another layer of information: in case the lights and the truck weren't enough, I can tell that someone is definitely at home. And that's all this early bit of surveillance was about. If he is here, then he is *not* where Virginia Martin is. Which means some of the threat is removed from her and I can take my time about moving forward on Donegan/McPhee. I can breathe. There is a part of me that wants to move now: get it behind me. But it's been a long day and I don't want a misstep. The work I do is best executed with a clear head. I mean to get it right. It's not like I'll get a do-over.

So now that I am certain Donegan is at home, I head for the motel I'd watched the PI surveil earlier. It is, after all, the only one in town and, while I check in, I try hard not to think of all the trysts and nefarious business that must go on here all the time, because there is no other option.

I am grateful that I don't recognize the old woman who checks me in. Old woman. I realize enough time has passed that she may well be someone I know, or know someone I know: a friend's mother or some other faint connection. Someone who once sold me shoes, or served me a drink when I was underage. But I don't look at her directly, and when we're done with the check-in, it feels very done, especially when she reminds me to be out by 11:00 a.m., "or else." I don't think about that "or else" with either mirth or apprehension, which goes to show how far away from my usual self I am. I don't often resist opportunities like that for a zippy rejoinder, but I have today. My head doesn't have room. My heart. I feel something cold and rocklike inside me right now. Hard. I let it go. I don't always do it, but I have learned that kindness must begin with oneself. Self-care. I'm not always the best at that. At all.

I know what the room will smell like before I open the door. Cheap sanitizer and cleaning products, old carpet and mildew. It's not an appetizing cocktail. You know what the room looks like, too. You've seen it before. A queen-sized bed with a nubbly bedspread and two pillows, much thinner than when they began. A fridge. An apparatus for the creation of coffee. A television: not this year's model. Not even this decade's model. An ancient yellowing phone on a scarred nightstand. A desk. A bathroom laid out with cheap soap and personal products. Thin towels and one extra toilet roll. It's a room not designed for long stays yet these days, in a town that is seldom anyone's destination, I'm guessing that long stays are almost all that turn up. I look around and realize I don't even want to put my bare feet on the floor, and the thought of climbing between the sheets makes my skin crawl.

Before I plop myself onto the bed, I pull out the sheets to expose the box spring. I am looking for signs of bedbug infestation: I know what it looks like and what to see but, fortunately, there are no signs of that here. Small mercies.

After that I relax, or rather do the thing that looks like relaxing for me, all the while calling Dallyce Bayswater, the PI, again every fifteen or so minutes to see if he'll pick up. He doesn't. Finally, I get the idea to use the motel's in-room phone. He still doesn't pick up, and I make my voice flat and unemotional as I leave a message.

"Hello, this is Sally Smith of Foxtrot Drive. I think my husband is having an affair. I would like to talk with you about retaining your services."

I turn on the TV and slip mindlessly through the channels. Local news. National news. Ancient sitcoms. Nothing that holds my attention beyond sixty seconds at a time. I know I want to do more thinking about what I know of Donegan/McPhee, but I also know I have to get this business with Bayswater out of the way first, if I can. My focus can only take so much distraction.

CHAPTER THIRTY-FOUR

I AM THINKING of heading back out in the direction of the crappy trailer at the forest's edge when my phone rings. And it's a local number. No guessing this time. I'm pretty sure even before I pick it up that it will be the PI, Dallyce Bayswater, returning my call. Who else would it be?

It is ten minutes after I left my potential client message. I am surprised and also unsurprised. He must be hungry.

I give him no more information than I'd given in voicemail. I tell him I will meet him and pay him his retainer. He asks for cash, and I roll my eyes but leave my voice blank. Five hundred dollars seems like a lot of money for what I am buying. He assures me it's on the low side for his industry. I give him the name of the motel and he tells me he knows it—of course—and will meet me there in an hour. As soon as I'm off the phone, I head out to find a cash machine so I can get him his loot. By the time the appointed time rolls around, I am back in my room with five bills in an envelope.

When I see him pull up, I leave the five bills on the bed, but I duck into the bathroom. I have the feeling that when he identifies me, he will opt out, so I make sure I'm out of sight when he arrives. I want to see to it that his opting out is not an option.

He's sitting in the chair next to the desk in the room when I come out of the can. He's eyeing the five C-notes, but his expression changes when he sees me.

"Oh. Shit," he says, lurching to his feet.

"Sit," I say, showing him the Bersa. Never hurts to have a bit of chrome, that's what I think, even if it can be a bit dramatic.

"Fuck," he says, but he sits as requested. I nod. Oddly, I'm not feeling anxious. I feel like I should be, but I'm not.

"Sorry for the tactics," I say as a way of starting in. And I mean what I say.

"Sure," he says nodding. He could be agreeing or disagreeing. I can't tell from his tone. But he's at the wrong end of my gun. Again. So he's not going to argue.

"I didn't know if you'd come if you knew who was inviting you," I say.

"Could be right," he says, his voice flat, and the words don't inform me much at all.

"Still," I say, "what I'm wanting is simple enough. Well within your stated services."

"That right?"

"I want you to find out why my brother hired you."

"I told you already. He wanted to know where you were."

"I think there might be more to it than that."

"I'm sorry," he says. And I can almost feel the backbone growing. "I'm not sure that's ethical."

"Ethical? Don't you think it's a little late in the game to start worrying about that?"

"Seriously. He's my client. And part of what I am doing for him was trying to find you."

"*Am?*"

I see a bit of delicate color creep up his cheeks. I know it isn't because he's bashful. Rather he has realized that he said too

much. And now I'm getting annoyed. I'd brought him here because I wanted to hire him. Now I don't want that anymore. I
prod him a bit with the muzzle of the Bersa.

"You know enough about me to realize I'm not afraid to use
this thing." He grunts. "So please don't fuck with me. I realize
there is such a thing as client confidentiality. We're going beyond that now." Another grunt. "You're going to tell me what
you are still doing for my brother."

He lifts his eyes to me skeptically, but doesn't say anything. I
pretend I haven't noticed and go on.

"You're going to tell me, and if I don't like the answer, I'm
going to kill you."

Do I see him blanch a bit as I say this? Wince? I'm not sure.
Small-town private dick or not, he's cucumber cool. I'm guessing
his balls were formed by real action. Right now, he's made his
face into a tough mask. I can see that it's not for show.

"You said you wanted to hire me," he says finally. It's a weak
attempt and we both know it.

"I did. I'm not sure I do now."

"I could be helpful."

"Like you said, you have an ethical problem. Conflict of
interest."

"Still. I can help you. I figure . . . I figure I already know what
you're looking for."

Now that's got my interest, since I'm not even sure myself.
"Oh?"

"Yeah. You want to know what happened to the trust."

I don't ask him what *trust* he's talking about. I don't let my
face say it either. But I have no idea. Instead of saying anything,
I nudge him again with the gun. A picture is worth a thousand
words. I'd hoped it would keep him talking. It does.

"When your mom died, your brother wanted to know if part of it would come to you. Since he'd already invested against it . . ."

"Against it?" I have this sinking feeling. I'm not sure why yet, but I don't like the way this is going. The only love I have left in the world, that's what I'd said to myself. And now? Now maybe I'm finding out it isn't even that.

"Yeah. So he had to find out if you were alive."

"Because the portion of the trust that came to him would be altered if I was?"

"Yeah," he says again.

"So what did you tell him when you found me?"

"The truth. That you were alive, but living under an assumed name and so unlikely to reappear in your birth identity."

"Good answer," I say.

"Particularly since he'd had you declared dead."

"What part did you play in that?" I leave my face blank, but the fact that my birth identity has been declared dead is news to me. But it did explain why Lucinda had looked as though she'd seen a ghost when she saw me. From her perspective, she had.

"What part did I play? Zero. It was before he hired me."

"So that's odd, right? He hired you to find a dead person."

Dallyce shrugs. "It's not my job to ask questions. Not ever."

"C'mon. You're telling me you were hired to find someone who was legally dead. Didn't you think that was weird?"

"I mean, sure. But again: I'm in the business of minding my business. He was paying me, so I did what he asked."

"Fair enough. But I don't get it. I thought someone needed to have disappeared for seven years or more before they could be declared dead."

He brightens at this. He's a private investigator. He knows about this.

"That used to be the case. Still is in some states. But in many it's now down to four or five years. As long as the person hasn't been in contact with anyone and no one has heard from them."

And, of course, no one had heard from me. At all. I had packed up my soccer mom car one day and driven away. Never mind not looking back: I'd worked hard not to look back—it hurt so much to think about any of it. And now, here I was again, and it was all around me.

"I didn't know that," is all I say.

"Listen, lady, I don't know much, but I know enough to see why you'd think something is wrong with all of this. I'm going to tell you another thing. It's unethical for me to say it, but, hell, look how deep I'm in here, all right? And you basically threatened me at gunpoint, so . . ."

I'd forgotten I still had the Bersa less than a foot from his temple. I drop the muzzle now. The gun in my business hand and loose at my side. It looks casual, but we both know I could raise it and shoot him with no notice at all. Still, his eyes register relief at my response to what he'd said and, I guess, the fact that a gun is no longer pointing at his brain.

"Go on," I say.

"There was an insurance policy on you."

"What?"

"On you and your family. Your husband. And your kid. I have the paperwork on file at my office." He meets my eyes, and I can tell he is about to convey a thing I don't want to hear. "You were the beneficiary."

"Me?" I try to comprehend what he is saying. It doesn't make sense. I'd had some insurance through work, but it was your usual run-of-the-mill sort of policy and not in an amount anyone would really care about. He is implying a different story altogether.

"Yeah. So . . . ummm . . . what if you weren't around to collect?"

"Like if I was dead."

"Yeah."

But still.

"My brother couldn't buy a policy like that on me. How could he?"

"Not him," Bayswater says, not meeting my eyes. "Your husband."

There is an intricacy here that I almost cannot face. I look at Bayswater. See what he sees. Realize there is more at play here than I could possibly know.

"Spell it out."

He shrugs.

"I don't know anything," he says matter-of-factly. It makes sense so I believe him. It's not the sort of thing a client would share. I accept what he was offering. "But, yeah. As it turned out, a policy like that would cast some . . . aspersions; it could be put like that."

"Right," I say, trying to keep it far from me. "But my husband ended up dying. So . . ."

"Yeah, I know. Maybe his dying wasn't the plan."

I think it all through. About what had happened. How it had all gone down. Maybe my child wasn't supposed to die after all. Maybe it hadn't been the will of God, or whatever the hell other platitudes everyone had kept saying to me right after the accident. Things said that were intended to make me feel better that never did.

Maybe the devastation that happened had not been an accident at all but an attack on me gone drastically wrong. Even glanced at sideways, that was a thought almost too tragic to bear. What if it hadn't needed to happen? Hadn't been fate or kismet or whatever the hell else I'd been telling myself all this time. An attack on me gone wrong. And my child had been collateral damage.

I have a sudden urge to get up, go to the corner, and curl into a ball. Cry. And maybe? Maybe I would do that later: curl up and die. But right now, I have a PI in my motel room and I can't keep him—don't want to keep him. I have to think about my very next move. Later I would cry. Maybe I'd even hold it until I was back in the forest. I'd take all of this out and examine it and lick my wounds then. For now, though, I have to decide what to do with Bayswater. I mean, I'd threatened his life. Likely he'd agree with anything I say. Right now. Once out of my sight though, he could do whatever he liked.

I toy briefly with the idea of killing him: launching a bullet into his skull right there. But I'd never been in the habit of killing people for no reason and, in any case, it doesn't go with what I am thinking now. I'd told myself I was done with killing. Taking out an innocent—even if irritating—PI didn't go with that program.

On the other hand, if he said he'd work for me, could I trust him? Probably not. Maybe counterintuitively, and despite all the conclusions I had come to, I decide to leave it up to him.

"What would you like to see happen now?"

"Pardon?" he says, blinking at me hugely.

"Well, we've been chatting. We maybe understand each other a little better now. What are our next steps?"

"Chatting? I've been sitting here at gunpoint."

"That's true," I say, nodding agreeably.

"You're the one pretty much calling the shots."

"Fair enough. Okay. Cards on the table time then."

He blinks at me, wide eyed. I figure he suspects how close he had been to a decision that would end his life.

"I'm not going to kill you," I say matter-of-factly.

"If that's true, why do you still have your gun on me?"

"It's not exactly *on* you," I point out.

"Still," he says. "We both know you could take me out from that position."

And, of course, he's right about that. Not an accident.

I think for a moment before answering. Instinct has been guiding me. And need. It takes a second to put it all into words.

"You're bigger than me. The gun evens us up. And anyway, I'm saying the outcome of this meeting will not be me deciding to kill you."

"Thank you," he says so solemnly it makes me smile. He smiles back. It isn't exactly a connection, but it feels like a step in the right direction.

"I came here hoping to hire you. I can totally see the potential conflict of interest," I say quickly, before he can interrupt, "but you're in such a good position for this assignment. You're half-way in. Or more."

I can see he is paying attention, not shutting it down, so I press on.

"And you could handle it any way you wanted," I say. "Your call. I don't need to know. Potentially two fees there: one from him, one from me. But, again, I don't need to know."

It is a calculated risk. I have the feeling that whatever he decides he'll be solid with me.

"Okay," he says after a pause. We already liked each other, he and I. Until I'd pulled a gun on him anyway. Once this difficult moment has passed, that might be enough.

"Okay," I repeat. "I have the $500 you told me to bring. If you agree, that can be a down payment, with another $1,000 to follow immediately. This is not the sort of job where a $500 retainer is sufficient." I've seen his office. Seen his shlubby old car. The fact that he's a bit hungry won't hurt my cause any.

He nods, and I'm not sure until he speaks if it is agreement with the numbers or the concept.

"Your plan is workable," he says after a pause. And I can see the hunger I suspected reflected in his eyes. The offer of real money has meaning. "I can get you the information you need. You're right: I have access."

I nod then put the gun down cautiously, but he makes no fast movements that cause me to regret my impulse. We shake on our agreement, and I allow myself to feel a flutter of optimism. I now have more than I started with. Since this chapter of my life had begun, it had always been me against the world. Suddenly, I have staff.

*   *   *

After Bayswater leaves, I decompress for a bit. I put the television on. Anybody looking at me would think I was watching what was on the screen, but really the sound is background and I'm listening to the voices in my head.

What are they telling me? Oh: so much.

I have a lot to process. And I have a lot to do. After a while, the voices are competing with the sound so I snap the TV off, put the thinking on hold, and get back into the action that will set me up for whatever needs to happen the following day.

I'm pretty sure Bryce Donegan lives alone. I know he holds a relatively small number of shares in several companies.

Online, in any case, he is aggressive, even abusive, but I haven't seen any sign of that so far in the man himself. Certainly on the phone, he sounded very rational and "normal." Thinking about that gives me an idea.

I go to the GML user forum. To my relief, it looks like a quiet day: no new rants or threats, in any case. I create a user identity. I hesitate a few minutes thinking it through, then I register as McPhee Slayer. Which maybe seems a little too on-the-nose while also being both in your face and juvenile, but that's the sort of mood I'm in.

Because you have to use a "real" name and email address in the registration process, I use one of several aliases and email addresses available to me, suspecting that the checking won't go any deeper than an email link to determine I control the address. I do, and a few minutes later I'm allowed access to the forums.

A fast reading shows me he's made a posting in the last few minutes. I check the market and, yes: the price of GML shares had dropped earlier today. Not a great deal and not in response to any actual news the company had released; maybe in response to the overall market. Donegan, though, had taken the opportunity to write yet another horrid note.

Twinkle, twinkle, little bitch

While you laze you're getting rich

Meanwhile all the suckers wait

Taking your kicks and your bait

Unless the stock gets a reprieve

Tomorrow could be your last to breathe.

I read the words with a growing feeling of horror. Then I read them again, and while I do, I feel a chill creep up my spine. Someone walked on my grave, we used to say when we were kids, Kenny and me, when we'd get weirded out. And there is no mistaking the meaning. Or the intent. This is a threat to Virginia Martin's life, plain and simple. And it doesn't feel like the distant future. From my reading, it seems like he's threatening to take some kind of action the following day. I rethink my plan. It's possible I have no time to lose.

CHAPTER THIRTY-FIVE

I THINK IT all through very carefully. This next move. Everything depends on it.

I had thought to post some sort of taunt, calling him out. But then this:

Tomorrow could be your last to breathe.

That is too pointed to take lightly. And so I don't.

Even though I had thought I was ensconced for the night, I get myself up and head out. I don't want to chance that he is even now heading in to the city to kill Virginia Martin while I recline in my crappy motel room not even watching bad television.

By the time I get back to his trailer, it is well after midnight. I am relieved to see the shiny red truck is in the same position it was in when I was there a few hours earlier and smoke is still trailing out of the chimney. He is still at home, possibly in there right now crafting still more puerile notes to his various forums.

I once again have parked somewhat down the road, then traipse through the forest, this time in darkness. It's not my first dark forest, either, though they never seem to get less scary. You can *know* that the loud cracking coming from the darkness over there was probably made by a deer or some other harmless animal, but in real forest dark, your mind can paint a very different picture. I try to shut off my imagination and move.

Out of the trees, I skulk as silently as possible toward the trailer. Dreading a dog sounding the alarm or, even worse, Donegan himself spotting me. But the trailer is quiet, there still appear to be no dogs, and I reach the front door without detection.

Once at the front door, I debate my point of entry. Should I try that door? It doesn't seem likely he'd have an electronic watching device on it, but one never knows. Or should I look for an open window, as I would usually do in a house? Or try another door altogether. But the windows are too high for me to reach without a ladder, so in the end, I opt for that front door. It's right there and, anyway, it's late and everything is quiet. It seems likely to me that he will physically be nearer the back door.

I am unsurprised when I try the door and find it unlocked. It's the country. Most people don't bother locking their doors in areas like this where entering the property means showing yourself and there are limited ways of getting away.

Inside the cramped living room there are no surprises. The first thing that I encounter is the smell of food fried several hours ago. I identify it from a place I can't even recognize. Some ancestral memory maybe? Or a trail of scent from childhood, once coveted and now all but forgotten. I silently slide open the window over the kitchen sink, then move more deeply into the mobile home.

Donegal's computer rests on a worn dining table right outside the kitchen. It is of such an age that, in perfect condition, in big cities that table would sell for big bucks at a vintage store. But it is not in perfect condition and we are nowhere near one of those shops, so it sways under its scant weight, in poor enough shape that earlier eras aren't even brought to mind. Squalor and desperation. And other feelings that don't evoke the finer things.

I hesitate when I get to the living room. What do I imagine I am doing here? Am I going to kill him? Do I have any kind of plan? But I've never been much of a planner. Historically, my life has usually indicated the direction in which I should go. And now, I hesitate, awaiting some direction, but it doesn't appear. At least, not right away.

I move more deeply into the trailer. Down a hallway that seems longer than it should be, considering the appearance of that swaying middle I peeped at a distance. I keep moving, though, until I am standing in a corridor looking into a bedroom looking, finally, at an empty bed.

A bed without a sleeper in it is not definitive. There could be other beds. Other locations for sleepers to be sleeping. But as I go further down the corridor, I find . . . nothing.

"Fuck," I say softly, but aloud. And I know instantly that no one else hears my curse.

I walk over to a bookcase at the far side of the room. I begin to thumb through the well-worn volumes, picking up a copy of Raymond Chandler's *The Little Sister*, but even while I do so, I am thinking about my next move. There is no reason for him not to be here, and yet the trailer is empty—when I was certain he was there earlier—and he is not.

When I go to leave, I step outside, and all that I hear are the voices of crickets in a perfectly still blue night.

CHAPTER THIRTY-SIX

So Bryce Donegan has gotten away. I know I should be more distressed about it than I am, but by the time it happened, I had already determined he wasn't a threat to anything but maybe the stock price. Maybe at a subconscious level I'd even wanted him to get away so I didn't have to do the thing I had maybe gone out there to do. From a purely practical standpoint, killing him was the right option. Eliminating him. I had no real reason to *know* he was not a threat to Virginia, even though, at a certain level, I knew it absolutely. But he had gotten away. It was out of my hands. And so, for a moment, I just breathe.

It is now three o'clock in the morning and I am deeply sorry I have rented a motel room and left some of my things there. I certainly don't feel like going back to it—the nubbly bedspread, the stale smell—but I do because it's the middle of the night, my stuff is there, and I don't have a better idea.

I don't sleep well. Partly because I'm worried about the dog. Partly because I'm worried about outcomes. But the greatest part is the lumpy mattress: I am uncomfortable and I am cold and I toss and turn for a few hours, wishing for sleep and also a time of the night when it will make sense to break camp. Finally, at six a.m., I can't stand it anymore and I pack up and head out, getting on the road with truckers and commuters, making a single stop for some second-rate coffee and first-rate biscuits and gravy at a truck stop off the highway.

By the time I make town it is in the full light of a sunny morning. I choose a hotel near the Greenmüll offices. It's a weekday and things at the hotel must not be busy because they let me check in at eleven: unheard of at times when things are in high demand. The early check-in gives me the time to unpack and regroup. I have this sense of getting down to business. As though everything that has gone before has led me to this juncture of get or be gotten.

The room I have booked is large and comfortable and it is all soothing pastels: mint and yellow, like the underside of a tiny bird. It's soft like that bird might be, too. And there's that softness again. Softness being a goal I never had and certainly never knew I wanted before and now seem to be attracting to myself in abundance.

I like the room. I seem to have a better idea now of what I need and want. We should all have that in our lives, I think. A growing understanding of what we require for personal satisfaction. We might not always be in a position to act on it, either. But it's the knowing: that's the thing. Whether or not we get what we want and need is second to the actual knowing. A lot of people go through life and never know. Not really. So even if they get it, they can't appreciate the depth of the gift.

I feel like I've hit some sort of milestone: I know and have acted upon the knowing in a way that has made it come to pass. I sent energy into the future of this trip: may this booking of the perfect room be an omen for the balance of my mission. Or my life.

I take a long shower in a bathroom that is made for speed and comfort. Sun shower. Heated towel bar, heated floors: all the comforts you wish you had at home. I stand under the shower a good long time. I'm not really washing much of anything. I am standing; feeling; thinking. The water is slightly hotter than comfortable, yet not hot enough to be dangerous. It's like I am cleaning some part of me that shouldn't even be dirty. Am I sluicing off road dirt? Crappy hotel dirt? Sure, there's that. But also, I am clarifying something, I think. And making ready another thing. It's a process, that's how it feels.

After I am dry and the appropriate makeup has been applied to my face, I dress in investor-appropriate garb and head for Greenmüll.

I don't bother observing from a distance. Instead, I park in the lot and stroll up to the front door. The same young man who was parked in the reception area last time is there again today. When I manage to pull his attention from his screen, I give him the spiel I have prepared. "I'm looking for Dr. Martin. I thought I might have a word with her."

To my surprise, he doesn't ask if I have an appointment. In fact, he barely looks me over before pushing a buzzer and indicating which way I should go.

I sort of remember the direction of the lab, so I follow my instincts until the office corridors widen out into the larger plant space. A direct walk and then a couple of turns bring me to Virginia Martin's lab.

Unsurprisingly, she is busy when I enter. Her head is down in deep conversation with a couple of employees, neither of whom I recognize. I move forward while also trying to hear what is being said. I don't manage to decipher even a tiny bit of the conversation, but Virginia Martin's eyes widen when she sees me. She doesn't say anything at first. I can tell that, once again, she can't quite place me. The distracted disconnect of the fiercely brilliant, that's what I think I see. The first thing she says confirms what I have surmised.

"You are familiar to me."

"Ya. We met the other day. I'm . . . I'm in finance. We didn't have lunch."

"Oh. Right. Cool," she says, but she doesn't seem that interested. At first. And I get it: meeting people is part of what she does. Part of what she needs to do. She's not required to remember us all. Likely since inception there have been a lot of financial types through these doors. Looking at her, though, it's like she has been thinking about other things from a long way away and it takes her a few minutes to come back. And maybe she would prefer it if she didn't have to. I don't blame her. The real world can be so very tedious.

I take this woolgathering time to look around. I am relieved not to see yellow-haired Matt Sundstrom from the bar, though I'm not entirely sure why I'm glad he's not there. It's like we have a secret together, he and I, and I'm not sure how bland I could keep my face if he were looking at me.

The lab itself looks much the same as it had when I was there. I've been standing there for a while, looking around, when it finally occurs to Virginia to ask why I've turned up.

"Well, Rance is wanting me to make an investment, right? I was in the area and thought I'd see the operation when the spotlight isn't on you."

"You didn't have an appointment," she says, her confusion clear. It's as though she thinks there might have been one that she's forgotten. "That's . . . not . . . done."

I smile. Of course she is right. But I'm a potential investor. I figure she'll indulge me. It ends up I'm right. And I'd implied I had a whole whack of cash that might be available for investment. Rance would have shared that. I can see her considering her options and can pretty much gauge the moment she decides to play nice.

"There's not much to see at the moment," she says, heading more deeply into the lab. "But come on in."

And so I do.

As I follow her, I consider how to maximize what I have seen as well as all the things that I know. Things observed in backpacks. In files. On people's faces and from their mouths. Things observed.

"I'm so interested in the beta families," I say. "How they are selected and what type of gear they might be getting next month."

I see her blanch a bit at this. And then, "Next month." It's a comment, not a question. "Is that what they told you?"

I nod. Keep my voice neutral. "Right."

"That's . . . optimistic," she says carefully.

"Oh yes?" My voice is still neutral. And then I don't say anything more. She's forced to speak to fill the dead space that grows between us.

"Right. Well. Yes. That was our original schedule. I can see why they might have told you a different date. I'm not sure . . . that is . . . umm . . . realistic . . . anymore."

"Oh?" The same mild understatement. After all, I've got no place to be.

"Right. Right," she says hurriedly, filling in the blank space. "That was our original schedule. They were totally right to tell you that." She hesitates and I still don't say anything. I fix her with an expectant look. She continues, as I'd thought she might, looking nervous and filling in the dead air. "We had no way of knowing *exactly* where we'd be at this stage when we made our schedule."

"It was tentative. Sure," I say. "That makes sense."

"Tentative," she repeats, seizing on the word. "Yes. Exactly. So we're a little behind schedule." That big, warm, somewhat famous grin. "But not a ton."

"Okay," I say, feigning an understanding I don't possess. "You're thinking . . . what? An additional month? Two? Or are you giving it a date yet?"

She moves her hands in front of her as she stands. One hand catches the other. Releases. Then begins again. A nervous gesture she's probably not even aware of.

"Yes. I think so. That is, that's what we are currently projecting. In that ballpark," she says again, the repetitiveness of her speech putting my hackles up as much as anything. Even so, I smile at her reassuringly.

"That sounds perfect," I say. "But what was the holdup?"

She doesn't answer right away. I've caught her unawares. And I see her struggling with the answer: trying her best to choose the right one. And that concerns me. When answers can be chosen you have to surmise that some of the available options are untrue.

"What's the holdup? Well. That's difficult to isolate." And I know I am hearing the Ivy League steel in her voice.

I don't say anything. I stand back with my eyebrows raised. She notices and hurries on.

"So. Yeah. Why, it's hard to say."

"Hard," I say, echoing her tone. She's brilliant so she notices.

"Difficult," she amends. "Yes. Well, Evan has pointed out to me that missing our deadline by a few weeks would be better than shooting for it and not getting it right."

"I can see that," I say. "And do you think that's what would happen? If you shot for it, I mean. Do you think there's a good chance you would miss your targets?"

She seems to consider my words but, on a certain level, I can see they don't need considering at all.

"I don't think so. But I do understand Evan's apprehension. He has a lot riding on this."

"You all do."

"Oh sure. Yes. But Evan even more so. He's got everything into it. It means so much to him."

"But I've read all about you, Virginia. You personally. And your tech. All those things you said could be said of you, as well."

"Sure, and that's right, too. But I'm a scientist so it's different for me."

"Explain."

"There will always be another summons for me. Of science, I mean. Another mountain to climb. Some other obstacle or challenge. No matter the outcome here—and I believe it will be good—there will be other windmills for me to tilt at. It's the nature of my business: finding answers. I'm not here for the money. You can probably sense that about me. I'm here for the questions and because Greenmüll gives me the toys I need to look for answers. No matter how all of this turns out, someone will always give me toys, because they know I have the skill set necessary to solve problems."

"But it's different for Evan." There is a part of me that wonders why she is being so forthcoming. Another part, though, has the answer. I'm not even totally sure that, at this moment, she sees me in front of her. She has warmed to her subject; probably one she spends a lot of time thinking about. And so she is airing thoughts that are often on her mind.

"Right. All of this is everything to him. There isn't anything else. And he's all in. If this doesn't work, he's sunk."

"Forgive me for my candor," I begin, "but—from my perspective—that seems a somewhat naive observation. To me. A relative stranger. It has me wondering about your motivation."

She laughs then, though it's not a particularly humorous sound. "You asked the question," she says. "And there is no motivation other than the obvious: working our way through the American web. It's a changing landscape."

"He seems so capable though."

"And he is. But when I say he has everything in, I mean *everything*. If this project were to tank, he'd have no place to go. So it can't tank. You see? That's what I'm getting at. His very vulnerability will make sure he always has everything in. And me? Well, look at my track record: I always have everything in no matter what."

Corporate invincibility, I understand that is what she is trying to convey. But I feel I am understanding a different story, beyond the one she is trying to tell. As she speaks, it strikes me that, with Virginia out of the picture, Evan would not have to deal with that potential failure. If she were lost, it would be tragic, of course. The loss of so talented a young woman. And Evan and company would be forced to struggle along without her. And they would continue her work, of course. Just somewhat slowed while they got their feet under them, finding their way without their technical leader. It seems the perfect solution for a unicorn to deal with flawed tech. The hang-up: the CTO has to die.

And I realize, of course, that none of this is the message she meant to leave me. That message—the company line, as it were—was one of hard work and infallibility. But I took away a different story.

We talk a while longer, but I break things off as soon as I politely can, taking myself back out the way I came in. I might have stayed longer but I know there is some place I need to be. And, as it happens, life makes it easier for me.

CHAPTER THIRTY-SEVEN

WHEN I GET to the parking lot, I see Evan's giant vehicle slide out and away. I rush the last few feet to the Volvo and get in motion, managing to catch up with the huge rear end of Evan's car as he rolls onto the freeway.

I realize that, other than the day I followed him and Rance to the restaurant, Evan has not seen my car. And the car is nondescript enough and in a neutral enough color, he could have seen it every day and he probably won't see it now. Like me, the car works at being invisible. It's possible to look right at it and not see it.

So I follow him. After a while he stops in front of a sushi joint and goes inside. I park at some distance and wait and watch. In a few minutes he comes out carrying a couple of bags, then he gets back on the road. I wait a minute before beginning to follow. It's late so there isn't a lot of traffic on the street. At the same time, I'm not too worried about being spotted. Evan has not struck me as someone who would be overly observant. Rather, it seems to me, he would be pretty self-absorbed. I keep my distance anyway, to be on the safe side.

His house is in a good neighborhood. One of many handsome piles in a development of them. His garage door opens at his approach and I keep going as he pulls in and parks.

I stop in the next block. And then I wait. I want to give him time to settle in before I move.

For a little while as I sit in the car, I think about nutrition. I don't want to study the subject right now, fearing the light from my phone will draw unwanted attention out to the street. But I think about what I've been learning. I've been reading about how nutrition affects the nervous system. So crazy. It's not a connection I would have made. "You are what you eat." Who would have thought that all this time later I would discover that my mother was right?

I read about the impact of various B vitamins on the brain, on the health benefits of eating avocados— "an avocado a day . . ." —and the importance of hydration.

I chill there in the car for about an hour. Having taken nutrition as far as I can without an actual text in front of me, I think about what I'm going to do, here in the real world. With Evan eliminated, so will the threat to Virginia be gone. Having spent some time with him and examining things carefully, I can see how getting Virginia out of the picture surgically would be helpful to Evan. Plus, temperamentally, it seems to me he is capable of it, if not by his own hand, then with the help of a hired one. Another benefit, of course, I'll be able to go home secure in the knowledge that I won't have to come back. It's not the most elegant solution. Nor is it the one most in line with the morality I am trying to pursue, but I don't have any better ideas and I can't stay in this town forever, waiting for Evan to successfully kill Virginia.

After a while, the house goes entirely dark and I pull on the flesh-colored gloves I usually wear when on a job. I grab my Bersa-heavy purse plus ammo, then head toward the house.

A window has been left open at the side of the house, probably a bathroom judging from the size. I slide it open as far as I can and as quietly as possible to make a good wide and easy opening. I am about to pull myself up and in when I get the call. The ringer is turned off on my phone, of course, but I feel the familiar vibration. I'm tempted to ignore the call—deal with it later—but, truly, so few people have the number, every call I ever get has its own urgency. No one calls me casually, simply to chat. Anyone that puts my digits together has some sort of business on the brain.

All of this is further confirmed when I glance at the phone and see that the call is coming from Reykjavík. Since I know virtually no one who might be in Iceland—I don't even know anyone who might know anyone who would be—I figure I know who the caller is—and I realize that she is the only one whose call I would answer right now.

I back away from the window and retrace my steps to the sidewalk. I move casually, as though out for an evening stroll, and manage to accept the call as it is about to go off to voicemail.

"Iceland, is it?" I can't help the prod.

The wispy voice laughs. It's a warm sound. "I know. I can't help myself for some reason. You obviously can't be allowed to know where I am."

"For so many reasons."

"Right. So this bit of subterfuge is fun."

"It isn't simply subterfuge either, is it?" I'm far down the block now, heading around a corner, so there is no fear of being overheard by my target.

"No, no. That's right. My call is being routed through Reykjavík. That's what you mean, right?"

"Yeah. That's what I figured. Fun. I've never been to Reykjavík before. But now my voice has."

"This isn't what I called about."

"I figured that, too."

"I have a name for you."

I'm outside and walking, but inexplicably the words make me walk straighter. She's decided to play ball after all.

"We are at a different place now," I say.

"We were hired by Evan Hollingsworth to look out for her and protect her. Considering the circumstance, it was not the worst option."

I surprise myself by asking: "You're sure?"

"Sure I'm sure."

"Wow." I know there is disbelief in my voice, but I don't doubt for even a minute. Sometimes you know when you hear it that a thing is true. Before she draws breath, I've turned around and am heading back to my car.

"That surprises you," she says. "Your surprise surprises *me*."

"Does it really? I'm not sure why. For one thing, you told me *you* were the client." And I realize, but don't say, that I have been surprised by another thing: I nearly killed someone for no reason. My reaction had been like instinct. The way most people kick when the doctor knocks them on the knee with a soft little hammer. Reflex. My instinct and my reflex had been to kill Evan Hollingsworth. And now I have been told that killing Evan isn't the right answer. What have I become? Who am I now that, even when I don't want to kill, my instincts lead me in that direction?

And then I let it go, for the moment. I let it go because I have to. I feel dangerously close to not being able to live with the answer to the question of what I have become.

"A white lie," she says. "That I was the client. And not entirely inaccurate. But you had Evan figured for the culprit, didn't you?"

"I did."

"That's what I figured. It's why I had to let you know." And the timing of it, that's the thing. The timing of her call makes me wonder. Did she know something? Or are her instincts so sharply honed that she can feel when all is not quite as it should be? If she'd called half an hour later, the story would have had a different ending.

"Is she even your daughter?" It has to be asked.

"She is," she replies with no hesitation.

"What you've created here," I say, "it was a narrow call."

"Pardon?"

"Never mind," I say. I am getting into my car. Preparing to drive away. "It doesn't matter now."

And then I realize that it doesn't. The phone is dead, but I know that, for a short time anyway, I have been released.

CHAPTER THIRTY-EIGHT

THE NEXT DAY I go back to the salon. It is less hectic on my second visit. I am running out of ideas and need more people to talk to. I figure Minerva might have some insight . . . maybe something that I've missed. I hope so anyway.

This time, though, there is no throbbing line of customers. Minerva has her long blond hair pulled up and secured with a chopstick, a neat trick I've always admired but have never been able to quite pull off. She is sitting at her station, poring over her computer with a spreadsheet showing up on the screen. I notice, also, that she is alone in the salon.

"Business day?"

"Yup. I'm in the doldrums today, all right," she answers as she looks up, and I can see right away that she recognizes me. "Hey, what are you doing here? I got the feeling you were going to be a once-every-two-years-whether-you-need-it-or-not kinda customer."

"Ha," I say. "Ha ha."

"Yeah, but I'll bet I'm not far wrong."

"I've gotta be honest: what you did looks and felt so good, I think it's possible I'll be getting hair attention more often."

"Hmmm," she says skeptically but with a smile, "we'll see."

"I'm not here about hair today . . ."

"See?" She says it smugly.

"I'm here about Virginia Martin." I feel as much as see her sit up straighter at this. It was clearly not what she had expected me to say.

"What about her."

"I believe she is in some danger."

"Who are you to believe such a thing?" Drawbridge up. There was probably a better way for me to have approached her, but I don't know what it was.

"That's a perfectly reasonable question." I wasn't sure I had a perfectly reasonable answer. I decided to go with a reply that felt close to the truth. "Her . . . her family contacted me. Out of concern. They had . . . reason to believe she was in danger."

"That's what you said."

"I guess . . . I guess I have reason to believe you know that as well." She arches her eyebrows in my direction.

"Me?"

I look at her for a moment. Directly. And she has the good grace to color gently.

"So what you're saying is, when you were here before, it wasn't for your hair at all."

It is my turn to color. "Yeah. Yeah, I guess that's right. I loved it though. Truly."

She smiles, but her voice is still stern. "You were here to, what? Watch Virginia?"

I nod. "Yeah. Protect her and also try and figure out who might be trying to hurt her."

"Well, I might be able to help with that."

I didn't know I'd been holding my breath, but I release it now. She believes me. It hadn't been a forgone conclusion. She believes me and she has input to add that might illuminate part of what is still dark. It's better than I'd dared hope for.

"Tell me," I say quietly.

"Last time I saw her, she told me Rance was shorting the stock."

"How could she possibly know that?"

"Hattie. Hattie works with Rance."

I look at her as though she is speaking a different language.

"Hattie? Why would that matter?" I can't see the connection between Virginia Martin and the person I had supposed was Rance's lover.

"Wait: you said the family hired you. Do you really not know *anything*?"

I shake my head. "I guess not."

"Hattie and Virginia are partners."

"Like, business partners?"

"No. Not like that at all."

CHAPTER THIRTY-NINE

I AM BLINDSIDED by this news. I always imagine myself to be so perceptive, but I'd missed this altogether. I feel I should have seen it. But now so much else makes sense.

The fact that Hattie had been at Virginia's house. She wasn't snooping around at all. It was her house, too. She was coming home. And the two breakfast plates. And the tidiness of the space. Virginia was working almost nonstop right now. She barely had time to eat and sleep, let alone prepare food and plate it. I was guessing Hattie would deal with some of this while Virginia was off spending impossible hours in her lab. Because they are partners. Because that is what lovers do: look after each other.

Once I reel in this news for later examination, I get back to the other thing Minerva told me: Rance has been shorting the stock. Here was an additional piece of information that, when added to what I already had, made the whole picture somewhat more complete. Hattie had not been removing stock documents, that's what I figured now. She likely had been bringing them home to show her partner what Rance was up to.

But what *was* he actually up to? And what far-reaching implication might shorting the stock mean in this situation?

Since Minerva seems to have nothing more to add to my knowledge, I begin to take my leave, but she stops me.

"Be careful, please," she says. "And take good care of Virginia. She's very special to me."

I tell her that I will. That I'm trying. And I thank her again for my beautiful hair. She shoos away my thanks. "We were working with good material," she assures me. "You don't do anything dumb to your hair to damage it. Your hair merely needs coaching more than anything." And I am left with the idea of a sports coach with a whistle and hair that can be unruly and undisciplined. It's a funny image.

I have a lot to think about, so I head back to the hotel to poke through the tidbits I have put together.

The day is bright and clear and there are a few solid hours of sunshine left in it. I change into sweats and head out for a walk with a painful void at my side. I miss the dog, and also, I feel oddly guilty to be going for a pleasant walk without him: he loves them so. After a while, though, I let it go: there's a lot right in front of me that needs to be dealt with. Walking will clear my head; help me think. And it does. When I get back to the hotel, I have a clear course of action.

Rance is shorting the stock. What does that mean? I Google a little bit, and then I pick up the phone. To my surprise, Curtis answers on the first ring.

"Did you change your mind?" His voice sounds earnest.

"About what?"

"Dinner, of course."

My mind is so far from that it takes me a minute to pull it back.

"No. I mean, geez. I'm sorry. If it were at all possible, I'd love to. But I'm nowhere near LA right now."

"I could send the news helicopter."

That stops me in my tracks for a minute. News helicopter? What?

"No, you couldn't," I say.

"No, that's right. I couldn't. Fun image, though, huh? Dramatic. Gallant."

"Yes."

"Good. I do like to see myself that way."

And I laugh, despite myself and everything I have on my mind, because it is Curtis and that's how he does the world: with joy and laughter. And it's so different to my approach to everything these days, I can't help but feel somewhat joyous, too. Even when simply talking on the phone with him. I realize that though there were others I could have called, all of this is why I reached out to him first. Which reminds me.

"I have called with a specific purpose," I begin.

"I guessed that," he says. "What have you got?"

"Explain to me, please, the term *short selling*."

"Sorry?" I can tell it's come out of left field.

"What is meant when someone says, for instance, that someone else is selling short a stock."

"It's complicated."

"Why do you think I called you?"

He laughs at that, but I can tell he is laughing near me, not at me, so I let it go.

"It's a stock thing . . ."

"That much I've got," I say.

He ignores me and continues. "In a short sale, a trader opens a position by borrowing stock shares he believes will decrease in value."

"Decrease? And that makes sense?"

He laughs. It has a genuine sound. "What? You want it to make sense, too? It's the stock market. But you're missing the salient bit," he says.

I think for a minute.

"The borrowing part?"

"Right. Exactly. The short seller *borrows* shares of a security from the market, basically banking on the idea that the share price will go down."

I think about this for a minute, even though my head is spinning.

"So let me see if I have this straight. The short seller borrows the shares, effectively selling someone else's shares at a high price. The shares then go down and the short seller buys those shares at the lower price as the price goes down in order to repay the shares he borrowed."

"Four stars," Curtis says, sounding genuinely pleased. "You'd call it 'market price shares,' but what you're saying is absolutely accurately. That's the heart of this: when someone dumps a bunch of shares, they are essentially leading the market down. That's the hope, anyway, in a short sell. That it keeps going down and down. And the further down it goes, the more you profit."

"But wait. What happens if the stock doesn't go down? What if it goes up instead?"

"Four more stars," he says. "That's an important bit. And it's called a short squeeze. You have to cover the shares you borrowed. If the stock price goes up instead of down, you still have to replace the borrowed stock, so sometimes it's best to buy it early as it rises, hoping it will decline."

"Because it might never come back down."

"Exactly. All in all, it's a pretty dangerous business. You have to be relatively sure the stock price is going to drop before making that investment."

I sit with that for a minute. Feeling it. Formulating.

"So if you were in a position to assure a short sale, maybe that's what you'd do."

"Make sure it went down, you mean?"

"Yeah."

"Maybe. Maybe, indeed. But that would be insider trading. But take this in: short selling is a legal way of playing the stock market. It might not be the most ethical, but it isn't, strictly speaking, unethical, either."

"So you're telling me to chill."

"Most certainly not. I don't even know what you're up to. But if you need a hand, I will definitely be to your location by Friday." And then the phone goes dead.

I sit there with it for a minute. I am certain I had not told him my location, yet he is on his way. I wasn't sure what it all meant, but I was not surprised.

CHAPTER FORTY

IT DOESN'T MATTER where I am. There are parts of my life that are easy. And that's a good thing, because many things are hard. Difficult.

In this heartbeat, I focus on my material from Cornell. I am by now deeply into the coursework and doing a section on plants that support respiratory and cardiovascular health. It's extremely interesting, but I find my mind keeps wandering back to other things. The shorting of stock. A CTO confident of outcomes, but with maybe too much against her. A rogue heckler out there, perhaps ready to spring up again and put a kibosh on so much. A friendly neighborhood investment manager maybe trying to burn down the castle so he can make a buck. A lot of bucks.

But nutrition. That's the thing that is right in front of me now. I breathe myself to a peaceful space while I struggle to keep everything else at bay. Just for a while.

On the coursework front, I discover that it turns out that grapeseed promotes cardiovascular health. Grapeseed. I have to stop and Google that one. Could they mean actual seeds of actual grapes, or is it some kind of code for something else?

But no, it turns out that grapeseed is the actual seed of actual grapes. I find myself lost for a while, trying to figure out how anyone discovered this thing—eat this part, throw this part away seems pretty straightforward—but I can't even begin to parse it. And there is grapeseed oil. That's a source. Who would have ever thought that grapeseeds were even oily? They seem like the driest, crappiest things ever. Yet here we are.

Garlic, dandelion, hawthorn berries. All good for cardiovascular systems. It's fascinating. I know at first read that it's all going to be life-changing for me. It will, that is, if I can pull my attention away from the business at hand long enough to absorb some of what I am supposed to be learning. You want a degree from Cornell? You focus, focus. You have to stop thinking about killing people. You have to stop thinking about people getting killed.

And then, because that's the way things like this go, the phone rings. I am informed that the call is coming from Uzbekistan, which of course is stupid. There is no one on the planet who would be calling me from that place. I wasn't even sure they had phones.

"I'm not going to give you a name," she says without preamble. "There is the chance that I am incorrect in my assumptions. I don't have the whole picture. The picture you have is likely more clear than mine."

I murmur a few agreeable words but, if I'm honest with myself, I have no idea what happens next. I say as much.

"So where are we?"

"I wouldn't like to lose her," she says.

"I know."

"She is dear to me." And I don't mention that she is the second person to say that to me on this day.

"There is a possibility that the technology doesn't work." There. I've said it. Laid it down.

There is silence on the phone. It echoes deeply between Uzbekistan—or wherever she actually is—and me. I can't decide what it means so I wait it out.

"The technology," she repeats finally.

"The tech as advertised," I say, hoping that clarifies it.

"I don't have that answer," she says. There is no expression in her voice.

"Would that change the picture as you understand it?"

"It might," she says. "It would present . . . other possibilities."

"I'll let you know how it all goes," I say. This time I'm the one who terminates the call.

CHAPTER FORTY-ONE

I WORRY ABOUT the dog. That's the downside. He's on his own and I can't call him on the phone and check up on him. I know he is fine, but I don't *know* he is fine. I tell myself to stop being a dork and get on with the business at hand. Meanwhile I decide I need to back-burner a way to make sure he's okay when I'm not there. Some kind of video setup, maybe? That's never a bad idea. I can't do that now, obviously. But at some future point. Future jobs. If there are future jobs. I hesitate there. It's such a big question.

I am missing pieces. I'm sure of that. And I have Googled everything as far as I can go: there's nothing left to search. The information I want is out there, but I have to go and fetch it myself.

And so I change. I put on black tights, a black T, black hoodie, black sneaks. I know I look like a dancer or an art student or a cat burglar, but there are few environments in which I would not be almost invisible, so I figure how I look doesn't matter.

When I return to the industrial neighborhood where the Extreme Angels building is located, it is after two a.m. and everything looks deserted. I circle the block a few times and cruise the neighborhood to be sure. I am trying to gauge what obstacles I might encounter, but also I am working on my courage. A scary part of town and a difficult task are ahead and I am not sure I have the jam. At the same time, I can't think of an alternative. I am back here now and I have to begin. This is the starting point I'd selected. Once again, I put my head down and press on.

There seems to be no reason to announce my whereabouts and intention, so I park a block away and skulk back to the building, keeping to the shadows. The only other souls I encounter are people of the night, and I am clearly not part of their business.

It doesn't make sense to me to go pawing at the front door—I don't think anyone is there and, if they are, I don't want them to know that *I* am—so I make a beeline for the back alley. I have no idea what I'll find there, but it seems a better starting point. I make my face a fierce mask and hope that the occasional vagrants I encounter will leave me alone. They do. The Bersa in my bag is a great backup and maybe gives me additional courage, but the thought of using it on an innocent in an alley because they scare me does not sit well. Someone hoping to shake down a couple of bucks for a score does not deserve the finish I would be forced to give, so I keep my face severe and press on against all comers. It works. After a few minutes I stand at a back entrance and the coast is clear.

When I try the back door, it is pure form: I do not expect it to open and it doesn't. A piece of luck as big as a back door left unlocked is too much to hope for, and there is no surprise for me there: the sturdy metal door doesn't budge and whatever lock holds it is on the inside. There are windows high off the street. All are closed except for the farthest one, which is high and completely unreachable from where I am. Unless.

There is a Dumpster across the alley. It is on wheels. It seems to me that if I were to push the Dumpster under the window, I'd be able to shimmy up and in. Even as I approach, I realize it isn't an original thought. Have I seen this move in a movie? Maybe more than once? With that in mind, why do they even still put wheels on Dumpsters, if ne'er-do-wells were just going to use them to break into buildings?

Once there, my hopes are dashed: the Dumpster in question is secured in place by a padlock and chain. I try to think of another plan, but I am stymied. I'd been through that front door: there is no way I'm going to be able to get in that way without someone inviting me in and there is another building on each side, so no possible entry through a side window. There aren't any. I examine the padlock thoughtfully, an idea forming. It is foolish enough that I feel it has no possible chance of success, but I also don't have any other ideas.

"What the hell," I mutter, drawing out the Bersa and screwing on the suppressor. I stand back slightly and take careful aim. I am going to shoot out a metal lock. Or try. A ricochet off the metal is possible and also potentially dangerous—even lethal—to me. After a while, though, I stop trying to calculate the odds and let 'er rip. I am relieved and unbelievably surprised when everything goes even better than planned. The suppressed shot is little more than a "pop" in the quiet alley, but the lock explodes when the bullet hits it, folding back as though it is made of rubber. I have a moment of pure elation before I realize unlocking the Dumpster was step one: I now have to push the thing across the alley, climb on it, and see if I can get through the window. Several times in the course of doing that, I question my own plan. Why the hell am I doing this? But since I can't come up with a better idea, I press on. If not this, then . . . what?

It takes a long time for me to get the Dumpster across the alley and close enough to the window for me to attempt to bridge the distance. Moving the thing does not happen without mishap. Getting on top of it taxes every slim bit of athleticism I can claim. The thing is, from a distance, getting to the top of a wheeled refuse container looks quite manageable. But they are much taller than they appear. I feel like a jockey trying to mount a very tall and recalcitrant horse.

Finally in the saddle, I try to push aside my instinctive fear of heights to turn my attention to the window. Up close the window is smaller than I'd taken it to be from the street: sort of opposite of my dilemma with the Dumpster. It is open and unbarred and it is large enough for me to squeeze through. Then there is a long drop to the ground on the inside. Before I take a run at it, I push away the vision of me sprawled on the floor with a broken leg, helpless and trapped and in desperate pain.

"Stop it," I hiss at myself. That would be the worst possible outcome. It seems to me that the odds are against the worst outcome, but what the hell do I know?

I see a vagrant shambling down the alley toward me. If I'm going to do this before he gets too close, I have to do it: now or never. I modify as I push off early, hoping for the best—breaking my leg at the bottom of the fall would be *one* of the worst possible outcomes.

Because the window is small, I am forced to go through headfirst, twisting myself around as best I can as I drop. I land on my back. Not the worst possible landing, but the wind is knocked out of me. I recover quickly and thank whatever goddesses are looking out for me. Clearly the outcome upon impact could have been much worse.

Once I go over the damage and find myself intact, I sit there for a moment, catching my breath while assessing my condition, my surroundings, and the silence.

This last is the most important piece. It is complete, that silence. I am relieved. The possibility that someone might be here—working late or camping out—had not occurred to me until I landed hard on my back.

When I collect myself enough to look around, I realize I am in some sort of storeroom. Warehouse shelves are filled with various types of supplies: file folders, coffee pods, a tool kit, paper towels, a mop and bucket and all the other things needed behind the scenes to run a large business.

With my breathing restored to normal and reassured by that deep silence, I head for the door. It doesn't open when I pull on the handle.

"Fuck." It is a whisper that holds deeper and more threatening resonances. It settles on me slowly that I have broken into a locked room.

"Of course I did." Giving voice to it doesn't help. Yet somehow it does.

So the door.

My first instinct is to take out the Bersa and start blasting away. It had worked on the Dumpster, after all. But I can see that with this particular lock all that would accomplish is a mess. Possibly worse. I look around the storeroom and see again the toolbox, neatly stacked among the supplies.

Faced with no other possibilities, I note that the hinges are on the side of the door that I am on. That means it is possible for me to take the door off its hinges. I've never done that before, but I feel capable of it. With help. I draw out my phone. Google. And am relieved to find, almost instantly, a two-minute You-Tube video showing you how to remove a door from its hinges with "two simple tools: a hammer and small screwdriver." As long, I am warned, as the door has removable hinges. I check and am relieved to see that, yes: the hinges do appear to be the removable sort shown in the video. Additionally, assorted hammers and screwdrivers are among the things to be found in the toolbox. I set to work.

One of the things I have discovered, living alone in my house in the forest, is that nearly any handyman-type job you might set out to do proves to be more difficult than it at first looks on paper . . . or in a YouTube video. It is demonstrated: one, two, three. Easy! In reality, every numbered step takes longer and proves to be more challenging than illustrated. It's the way of the universe, I think.

I set to work and discover almost instantly that in this very old and remodeled building, the hinges have been painted and repainted many times. That's not a dealbreaker, but it does make the whole process more difficult and I'm already hampered by my pathetically girly weakness. That is, I can know how to do a thing, and I can take a proper run at doing that thing, but sometimes I lack the torque to complete the job.

That is almost the case here and, for a minute, I believe it *is* the case. But then I rummage around on the shelves and find a can of WD-40, which is a kind of lubricant that isn't, really. The "WD" part stands for Water Displacement and I have no idea how it works, but for getting stuck things to move again it does, in fact, work. Magic? Maybe not. But when I blast the hinges with it, after a few minutes I am able to get motion when I couldn't before. It is another fifteen minutes before I have the hinges fully off the door. And another several before I have the door out and set down inside the room.

When I look at the mess I have made, I feel panic and amusement. There is no way I'll be able to get that door back on: they're going to know they had a visitor.

Since I came in the back way, as it were, I know I am at the back of the building, a part I haven't been to before. I need to locate Rance's office. Where else to find what I need? Since I don't even really know what I am looking for, it seems as good a place to start as any. But where to find it?

I am in an old building and so there are many corridors and all of them seem to lead to rooms I've never seen before. I find a bullpen—a dozen desks with a dozen computers and a dozen phones. I hadn't necessarily expected that here, but neither is it a complete surprise.

I keep moving.

Down another corridor I find a lunchroom. The scent of toast and greasy microwaved food lingers on the air. Next is a media room. I know I am getting closer and—yes—Rance's office was one of those that was accessed from the media room. I remembered that much from my visit. Financial videos and investments and sign here please on the dotted line.

When I reach out to open the door, I am apprehensive I'll find yet another locked portal, but the door opens easily on Rance's empty office. I close the door behind me and lean against it and for a few minutes, breathe. And breathe.

The office is pretty much exactly as I remembered it, though I hadn't been there long enough to take in details. The large desk, expensive and expansive. There is also an executive chair and a bank of closed cabinets that I suspect would house the materials I am looking for. Not that I know exactly what I am looking for, but it seems like a good place to begin. Another cabinet holds books and trophies and other memorabilia, but I make a beeline for the closed cabinets. The move is rewarded when I open them and find neatly organized files inside. I begin in what I think is a logical fashion, finding the alphabetical area that would house information about Greenmüll and maybe Rance's shorting of the stock, but I find nothing like that there. It reminds me that filing is a very personal business. I myself would file contracts by name, but it was possible that Rance filed by project, which, though irrational seeming to me, was valid enough for some. But if it was all filed by project, I'd be SOL. So many projects, so many names likely cross-referenced by some master list, maybe on Rance's phone or some other similar place as inaccessible to me. Who knew? But contrary to what one might think, finance is a personal business. Filling it with personal idiosyncrasies made sense.

So projects: there are a lot of them. Rance has been at this business for a number of years. And it doesn't help that I sort of don't know what I'm looking for. It's needle in a haystack time and after a full half hour of desultory and sorta pointless-feeling searching I begin to wonder what the hell I'm doing there.

Greenmüll is one of the things I check, of course, but Extreme Angels has been working with them almost since the start-up started up, and there are multiple files on them: how the company was structured—who was doing what and why with whom—as well as documents to promote investment. When I come across a list of the investors and board members that existed up until the time the company went public two years earlier, I feel a small surge of elation. I'm not certain it will be at all helpful to me, but I photograph each page, then carefully replace them, then move from the files to the desk.

Sitting down at Rance's computer, I begin what I feel will be a useless sequence to boot the device. At first, I'm right, too. The start-up screen is password protected. I try a bunch of obvious blends of his names and birth date, which I get from his passport, also in the drawer. But nothing budges. Ditto on "pass-word" and "12345678."

So it becomes apparent to me that he has an actual password, and I can see absolutely no way of figuring out what it is: I don't know enough about him to even begin the process of guessing my way in. First address. Where he went to school. Mother's maiden name. I have no way of knowing any of that.

Instinct more than anything guides me to open his desk drawer. Along with the usual top office drawer detritus, there is a small notebook. I suppress a smirk. Wouldn't it be funny if?

On the first page of the book is Rance's name and a street address, not the location of the office. His home address? I photograph the page. On the last page of the book there is a column of notations. Some scratched out. I try the top one that is not scratched out and am astonished when the collections of letters and numbers hits. It seems I've found Rance's personal list of passwords, which both cracks me up and is logical. Why not keep them written down in your personal office where no one else ever goes? Why not, indeed. Before I do anything more, I photograph the page. One never knows.

Finding my way around Rance's computer proves to be like navigating a stranger's attic. Getting in had been easy. Digging through the accumulated *stuff* of two decades of business paper-work is more challenging. And, of course, no one has a computer for two decades. But upgrading and migrating to a new system these days most often means schlepping all the old things along. And since there is generally a larger amount of storage space on the new computer—a bigger attic!—it's easy to shove older files into new folders "just in case" rather than dealing with it now.

It looks like Rance has done a lot of all of that. I stumble across lots of files dating back a decade and more. If dust accumulated in electronic spaces, I know I'd be sneezing and knee deep in dust bunnies by now. All of that makes finding what I am looking for more difficult.

And what am I looking for? I'm not even sure of that, so I keep digging around in there, hoping that I'll spot a clue that makes some kind of sense.

Going through his browser history, I find a web page that loads his trading account. I figure I'll have to hit the password book again and hope for the best. But the computer is polite and well trained: as soon as the page finishes loading, the browser fills in the blanks for username and password and, even though the ease of it all astonishes me, I find myself in Rance's trading account.

And this is his personal trading account, I note, not that of Extreme Angels. I figure that probably they do their trades on a hardwired machine either somewhere else in the office or it may even be located at a different address entirely: a brokerage, for instance, where trade instructions are sent and an investment banker executes them. That is other people's money, and care has to be taken to get everything right. This, though, this is different: Rance's own trading account. I decide to have a look through his recent trades and see if I spot anything interesting. Almost immediately, I do.

In his account I can see that he has been holding several thousand shares of GML for the last few years, some of them probably even tied into his early development of the company's finances. But his trading account indicates that over the last few days he has put in sell orders for double the amount that he owns. That is: he has sold far, far more shares of GML than he owns. I'm not sure what it means, but I'm certain that it does have meaning. Could this be the short selling that Minerva had told me about? Whatever the case, it is my feeling from the beginning that something does not smell right with the data. I don't know enough about how the stock market works to know what's going on. I photograph several screens worth of data and move on.

After looking over his trading account, I still snoop around on Rance's computer, but after a while and with nothing more interesting unearthed, I get the feeling that I've found all there is for me to discover.

Thinking that I might find more of interest in Hattie's desk, I look around for it. But there are too many desks available to look through, and there is no way of knowing who they belong to without searching each one so, after about half an hour of searching desks and with many more still to search, I give it up. I've started looking over my shoulder, nervous that someone might show up and discover me.

I decide not to try and tackle getting up the wall and out the window to the Dumpster when I exit. After all, I reason, they are going to know they had a visitor in any case as there is no way I'll be able to put that storeroom door back on its hinges. I opt to go out the front door knowing that it may well trigger an alarm, but since I'm breaking *out* not *in,* I'll be long gone by the time anyone responds.

CHAPTER FORTY-TWO

WHEN I GET back outside, I feel a rich coolness and the air is filled with moisture. Purely pulling the fresh air into my lungs feels like a gift. Being outside. I feel somewhat more relieved than I should. I beeline back to my car and it starts and gets away without incident. As I drive into the night, there has been no police response, and by the time I am a couple of blocks away, I breathe again—and then again.

I don't wait until I'm back at the hotel before I call Curtis. He answers fairly quickly, but his tone lets me know he doesn't have time to chat.

"Sorry," he says, his voice barely above a whisper. "A press conference is about to start."

"Anything interesting?"

"Politics."

"Right. Okay. Call me later? I have more stock market questions."

"Sure, but it'll be a few hours."

I let him know that's okay, but it isn't, of course. I need another option and I need it as close to now as possible. The text I send is succinct:

I have discovered perplexing data and need expert advice. Call any time to consult.

I have only gone a few blocks before my phone rings. I am not surprised.

"Whatcha got?"

"Rance's trading account. It doesn't seem right."

"How did you get into his account?" I hear a begrudging note in her tone. Respect?

"It doesn't matter," I say. And truly, it does not. The end result is all that will count. In all of this.

"Okay," she says. "Fair enough. We need a stock market person for you to talk to? Tell you what you saw?" I continue to be surprised by how quickly she can assess a situation and move forward to what needs to be done.

"That would be great," I say. "Possible?"

"I think so. I have someone in mind. Let me see what I can do."

*   *   *

While I wait, I make another call. It's been on my mind but I've been putting it off. Why? I don't want to appear insane. Even to myself. Maybe especially to myself. But I put that aside for now. My sanity might suffer, but I need any answers I can get.

It takes me a while after I get back to the hotel to find a phone number for Lisa Jane Samaritano. I haven't stayed in touch with her, even if she had proven to be super valuable and her insight—or maybe it's purely called sight—had led me down unexpected paths. It seems worth another try.

I find that she is no longer employed by the psychic agency she was at when I first called upon her. I discover that she has since hung out her own shingle. Which makes sense to me—she's certainly talented enough—but it does mean it takes me a bit to find her. While I search, I take myself to task a bit. How desperate must I be to be looking again for psychic help?

"I have a mad request," I say when I manage to get her on the phone. I'm not certain if she remembers me and I decide not to call myself to her mind. If her psychic abilities are all they're cracked up to be, she'll remember me, or at least, she'll know how to help me. If they're not, well, it doesn't matter anyway.

"You are ever about the mad requests, I think."

It's innocuous. It could apply to anyone. And yet.

"I'm in a bit of a pickle," I begin.

"Of course you are."

"Excuse me?"

"Well, why else would you seek me out?"

Point, I think. It's a valid thought. I ignore the comment anyway. It's stinging a little too close to home.

"I cannot quite determine—yet—if the person I am looking for is as dangerous as they seem. How can I tell?"

There is a pause, but it's not super long.

"Danger is in the eye of the beholder."

I pause and chew on that before answering. It's fair, for sure. If vague.

"Please. I'm wondering if . . . should I be establishing relationships right now at all? Or going it on my own?"

She doesn't answer for so long, I think she's hung up. And then, "You know the answer to that question, I think. I'm not certain of the reason to ask it again now, other than to reassure yourself."

"That doesn't help me."

"Yes. I'm sure that's right."

"What's right?"

"That what I said doesn't help you."

"Excuse me?"

"Exactly," she says, and there is so much enthusiasm in her tone that it's hard to keep being annoyed with her.

"Still," I say.

"Exactly!" She says it again.

"Listen," I say, thinking aloud, "this is getting silly. Can you help me? Or not?"

"Of course I can. You know that. Okay, listen: let me give you what I've got. It's likely to make more sense to you than it does to me."

"Shoot," I say, letting her know I'm listening.

"You will find what you are looking for in the dark."

"What are you now? A fortune cookie?"

She laughs. "Ha! Yes. Maybe. You could say that." Then she sobers. "No but seriously: it will be dark when you encounter what you seek."

"Oh-kay. Anything else?"

She goes on as if I haven't spoken. It feels to me like she's listening—maybe to voices from a distant realm, I reflect—and sharing it as it comes up.

"Yes. Your answers will come from unexpected sources."

"But that's meaningless," I say. "That could be anything."

"I see a parking lot. Cars coming and going, even when they shouldn't be."

Greenmüll, I'm thinking. "What else?"

"Everyone is very well dressed."

"Please," I say, my patience thinning.

"This last part makes no sense to me."

I sigh. "Go on," I prompt.

"Not everybody lives."

*   *   *

The handler is less efficient in her response.

This time she appears to be calling from Belarus. I'm getting used to it now, though, so the outlandish address barely gets me to crack a smile.

"I have what you requested. A person with answers for you. I'm texting you his number. Please call him in a quarter of an hour. He'll be expecting you."

It all seems a little cloak and dagger for the straightforward questions I want to ask, but then I started the whole thing, so I go along. I mean, I could have Googled, as I quite often do. But Google answers can be one dimensional. This time I felt I was asking a question that needed a more full and complete reply. I don't want to get this wrong.

"Why would someone sell more stock than they own?" That's the first thing I ask.

"Of a single security, you mean?" The voice on the phone is not what I'd imagined it would be. If the kid is sixteen, it is a lot; his voice is not quite settled and it breaks occasionally. I wonder about his relationship to the handler. Grandson, maybe? The offspring of some other offspring? I know it doesn't matter, though. For one thing, it becomes apparent almost right away that this kid knows the stock market. Even his tone inspires confidence and betrays his deep knowledge.

"One stock, yeah."

"That would be a short sell. It's pretty common. You sell stocks you don't own—basically borrowing them from the market—because you're banking that the stock price will go down."

I sit with that for a minute. Digest it. It was pretty much what Curtis had said—it had been different actually seeing the move in play.

"Let me make sure I have this perfectly straight: In this case, you're investing in the hope that the stock price goes down, not up?"

"Well . . . kinda. Not exactly. Because you're not truly investing, do you see? You're selling stock you don't own."

"Oh-kay. Let me run it back. I sell stock at one dollar a share."

"Right. Borrowed stock."

"Okay. I sell borrowed stock. The share price drops to fifty cents. I keep the fifty cents between what I sold it for and what I then had to pay because I said I would buy it?"

"Pretty much, yeah. Because you were selling shares you had borrowed in order to sell them at that higher price."

"Wow. The stock market is a pretty screwed-up business, isn't it?"

"Pretty much."

"Okay: let me run a scenario by you. If you were doing a very large short sell . . ."

"High price or many shares?"

"Both."

"Okay."

"If you were doing that, and you had it in your power to make sure the share price went down, you'd do it, right?"

"That's a pretty open-ended question."

"Yeah. Sorry. I guess it is. But that would be the ultimate short sell, right? If you could control the downward . . . plunge."

"Yes. I guess so." I can hear him thinking. "But it wouldn't be
. . . honest. And it would be the very definition of insider
trading."

"What could cause a stock price to go down?" I ask, knowing
it will be a crowded field. His response let's me know I'm right.

"Oh! So many things. I wouldn't even know where to start.
Sometimes it's a whisper, like in the forums. A rumor, you
know? Sometimes a share price will even drop on news of good
stuff happening. People choosing a high moment to cash out."

"What about if there is bad news?"

"Well, depending on the news, the price will bounce. Not necessarily drop all the way down. Like, again, a little bit of bad news
might end up raising the stock price. If the price starts to drop,
people might start putting in buy bids. But if super bad news gets
out, like the bottom has dropped out of a particular market, say,
or the technology has been replaced by better or newer tech, or
regulation is coming out that will make it impossible to do this
piece of business, that will make the price drop, sure."

"What about if someone dies?" I'm mulling as I ask it.

"Pardon?"

"Well, let's say, for instance, a company whose developing
technology is dependent on the brilliance of one person. Say
that one person dies."

"You're talking about the proverbial irreplaceable person,
right? Without this guy the show can't go on?"

"Kinda like that. Yeah."

"In that case, yeah, I'd say the stock would tank."

"Tank as in drop through the floor?"

"Yeah. Potentially. Again, it would depend on how much the
whole enterprise depended on this person."

I thought about Greenmüll and how Virginia Martin's technology was all anyone ever talked about. It was going to change the world. But even with her there, the forward motion seemed limited. With her gone, I couldn't imagine anything but a full stop.

"If it depended on them entirely."

"Yeah," he says. "Then I'm guessing it would pretty much bottom out. I'm getting ready to sell mine and I don't even know who you're talking about. Want to slide me a hint?"

I thank him and say good-bye, leaving him hintless.

CHAPTER FORTY-THREE

I HAVE THIS awful feeling. Call it a premonition. Call it a goose walking over my grave. Whatever it is, it is not good. It is, rather, a feeling that should not be. I feel sure of it.

Having been there very recently, I know that Rance is not at his office. I suddenly find myself wishing I knew where he lives, then realize I think maybe I do. I check my phone: the photo I took of his notebook. First page. Sure enough: it shows a residential address. I program 1536 Foxtrot Drive into my phone and head there, not at all sure what I will find, but feeling an unfamiliar roiling in my gut.

The address leads me to a beautiful midcentury bungalow in what even in the dark looks to be a generously treed neighborhood. The house has been exquisitely restored, every detail looks authentic to its period, right down to the open carport, which I note with interest but no surprise is empty right now: the Taycan is not here and the house is dark. I have a sinking feeling, too, because it's the middle of the night and he isn't where he's supposed to be. Does that mean he *is* where he isn't supposed to be? I figure I have a hunch I know where that might be.

* * *

At first glance, I think that hunch is wrong. When I roll up to Greenmüll, I see no vehicles at all. And I sort of can't believe it: I'd been so very sure.

I'm so disbelieving that I drive around back to the loading docks and, sure enough, both the Land Rover and the Taycan are there, at the back of the building. I sit there and blink at them for a minute, almost not believing my eyes. Had I not followed my instincts, I would have figured no one was there. And, clearly, I would have been wrong.

I decide to set up yet another little stakeout in my usual spot. Sitting there outside the plant feels like old home week. Everything is familiar. Even though it is full dark, so many of the things I am feeling are exactly the same. The way my butt feels on the seat: familiar, yet unrelenting. The way air sounds, filling my ears with the quiet hum of nearby industry. The way my car smells at rest: aging leather and clean vinyl and the familiar scents associated with an internal combustion engine.

I have tucked in there in the familiar position because I'm not quite sure what to do. I know it is idiotic to just sit in my car when the vehicles are out there, clearly telling me who is inside the building. It is three in the morning. It's late even for Virginia Martin, but what is the Taycan doing here? I am thorough in my indecision. I don't know what to do.

My instinct, though. It knows the moment has come.

I get Curtis on the first ring.

"Can you drop what you are working on?"

"Maybe. I think so. Yes. What do you have?"

"A story. Significant, I think. How soon can you get here?"

"Where are you?"

I tell him.

"I can be there first thing in the morning."

"That might be too late."

"I'm on my way."

"Bring a crew."

* * *

There are times for waiting and watching, but when I get off the phone with Curtis, I realize this isn't one of them. I have a sense of questions about to be getting answered. And that won't happen with me sitting out in front of the building.

I park between the Land Rover and the Taycan and climb up to the loading bay doors. Locked, of course, and though there are windows in some of them, I can see nothing but darkness inside.

As I peer through the windows in the loading bay doors and into the empty plant, I wonder if I might be mistaken in my thoughts and apprehensions. Maybe Virginia and Rance had business together and they've gone off. Maybe they are lovers. But I reject both of those thoughts in fairly short order. My instincts aren't always completely right, but they are seldom so far wrong either.

Instinct or not, the locked plant proves to be a fortress. No second-story windows to climb through here, either. There is no recourse available to me beyond trying the doors, and they all prove to be securely locked. Of course.

I am about to leave. It was an instinct, after all. It's not like I have any real knowledge and, clearly, I can't get in. And, once again, I try to convince myself about all the places they might be together, having both left their cars behind. And though it seems thin, I know it is possible. I'm about to convince myself, but then I hear a sound. I don't identify it as a scream—it is too indistinct for that—but a primal part of me recognizes the sound anyway. A human in distress.

I look around for some way—any way—to get inside the building, but it is a well-protected high-tech facility, so it is very secure. Extreme measures seem warranted, and I have a moment when I consider driving my Volvo though the loading bay door. That moment passes when I consider the height of the door. It seems possible to me that hitting the door with the car might total the car and possibly trigger an alarm while still not getting me in.

I am considering all of these things when more lights come on in the plant. It startles me enough that there are a few beats of my heart where I don't move at all.

Deciding.

Lights have been added, but there is no more action than before. I find myself desperate to discover a way in.

There is a forklift sitting on one side of the loading bay. It seems like a long shot so distinct that I almost don't try it. But then I realize I don't have a single other idea. I walk toward it, starting off wanting to check the visor for the keys, before I realize that there isn't one. I check under the seat, in a door pocket. When I get to the ashtray, I hit pay dirt: a key had been stuffed in alongside gum wrappers, but thankfully no cigarette butts.

I stick the key into the ignition and the electric motor comes to soundless life. I consider the sanity of what I am about to do, but then I force those thoughts away. This is not the time for a dose of reality, I tell myself. Or sanity. Instead, if there was ever a time for magical thinking, this is it.

Because it is an electric forklift it isn't terribly powerful, but it's heavy and strong. It can't go fast, but I have the feeling there's not much that can stand in its way.

And all of that is pretty much how it goes down. I advance on the door at top forklift speed—maybe five miles per hour—and the door is like melted butter under the weight of the cumbersome electric vehicle.

It turns out not to be a quiet approach, but it is not like the sound of a car accident, either. It happens so slowly, it's not like the sound of a high-speed impact. On the other hand, there is not much that is subtle about it. Once I'm inside the door, I pitch myself under a nearby table to see if anyone will come running to investigate the sound. I give it a few solid minutes—waiting for someone to check out the noise—but no one comes and nothing happens, so I decide to press on.

When I poke out from under the table, I have the Bersa ready, should the need arise. But all is so still and quiet. The Greenmüll plant is a big space, so at first I'm not sure where to go. Then I think about it. It's the middle of the night—or super early morning, depending on your perspective—and some weird goings-on are going on. I think I'm going to find what I'm looking for in the lab, but I progress quietly.

Despite my showy launch in the building, I enter the lab with stealth and caution. When my intentions are examined, it's the only way to go. I want to end all of whatever this is and no matter what it takes. I figure that asking for a warm welcome is too much.

As I make my way toward the lab, I feel my nerves jangle. Something here is not as it should be. And while I admit there might be many things not as they should be, I am on the alert for a single one. It takes me a few minutes to spot what beyond the obvious is different about this visit. When I do, I am surprised I didn't identify it right away. It is quiet. Absolutely still. And I realize that on previous visits there had been more noise than I was aware of. The roars of the machines, of course. And the comings and goings of many people. Phones. Trucks delivering and picking. But tonight, there is nothing. The quiet is disconcerting.

When I get to the lab, I realize that my quiet is also unnecessary: there is no one here. It confuses me. I'd been so certain of what I'd see, I don't believe my eyes at first. How can there be no one when I had expected that there would be? Also, I'm confused. If not here, then where? Where are they? Where could they be? Or maybe they aren't here at all: their cars here left behind. And though that doesn't make thorough sense to me, it's still a possibility.

One of the challenges is in simply and honestly moving forward. Every minute I spend searching around increases the chance of detection, even though I'm fairly certain that whatever is going on, they're not going to be anticipating someone catching up with them.

I'm about to go search the executive offices when I hear a loud clanging coming from the plant. I hustle out there, toward the sound, as quickly as I can without making any noise. I'm shocked by what I see.

Rance is slumped in a chair. I can't tell if he is dead or out cold. Whatever the case, he's not moving at all. As I watch, Hattie and Virginia move to the chair and start dragging his slumped form between them. Nearby, an aluminum tray is on the ground, scientific tools scattered. I'm guessing that the dropped tray is the source of the sound that summoned me.

The two women are dragging Rance toward one of the high-temperature incinerators. The scene is so unexpected I'm not at first sure how to react. The first thing I think is that I should help them. I've never had any affection for Rance. But another, more human, part knows exactly what I'm seeing. In a heartbeat I understand that some of those who have gone strangely missing might have ended up this way.

The Bersa has been in my hand all along.

"Guys," I call. "What the fuck is going on here?"

Hattie turns around so quickly, she drops the part of Rance she was supporting, and I hear the wrenching of her high heel as she slides around, but she doesn't miss a beat. When she turns, it astonishes me to see that she has a gun in her hand. And then I correct myself. Why am I astonished? They have done what was right. For them. And now they are trying to protect themselves. It all makes a sort of savage sense. On a certain level it is all perfectly understandable. Law of the jungle.

For her part, Virginia stands off to one side. She's dropped her half of Rance and he's slumped on the floor in a sad, broken heap. Virginia stands there biting her lip, like there's a decision to be made. I'm not sure I even want to think about what she is deciding.

"What's this? A standoff?" I know I sound half amused, and I am. Lisa Jane Samaritano had been right: none of this was what I had expected. Honestly, had it been Rance standing there over a prone Virginia I would have been less surprised. At the same time, I am exquisitely sad. I am reasonably certain that Virginia Martin is one of the most brilliant scientists of her generation. And I feel as though, right here, I am looking at the end of her career.

"Put the gun down," Hattie says. I'm looking at Rance and realizing I might also be looking at a dead body. And I'm thinking about Matt Sundstrom, who I'd been trying to get ahold of unsuccessfully for days. And maybe even Bryce Donegan? The whole thing leaves a bad taste in my mouth and gives me the feeling that Hattie knows exactly what to do with the gun in her hand.

I move the barrel of my own gun to the left a few inches, which puts its aim straight at Virginia, and throw a careless grin I don't feel in Hattie's direction.

"If I go, I take her with me."

And then I have this moment of almost pure panic. What if she takes me up on it? There is no obvious move and I have this vision of ending up like so much trash in one of Virginia's incinerators. I am guided then more by instinct than intellect. From where I am standing, my lower half is protected by tables and machines and I am close to an exit back to the executive offices. A motion catches Hattie's eye and I see her take her sights off me for a millisecond. It's all I need. I drop down behind the desk, roll toward the nearest doorway, and then I run like hell.

CHAPTER FORTY-FOUR

I MEAN, HONESTLY, there is nowhere to run and I'm not trying to get away anyway. Not really. I'm trying to get out of the range of Hattie's deadly-looking little gun and I figure that with Rance on the floor and Virginia looking confused, she'll have her hands full there anyhow.

While I run, I also try to formulate: what to do now? I go through the executive offices, then charge out the other door to the plant, which leads me in a straight line back to where I left my car. I trot over the mess of glass and crushed metal I created when I broke in and I am out of there so quickly it astonishes even me. My keys are in my car and it starts instantly and I'm in motion in a heartbeat. Even though my hands are shaking, while I drive, I call 9-1-1, telling them there is a murder in progress at Greenmüll and letting the voice on the phone know it's urgent that they get there quickly. A matter of life and, more probably, death.

"Can you give me your name, please?" I had expected the question and am ready for it: I end the call, roll down my window, and pitch the phone out of the moving car. It will be found, but there won't be anything about it that's traceable to me, especially if it takes a few days or weeks to find it, which seems possible.

The light is coming up over the horizon while I stop at a 7-Eleven to buy a burner phone. I get cash from the ATM and when the guy behind the counter asks for my ID, I slip him a hundred on top of the price of the phone and give him a meaningful look. He pockets the cash and waves me and my new phone out the door.

* * *

I wait until I'm back at my hotel before I activate the phone and the first call I make is to Curtis.

"You on your way?" I say it without preamble and I say it knowing he'll have to orient himself on the new number, but he's a smart guy and I know he'll figure it out.

"I'm still an hour out," he says.

"You'll want to hustle. It's going down."

"What's going down?"

"Just get there," I tell him and give him the address again. His arrival won't make any difference to anything, but he'll end up owing me a favor, and I live a life where that can be a good thing. "And leave me out of it."

"I figured," he says, and I can hear the grin in his voice. I grin back and hope for a time when our paths will cross, but I'm pretty sure it won't be today.

I know that part of me calling Curtis had been wanting to put off the time where I must get in contact with the handler. It's her daughter. I don't know what I'll say. I leave a message in an email for her to call me and I leave the new number. Then I start to pack. I have not been driving long when the call comes and I sigh as I say hello.

"Tell me," she says.

"I don't know where to begin."

"Just begin."

And so I do. I tell her as flatly as possible and without embellishment. And I tell her without a hint of the grief I feel for her in my heart. Her daughter has survived, but it's not possible she is what her mother had expected and, whatever the case, her life will never be the same.

"And the police are on their way, you said?"

"I'm sure they're already there. It's probably happening right now."

"Will we ever know what really happened?" Her voice is flat as she asks.

I think about Curtis, already speeding there. I think about the cops, ripping the place apart. And even, I think about the handler herself, questioning her daughter, some day if not now.

"Yes," I answer her finally. "I believe we will."

*   *   *

When I get home, I am surprised when the dog does not greet me.

I find him sitting on the couch sulkily. He looks fine. He looks healthy. But he also looks exceedingly pissed.

"What?" I say to him. "I'm sorry. I should have brought you with me."

He turns his head the other way.

After a while, I give up. I go to the kitchen, make myself a coffee, then take it into the backyard to sip on. The dog follows me outside and puts his head onto my lap for a scritch. He has forgiven me. I'm more relieved about that than I probably should be.

After I finish my coffee, we take a walk in the forest. And I am astonished again by the healing peace all around me. And the green. For his part, the dog now behaves as though no time between us has been missing. I might not have left him behind at all. And I wonder again, as I have in the past, about the resilient nature of dogs. And also, how all of time seems to them to be parallel. No before and after, but a beautiful and continuous now.

It is evening before the call I have been expecting comes. I figure it's been a busy day.

"I owe you on this one, kid," he says without preamble.

"Right? I knew you would."

"Did you see the show?"

"Oh geez. Ha! I forgot. You were live broadcasting?"

"Straight up. But you know they'll be rebroadcasting this all day. Go watch it, please. Then call me back. It'll save some back-and-forth."

So that's what I do.

It doesn't take me long to find it. Curtis works with a network affiliate out of LA, but this is a national story and his network is carrying his live feed, even though it isn't live anymore. The wonders of television that streams.

I find him in a shot I know is taken from the Greenmüll parking lot. Bright sun is reflecting off the shattered loading bay doors behind him. Curtis himself looks a bit tired, like he's been up all night and maybe managed to throw on a bit of foundation, to give his face some color. He doesn't look quite as good—smooth and polished—as he usually does, but he still has that voice of authority you can't help but want to listen to.

"A few minutes ago, Virginia Martin, the chief technical officer of Greenmüll Technologies, and another unidentified woman were brought out from the Greenmüll headquarters, here behind me, placed into the back of police cars, and driven away. The police are declining to comment at present. We'll be following this story closely. Back to you, Jessica."

I stand there for a minute or so to make sure there is nothing more before I call him.

"That's *it*? You could have told me that much over the phone."

"I like to keep you in suspense."

"You've got more though. I know you do."

"Well, some. You could wait for my update in an hour, or—"

"Curtis!"

"Well, to be clear, there's nothing that I *know*. If I did, I would have added it to the report you saw."

"Gotcha."

"And, as I said, there haven't been any official statements yet."

"Right."

"But forensics have been in there all day."

"Forensics?"

"Yeah. And an ambulance left here not long after I arrived. I saw them bring somebody out on a stretcher. I don't know who. But they left in a hurry, so I think whoever was in there wasn't dead."

I figure that would be Rance. And if what Curtis is supposing is right, he had made it out alive. The way things were looking when I showed up, it's possible that my arrival was what saved him. I'm not sure how I feel about that.

"And, I dunno," Curtis is saying. "I don't think everything is what it seems. Like there's a lot here that doesn't make sense. Not only to the cops, but also to me."

"For instance?"

"Right, well, those loading bay doors. What happened there?"

"That was me."

"You?"

"Yeah."

"You going to tell me?"

"No."

"Okay. So well, there's that. And then, forensics. If no one is dead, what are they doing there?"

"Figuring things out," I said.

"That much I got. What I need to know is: why?"

That was the million-dollar question, wasn't it? Why. I had a better idea than Curtis did, but I decided to let him get to it on his own. It would be better that way, because if he came to the same conclusion I did, I'd know we were on to something.

CHAPTER FORTY-FIVE

By the time I get up the gumption to notify the handler of *anything*, a couple of news cycles have passed.

I send the text. She makes the call.

"I know," she says without preamble.

"Have you spoken with her?"

"No," she replies. "There has been no time that was opportune."

"I can imagine."

"It's a bad business."

"Yeah."

"Someone called 9-1-1. An anonymous tip. You?"

I hesitate before denying it. As I consider, calling the cops on the client wasn't my most politic move. But . . .

"No. Uh-uh. Wasn't me."

Even when I say it, I realize that, eventually, she will speak to Virginia and Virginia will describe me and the game will be up. And then I realize that it probably doesn't matter. At worst the handler will order a hit on me and that will be the end of . . . well, all of this. There won't be all of this to worry about anymore. I contemplate the possibility with both dread and relief.

"Really," she says. It's not a question.

I hesitate. Then, "No. Sorry. That was reflex. Yeah, it was me."

There is a silence so deep you could serve soup in it. When she speaks, her voice is clear. Precise.

"And you thought that was a good idea?" Despite the words, there is no judgment in her tone.

This time I think carefully before replying.

"I didn't think it through, to be honest. She tried to kill me."

"Virginia did?"

"Well, Hattie. Virginia was there. It all happened very fast."

"I'm sure it did," she says in a clipped tone. "We'll be in touch." And after a half minute of waiting for her to say more, I realize that the phone is dead.

I watch the news. They have cleaned out the incinerator. Sifted, I guess, through the ashes. In those ashes they found DNA remnants from at least three people. I think about it. Who is missing? Who had injured or threatened Virginia's goals in some way? Once again it seems possible to me that Bryce Donegan, aka Daddy McPhee, is a candidate. It would seem to me that Matt Sundstrom is another. I can't think of anyone else offhand, but there could be so many people whose paths have crossed Virginia's that might have threatened her in some way.

I stew on it all for a while. Take more forest walks. Then I call Curtis again.

"I've figured it out," I say.

"What?"

"Why she was doing it. Why they were doing it."

"Doing it." He sounds sleepy. Like I might have woken him. I check the clock. It's two a.m. Ooops.

"Killing people. They were killing people in that incinerator. Maybe not actually killing them that way, but getting rid of the evidence. They nearly killed me."

"I don't know this part." He still sounds sleepy, but he definitely sounds more awake than he did.

I hesitate. Then: "I think that is what was happening. Anyone who thwarted them got bumped off."

"'Thwarted'? 'Bumped off'? Who are you?"

I laugh. It isn't the first time he's ever asked me that.

"Fair point," I concede. "But look past that. These two women, they have been killing people, you agree?"

"It would appear so. Yes."

"And the people they have killed were getting in their way," I add.

"Wait. Are you saying you know who the bones belong to?"

"I've got a pretty good idea, yeah."

"And they wanted to kill you and Rance?"

"Yeah."

"Why?"

"I think maybe I got in the way."

"I can see how that could happen," he says a little too easily. I try not to take offense at his tone.

"Right," is all I say, keeping my voice flat.

"But what about Rance?"

"I'm not sure. All I know is he was shorting the stock. Do you think that might be part of it?"

"What? Wait. How do you know that?"

"I just know," I tell him. "But it's for sure. Why?"

"That's why you were asking about the stock market."

"Yeah. But why would he do that? That part I don't know. Another piece: someone wanted Virginia dead. Good authority says someone had been hired to kill her."

I can feel Curtis thinking it through before he answers. I don't blame him. There are a lot of moving parts.

"He was shorting the stock, then she dies? You think that was the plan?"

"Right. Yes. That's what I think was in play. Like I said: what I don't get is why."

"Think of it."

"I have been thinking. I don't get it."

"I think I do," he says thoughtfully. "If Virginia died, the stock would tank. I mean, she's the balls of that business, right?"

"I wouldn't put it that way . . ." I say.

"Okay. She's the heart of it, then. Her tech is what makes the world go around. Correct?"

"Correct."

"How much did he short? Do you know?"

I give him the number and he whistles.

"He'd make millions."

"I guess it'll tank now anyway," I say. "With her in jail."

"It's dropped a little, but not an all-out tank. Yet. It will all depend on how it plays out."

"Like life," I say and he laughs.

"Yeah, like that."

"When you say 'play out' what do you mean?"

"Like if she gets time or they cut her loose or whatever," he says. "For now, most everyone is hanging on to see which way it goes."

"How it plays out."

"Right."

That was it. They were wanting to see which way all this fell. Which way the profit would fall. Or not fall. I have a sense of multiple forces hanging in the balance.

"I'll let you know if I hear anything new," I say. "You do the same?"

He agrees that he will but by then we are both thinking there isn't going to be much more to say. Virginia is on ice for the moment. And me? I am home.

CHAPTER FORTY-SIX

A NUTRITION CERTIFICATE from Cornell will help you lead the longest, healthiest life possible, that is what I understand. And help you help others to do the same. I believe it, too. Having read through most of the material by now and done a lot of the work, I am astonished at how much I have learned. Amazed at how much I did not know. Before now.

Everyone blabs endlessly about their optimal health and weight and activity level, but they don't seem to realize there's a real science to all of it. It shouldn't be sitting around and throwing ideas against the wall like most people do. Seeing what sticks. It is possible to know things. Understand them. And to take the knowledge and understanding into the future. That's what I believe. That's what I have learned. We can eat ourselves healthy. We can eat ourselves sick. We have so much more power over everything in our environment than what we think we do. Not everyone is ready to know that. At all. It's a huge amount of responsibility. And no one to blame. Not all the time. That's a difficult thing to get your head around. We tend to like to blame people.

"Everything is a little different than we imagined." On the phone, Dallyce Bayswater's voice is earnest, and I believe what he is saying. Or, at least, I believe *he* believes what he is saying. I had called him, wanting to give my new phone number. I didn't realize he'd been looking for me, and was ready with an earful. "I'm pretty certain it was not your brother who was up to no good in this situation. With how it all happened, he became the beneficiary."

"How it worked out."

"Yeah. You were gone. Your family was dead. But I honestly don't believe Kenneth had anything to do with it."

"All coincidence, I suppose?" I know there is a sneer in my voice. I can't help it.

"Not exactly. I mean, honestly, with how it all worked out, we'll never know. But from what I can tell, it wasn't Kenneth who was a bad actor, it was your husband."

"No. I can't believe it. He would never have hurt our son."

"Like I said, we probably won't ever know. But what if he wasn't trying to hurt your son? What if you were the target?"

I don't have words for a while after that. I am in a sea of pain but also at the center of a cone of justice. Terrible justice. It all makes an awful sort of sense. My husband wanted me dead so he rigged an accident that ended up killing our son and leading to his own death, too. But for the collateral damage, it would be poetic justice. But the price. The price was too high.

Another unexpected piece: it explains my story as well, you see? It explains it to both of us: you and me. I am the walking dead. The one who was supposed to die and the only one who lived. I would laugh—laugh and laugh—but I am so filled with emotion I can barely trust myself not to cry.

"Thank you, Dallyce," is what I manage to say. "For taking the time. It all makes a lot of sense." Too much sense.

"What about Kenneth?"

"What *about* Kenneth?"

"Your brother has expressed a strong desire to see you."

"Yeah. I know. A part of me would like that, too. But I can't right now. Can you tell him that for me, please? Maybe some time. But not now."

Afterwards, I wonder about that part. He's my brother, after all. Maybe all of the family I have left. But I'm raw again. As raw right now as I was when it happened. And then I realize, also, that maybe I feel I need to be better to see Kenny again. Better than I am now. A better me. I need to not be who I am. If I could only be enough. Plus I wish I could stop myself from being too much.

It is the perfect diversion from this maudlin turn of thought when my phone rings. I glance at it and see that the call is coming from Kiribati.

I don't even say hello. "Kiribati? Really? Isn't that pushing things?"

"How so?" Her voice is filled with mirth.

"Oh, I don't know. For maximum impact, shouldn't they be countries someone has heard of?"

"It's not what I'm calling about."

"It isn't?" I leave the sarcasm silent.

"I wanted to thank you."

"Thank me? Not necessary. It's what I do. And I'm not sure I did my best ever by you this time. I mean, I tried. But . . . it was a lot. I'm sorry."

"No. Certainly no apologies. I spoke with Virginia not long ago. She's been released. There is nothing to connect her to any deaths. In fact, it's possible Rance will be investigated about the bone fragments they found."

"Rance?" I can't believe my ears.

"Yes. Do you know he broke in that night?"

"How?" I am hiding my face under my arm when I ask it. I know the answer but I don't know what to do.

"Can you believe he drove a forklift through a loading bay door? Who does such a thing?"

"Yeah. Really." My voice is flat.

"And there had been some kind of finagling with the stock, too. I guess he is not quite who he appeared to be."

"Who ever is?" It's all I can think to say.

"Anyway, as I said, I wanted to thank you. None of it came out as expected, but I know the outcome was much better thanks to you."

"Please. Again, thanks are not necessary."

"I know. But things were different this time. Things are different now. You know that, don't you? We are at a different place than when we began. Do you feel it?"

I realize instinctively she has started a new topic. A topic unrelated to how I've spent the last week or so. Maybe even the last few years. And her words resonate with me. I nod into the phone, never doubting, even if I don't fully understand. "I . . . I think so," I say hesitantly, ever knowing that a part of me understands very well.

"We began with commissions of one sort. Jobs that needed to be done. And now? We've moved beyond that."

I look at my phone blankly, as though I might see her in there. I understand her words perfectly, but I don't comprehend. Not completely. And maybe, in a way, not at all.

"Explain," I prod.

She doesn't answer right away. In fact, she takes so long to reply that, for a moment, I think our connection is lost. Then she speaks.

"There are things that are wrong with the world," she says finally. "We have the power to make some of them right."

I feel my eyes widen at this, the fullness of what she is saying coming home. It takes me a minute to think of a response, though when I do, I know it is right.

"That would be a different sort of undertaking, then," is what I say.

"Yes," she says. "I think so."

AUTHOR'S NOTE

IN HIGH-LEVEL BUSINESS and investment, there is always an exit strategy. It's just as it sounds: you will invest these dollars now and in time you hope to sell the company for twenty bazillion dollars. That's an exit strategy. In business, you don't make a plan to get in without also making one to get out.

In writing the book that now bears that name, the protagonist's personal exit strategy kept coming up. Her life has been difficult. She's not so sure she wants to keep doing it. Sometimes she thinks about checking out. And because the backdrops of this particular book are the worlds of high finance and tech start-ups, the idea of the exit strategy comes up a lot. After a while it became apparent that it was a pretty good name for this book: punchy and on point. And so that's how that happened.

The book itself happened a different way.

After *Endings*, it wasn't easy to know where to go. She was tired, that was apparent. Her heart was never really in killing people, and she doesn't need the money anymore. In fact, she seems to have abundance, in all ways but the ones that matter. So, as is my habit, I sat down with the character and her story in my heart and I started to write. The book that is now *Exit Strategy* is what came out.

But I didn't do it alone.

I am so grateful at this stage in my career to have a team that helps shape and create the books I write.

Bob and Pat Gussin at Oceanview Publishing are friends to many writers and I am so happy to be one of them. As almost anyone in the business will tell you, they are lovely people and so it is unsurprising that they, also, surround themselves with lovely people. Thank you, Lee, Lisa, and Christian for all the everythings you do.

More of the team: my agent, the wonderful Kimberley Cameron of Kimberley Cameron and Associates, has made good on all of her promises, and then some. My film and television agents, Mary Alice Kier and Anna Cottle of Cine/Lit Representation, are lovely and amazing.

I am similarly blessed in my home team. My husband, Anthony J. Parkinson, embodies faith and support. Additionally, Tony was the first reader of this book and provided invaluable details about start-ups and stock markets and all the business things he knows better than most people.

My son, the actor Michael Karl Richards, continues to be a terrific source of inspiration, information, and discussion about the arts and where they drive us.

Along with these two, Mike's lovely wife, Kristen Houser; my brother, Peter Huber; and his partner, Roger Chow have been having weekly "family dinners" via Zoom since the start of COVID. These have become fiercely personal family roundtables where we discuss everything that is important to us on a regular basis, even though we are miles apart. This core group keeps me balanced and on track. I think maybe I do that for them, too. We are so lucky.

Other friends, family, and colleagues have been likewise deeply supportive. Will Bass, Janet Bauer, Stephanie Parkinson Briguglio, Michéle Denis, Laura-Jean Kelly, Sarah Entz, Sheena Kamal, Jeannie Lee, Chris Newell, Jo Perry, Diana Welvaert, and Carrie Wheeler continue to provide support and inspiration. Thank you.

Now several books into what continues to be an interesting career, the thing I feel beyond everything else is gratitude. It fills me. Pushes me forward.

Thank you for your support and for caring enough to even get to this part of this author's note. Your presence here is everything. Thank you for sharing this journey.

PUBLISHER'S NOTE

We hope that you enjoyed *Exit Strategy*.

We wanted you to know that *Endings* is the first book in this series, preceding the story in *Exit Strategy*.

Endings, at its essence, is not a book about a female contract killer though, on the other hand, it is always that, as well. *Endings* is about redemption. And the struggle we all face as we try to find the light. And hope.

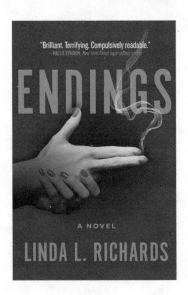

"Provocative and powerful, *Endings* by Linda L. Richards sweeps the reader from leafy suburbia into the strangely seductive underworld of a woman who teaches herself to kill for a living. Page after page, Richards ratchets up the tension, weaving tradecraft, disguises, and psychology into a riveting tale that peels back the layers of the soul."

—GAYLE LYNDS,
New York Times best-selling author

We hope that you will read both *Endings* and *Exit Strategy* and will look forward to more to come from Linda L. Richards.

For more information, please visit the author's website: www.lindalrichards.com.

Happy Reading,
Oceanview Publishing